On The Road
To Death's Door

M. J. Williams

On The Road To Death's Door

Copyright © 2011 Mary Joy Johnson & Margaret M. Williams

Cover Credit: The cover art for *On The Road To Death's Door* was created by Joshua Williams © 2011. Various images were used by permission in the cover art. We thank photographers Jeremy Bronson, David Jakes, and Randen Pederson.

ISBN-10: 1468065335
ISBN-13: 978-1468065336

To Mark,
whose unfailing faith in our efforts
and whose patience and encouragement
mean the world to us.

"Shells sink, dreams float. Life's good on our boat."
–Jimmy Buffett

ACKNOWLEDGMENTS

Many thanks to our critiquers who gave us such valuable feedback: Erin Williams Hart, Holly Johnson, Jean Joque, Larry Leffel, Chichi Melekos, Mark Williams, and Ann Wood. Special appreciation goes out to Kelly Joque for the lesson on firearms and for providing feedback to make the police scenes as authentic as possible. However, any errors of any nature in this book are the sole responsibility of the authors. We are also indebted to Fr. Andrew Greeley and to Capt. Jim Robinson, USCG, for taking the time to answer technical queries from novice writers. Joshua Williams' computer and artistic skills made the publication of our novel possible. Christine DeSmet served as our mentor and persistent cheerleader throughout the creation of this work. We cannot say it too often: *Thank you!* to all who supported us.

CHAPTER 1

The campground smelled vaguely of wood smoke and pine. Maple and birch leaves rustled softly, if unseen, against the mottled, star-spotted sky.

Emily Remington carried an armload of cut fire wood and dumped it next to a brick-lined pit in the ground. She looked up in time to see Stan and Malcolm clamber to the top of the ladder attached to the back of the RV. They looked like wraiths in the swaying light of the Coleman lantern Stan was carrying in one hand.

"Be careful up there, Hon!" Audrey shouted.

Malcolm waved her off. Stan grunted, more from the exertion of climbing over the lip of the ladder than from any kind of editorial statement.

The Winnebago was tucked into a copse of maple trees, and the two men had to duck to avoid being backhanded by a low-hanging branch. Malcolm pulled a handkerchief from his back pocket and swiped at his forehead. When he had tucked it back away again, he pulled a small bottle out of a front pocket. He offered it to Stan first. Stan grinned and accepted the drink. Standing on top of the huge vehicle, legs askance, he threw his head back and took a long slurp.

"Ahh!" He handed the bottle back to his friend, then surveyed the campsite from his new vantage point. Emily was busy arranging the dried logs into a teepee shape in the middle of the fire pit. Audrey bustled up behind her.

"This is so rustic!" Audrey exclaimed as she busied herself about the campsite, martini glass in hand. She picked up a lawn chair and swiped at it with a tissue while Emily, on her knees, blew at the growing licks of flame.

"One used carpet, ready to be delivered!" Stan announced.

The two women turned and watched as their men positioned themselves on either side of a six-foot long carpet roll. Emily grabbed her can of beer from the picnic table, enjoying the scene as if from a theatrical show.

"I still cannot believe you bought that thing at a garage sale," Audrey chattered. She took another drink from her stemmed glass. "That is just sooo...quaint."

"Man, this thing is heavy," Stan complained. "What did you do, Em? Hide a body in it?"

The two men grunted and heaved but couldn't get the carpet roll to move into a controlled position.

"How about we just shove it off?" Malcolm suggested.

"Sounds like a plan to me," Stan said, breathing heavily. "Hey, ladies! Heads up! It's raining carpeting. On three," he directed.

Malcolm nodded, putting his weight behind the carpet.

"One, two, three!"

They shoved at the bundle and rolled it off the top of the RV...

"Oh, shit!"

...onto the awning...

"Damn!"

...which bent and ripped under its weight...

"Crap!"

...and fell to the ground with a THUD.

"Stan!" Emily shouted. "What are you doing?" She stared in dismay at the ripped awning with its bent support struts.

"I don't know, Em," Stan said, standing on the top of the Winnebago, hands on his hips, looking for all the world like king of the mountain. "If we gotta do this much work to get it down, what are we gonna do when it's time to get it back up?"

"I think you need to work those arm muscles a bit more. The guys at the garage sale didn't have any trouble getting it up there."

Stan signaled Malcolm to climb down the ladder ahead of him. He rubbed his hands against the sudden chill of the evening, then clambered down himself, eager to stand in front of Emily's already blazing fire.

"Okay, let's roll this baby out and see what we've got." He pulled out his pocket knife and cut the twine which bound the rug. He positioned a foot against one end of the roll and signaled Malcolm to do the same at the other end. "On my count again. One, two..."

With a dual grunt they pushed, hopped, pushed, hopped, unrolling the carpet one lump at a time. Finally Stan gave it one last mighty heave with his foot.

"What the—?"

They watched in horror as first an arm, and then a leg, and finally an entire body flopped out of the bundle. Stan, Emily, and Malcolm stared in stunned silence.

Audrey screamed.

CHAPTER 2

Earlier that same day...

"Come on, baby. I know you can do it." Emily caressed the steering wheel and tapped the gas ever so lightly. The RV lurched forward. "Damn!" She slammed on the brakes.

With a frustrated sigh she leaned her forehead against the wheel. Learning to maneuver this monster was going to take some practice. *I'm too old for this,* she thought. She glanced at her watch. Quarter to eleven. *And I'm not getting any younger sitting here.*

She gave it another try, jerking the big vehicle into a parking spot in front of the row of dilapidated houses that was never meant for anything with a wheel base wider than the family mini-van. She threw the transmission into reverse and eased the vehicle backward a foot.

She was grateful Stan wasn't in the seat next to her scrutinizing her every move or telling her how to do it. Of course, if he'd been in the RV, he would have been driving. Their unspoken agreement when they'd acquired the thirty-two-foot Winnebago was that Stan would drive, Emily would keep it running.

Not that Emily didn't enjoy driving. After all, she used to drive all the time on the job. But that was a considerably smaller vehicle: a Ford Crown Vic, outfitted with the usual emergency warning lights, radio, and other equipment found in your typical small town patrol car. But this thing. Yikes! Turning corners was challenging enough. Parking it was beyond reasonable.

She nudged the gear shift back into drive and moved forward an inch, regretting the decision to fit the Winnebago into this particular spot. She shifted yet again into reverse and touched the gas pedal ever so lightly.

The rear wheel of the Winnebago jumped the curb, and Emily lost sight of the blue Honda behind her in the rear view mirror. She hit the brakes. She'd have to pull ahead again.

She made a mental note to get one of those rear view cameras to mount on the back of the oversized bus. She shifted into drive again and crept forward another inch, straightening the wheel. She estimated the space between her and the bumper of the cranberry Explorer in front of her. Not enough to slip a shoehorn.

Again she thanked the spirits of the road that Stan was at the golf course and not here to witness her ineptitude. At the same time, even though handling this big baby was proving to be a challenge far greater than she'd anticipated, she knew without a doubt that she'd eventually master it. She was simply frustrated at this moment because she could see other people hopping out of their cars, hurrying past her on the road, and up into the driveways of houses hosting the garage sales. Emily glanced longingly at the tables piled high with treasures and grasped the gear shift with renewed determination. She edged the Winnebago back away from the cranberry SUV.

Satisfied, she reached for the key to shut off the engine. She was curious to see how far she was from the curb. She looked up to see a young woman in a too-tight t-shirt, jeans, and spangled flip-flops walk up to the Explorer carrying a large plastic laundry basket. A curly-haired toddler followed at her heels. The young mother aimed her electronic key and unlocked the doors of the SUV, swung open the tail gate and tossed the basket on top of other earlier purchases—a pair of ice skates, a small white painted end-table lying on its side, a milk crate filled with a mismatch of plates, bowls, and cups.

She scowled at Emily as she slammed the back end, then made a point of checking the sides and rear of her vehicle for dings and scratches, evidence of Emily's inability to handle the big rig.

The little girl—or was it a boy, it was hard to tell—stared up at Emily through the windshield. Emily waved her fingers at the child, who scrunched its face and grabbed its mother's leg. The mother yanked open the front passenger door and lifted and buckled the now wailing toddler into a car seat.

She seemed more concerned about whether her car had a few scratches and dents on it than about the safety of her child who should have been in the back seat. Emily grimaced remembering the time she'd lifted a limp child from the front seat of an accident, killed by the very airbag meant to save lives.

The young mother quickly climbed into the driver's seat and, without bothering to buckle her own seatbelt, pulled the big SUV out into the street, leaving a car-length space directly in front of the RV.

"Thank you," Emily said to the disappearing taillights. "But your timing stinks."

Emily glanced at the clock on the dashboard: 10:53. Already? She had only made four stops this morning, none of which had been very productive. All she had found so far were a copy of "RVing For Dummies" and an old book for Stan on the history of shipwrecks in the straits of Wisconsin's Door Peninsula—known to sailors as Death's Door. Most of the items for sale had been children's games, bicycles, old dishes and clothing that was too good to throw away, but nobody wanted to wear anymore. At least this stop, billed in the ad as a "10 family neighborhood sale," had lots of possibilities with only one need to park.

She'd been pleasantly surprised to discover that this small Door County community was as enamored of garage sales as her own small town on the Michigan side of Green Bay. Bailey's Harbor was, by all appearances, more of a working class community than the upscale tourist towns on the other side of the Door Peninsula, a favorite vacation spot for Wisconsinites and their Illinois neighbors. She noticed that the town's small harbor off Lake Michigan housed more fishing boats than tourist craft. And the few restaurants and shops in town seemed less trafficked than the ones she'd visited the day before in Fish Creek on the bay side.

Emily stashed her sunglasses in the visor pocket, then grabbed her wallet from her shoulder bag and stuffed it into the pocket of her jeans. Clambering down the steps of the RV, she checked her distance from the curb. Not bad. Only a foot or so away. She'd master this old crate yet. A cool breeze reminded her this was early October, despite the bright sunshine. She sighed. Reaching back into the Winnebago, she grabbed her hooded sweatshirt from the front passenger seat.

"Nice wheels!" a young man said as he lurched past her wrestling with a coffee table.

"Thanks. Gets me where I want to go."

Emily had not been thrilled the day the lawyer had called her and told her she'd inherited her aunt's well-worn Winnebago.

"I suppose we could try selling it," she had told Stan. "We might get a few bucks for it."

But Stan's eyes were already aglow. He was picturing himself behind the wheel, the two of them traversing the country like Charles Kuralt or John Steinbeck.

"John Steinbeck traveled with a dog," Emily had pointed out.

"We can get a dog." Stan smiled, knowing that's not what she meant. "And anyway, Charles Kuralt traveled with a camera crew. We have a camera."

Emily chose not to comment. He had an answer for everything, and it drove her nuts.

"Just think of all the nooks and crannies we can explore." He didn't know when to stop. "We're retiring, right?"

"Yeah?"

"Well, this way we can see the country. Tour the desert. Climb the mountains." Stan wrapped a loving arm around her. "Take Megan and the kids to the seashore."

Emily laughed. Her husband of twenty-nine years knew her only too well. "Admit it," she challenged him. "You're just looking for an excuse to take those grandkids to Bull Run and Tom Sawyer's cave."

"Just think of it, Emily, we'll follow Lewis and Clark's trail with Wynter, Allyn, and Annabell."

"Lewis and Clarke's trail?"

"Or wherever your little heart desires. Like...to see the grandkids?"

And so, Emily found herself the "proud" owner of a ten-year-old, thirty-two-foot Winnebago motor home with 58,000 miles on it. And that meant somebody had to maintain the thing. Stan was as clumsy with an Allen wrench as he was nimble with a search engine on his laptop. Maintenance would be her job. Stan was too much of a dreamer, a scholar, a gentleman to ever get his hands dirty keeping the old thing running. But he'd drive it wherever they wanted to go. Because that's what he loved doing. Driving. Driving and thinking.

"Hi ya," said a sixtyish woman with red hair too bright to be natural, sitting in a lawn chair.

Emily smiled. "Howdy to you. Great day for a garage sale."

"Nice Indian summer we're having." The woman turned her attention to an elderly gentleman handing her a dollar bill for a jigsaw puzzle.

Emily poked around the items on a long folding table. An old turn-table for LPs that no one used anymore. A stainless steel toaster missing its cord. A set of mismatched travel bags. Emily moved on to the next driveway.

It was a luxury for her to be able to spend an entire morning browsing other people's junk. Before her earlier-than-expected retirement from the police department in the small town of Escanaba, in Michigan's Upper Peninsula, she'd had to disguise her interest in garage sales by snatching quick five-minute expeditions during her long days on patrol. Unfortunately, the neighbors often got nosy, thinking perhaps she was investigating somebody doing something illegal.

The morning sun was beginning to feel warmer now that she was out of the wind. Emily unzipped her sweatshirt and tied it around her waist. As she entered the garage, her nose wrinkled. A waft of pine mist and gardenia, mingled with the odor of fresh oil and stale fish guts, washed over her. Breathing through her mouth, she scanned the shoppers and the offerings in the garage.

A table of glassware gleamed in the sunlight, but Emily barely gave it a glance. What she was looking for were bottles. Colored Avon perfume bottles to be specific, the older the better. She edged her way past an elderly couple studying the mark stamped on the back of a ceramic dinner plate.

Suddenly two boys around nine or ten years old, in jeans and Green Bay Packers sweatshirts, whizzed by her. Their movements weren't registering the way they should. They seemed to be gliding by as if they were on skateboards. But they weren't. They had on plain old sneakers (if one could call kids' footwear these day plain or old or even sneakers).

She watched them skim around a table and head off down the driveway. The taller of the boys was gliding on his heels.

There must be wheels in those shoes, Emily deduced. This was something else for store owners to complain about.

Emily focused her attention back to the sales tables. She picked up a bottle. It was Avon. Blue. The tall stoppered, vase-like perfume decanter was one she didn't already have. And definitely old. Stan would have an excuse to tease her about her "tacky" decorating taste. She decided that was a good enough excuse to buy the bottle. At fifty cents, it wasn't like she was out a lot of money.

Several boxes of books along the outer wall of the garage caught her eye. Her occasional purchases of old, used historical books was the only thing Stan didn't complain about her buying on her rounds. An ample woman in red stretch-pants four sizes too small waved two saucepans in front of the teenage girl guarding the cash box.

"I'll give you a nickel apiece."

"Sorry, lady. They're my Aunt Carmen's. If they're marked a quarter, that's what you'll have to pay. Unless you want to come back later when she's here to dicker." The girl worked a wad of gum in her mouth.

"It's a crime, charging that much," the woman complained. She turned toward the table where Emily was poking through bedraggled Christmas baubles, half-burnt candles, and old vinyl LPs. "It's a shame what some people wanna charge to get rid of their junk," she said to Emily as she pawed a table-top centerpiece of dusty plastic holly and red berries and a chipped, chrome picture frame.

A man in a blue plaid shirt, fishing vest, and jeans walked up to the cash box guard. "Your ad said you have some living room furniture. Is it already gone?"

"In the house. Mikey! Mikey! Come watch the money a minute, will ya?" The girl rose and beckoned as one of the boys wheeled to the table and plopped down in the chair she'd just vacated.

"May I see, too?" Emily joined them at the door to the house. The girl nodded, and Emily followed her and the fisherman into the kitchen. A smell of burnt coffee struck her nose.

"Shit. Forgot to turn off the pot again. Ma's gonna kill me." The girl flipped the button on the coffee-maker. "The living room's back this way." She gestured vaguely to her right, chewed on her gum. "Everything in there is for sale. Prices as marked."

They walked through a small, crowded living room. A blue and pink plaid sofa sat along the long wall of the room. It appeared to be in fairly good condition, even if the colors were god-awful. Tables and lamps were strewn about.

Emily wondered why she bothered to look—the Winnebago was fully furnished—when the rug she was standing on caught her eye. It was a beautiful dark red Persian design with navy and green paisley surrounding a central medallion of birds and flowers. It looked to be about six by eight feet, was a bit worn in spots, and had a coffee-colored stain that would have to be scrubbed out.

But Emily saw it as perfect for under the awning just outside the Winnebago. She'd noticed that other RVers often laid a swatch of that ugly green indoor-outdoor carpeting under their folding camp chairs. She imagined how nice it would be, sitting out in the morning, drinking their coffee, reading the paper, their own lawn chairs and collapsible breakfast table nestled on the colorful oriental rug.

"What are you asking for this carpet?"

"Thirty bucks." The girl blew a bubble with her gum.

"Would you take twenty?"

"Prices as marked," the girl repeated her earlier statement. Emily started to turn away. The girl shrugged, shifted her gum from the right side of her mouth to the left. "Aw, hell. Why not." She extended her hand.

As Emily handed her a twenty from her wallet, the girl said, "I'll get my dad and my uncle to roll it up for you. If you can wait a minute. Last I saw of them, they were heading down to the Murphy's to help them load a sofa or something."

Emily pointed out the Winnebago, instructed the girl to have the men tie the rug to the top, and headed off to the sale next door. There she found an ornate German beer stein for Stan, but that was about all. When she got back to the Winnebago, the men were just finishing tying the Persian rug into a lumpy bundle. They shoved it up and onto the top of her motor coach.

"Looks like you've been travelin' a bit," said the taller of the two men.

"Actually, this is our maiden voyage. First leg of a cross-country trip."

"No kiddin'. Where ya headin'?"

"Wherever the wind blows." Emily grinned. "I've always wanted to say that. Actually we'll be catching I-90 out to Boston."

"You stayin' at one of the campgrounds 'round here?"

"Moose's Leap. Over by Fish Creek."

"Up on the bluff there? I hear it's pretty popular. You know how it got its name, don'tcha?"

Emily shook her head.

"It's a known fact that back in the thirties, there was a herd of moose used to roam these parts. People say one winter night, when the ground was froze so hard you could chill your beer right outside the back door, something came flying outta the sky, something round and shiny with lights all around." He moved his hands dramatically into the shape of an orb.

"What? Like a UFO?" Emily asked.

"There's some folks say that's exactly what it was. Didn't make a sound. Just sat over them trees, spinnin' and shinin' its lights, in a pattern-like. Well, that UFO, or whatever it was, scared that herd of moose. Chased them right on up to the edge of the bluff. But they was runnin' so hard they couldn't stop. So over they went. Leaped right out over the bluff and into the bay. Except the bay was froze solid. And them moose splattered like bugs on a windshield."

Emily gave the man a skeptical look. He was grinning, and his brother was grinning even more.

"I didn't think moose ran in herds," Emily ventured.

"They don't anymore!" the man said, laughing. And his brother laughed even harder, slapping the storyteller on the back.

"I love the way you tell that story," he chortled.

Emily laughed, too. "I'll have to remember that one."

"Well, you have yourself a good trip. And enjoy that rug."

"I will."

Emily checked her watch and sighed. She'd be late picking up Stan at the golf course. Oh, well. He wouldn't grumble. He'd be ensconced at the bar, contentedly nursing a brandy manhattan with his friend Malcolm until she arrived.

As she climbed into the Winnebago, Emily waved amiably at the silver-haired man in the fishing vest who was trying to fit a battered ice chest into the trunk of his 1995 Cadillac. *A Fleetwood, of all things,* Emily chuckled to herself. *He could swim in that thing.* To Emily's great relief, he'd parked it with plenty of room between him and the RV.

Moose's Leap. She laughed out loud. She'd have to remember to tell Stan that one.

An obnoxiously tinny version of *Für Elise* floated from her sweatshirt pocket. Emily smiled as she pushed the "talk" button.

"Hi, honey," she said into the phone.

"Hello to you, too, babe," said a deep, sexy voice that was definitely not her husband's.

"Malcolm!"

"Looks like your husband's squawk box ran out of juice. Just checking in to let you know I beat the pants off him and you can pick us up anytime you like," Malcolm said.

Emily checked the caller I.D. on her phone's tiny screen and sighed. "If I could have a dollar for every time he's forgotten to charge that thing..."

"We'd go dancing all night long at the Starlight Ballroom. Your treat, babe, 'cause you'd be rich and sassy," Malcolm rumbled.

Emily grinned. She remembered now why she enjoyed Malcolm's company so much. He had a way of making a woman—even one who spent her mornings garage saling— feel sexy and appreciated

"I'll be there in twenty. Tell that husband of mine I expect him to buy me lunch."

CHAPTER 3

"I just made a date with your wife," Malcolm said, tucking his cell phone into his pants pocket.

"Hope you can handle her better than I can," Stan laughed. He swirled his manhattan in his glass and grinned at his friend. They had just finished a challenging eighteen holes and were in no hurry for Emily to pick them up.

Stan marveled at how their friendship, which had begun when they were roommates in college in the late '60s, had endured despite the obvious disparity in their careers and lifestyles. Stan was trying to figure out how to stretch his state pension from his job as a college history professor. Malcolm, on the other hand, had risen from the ranks of lab technician at a large Milwaukee chemical company to CEO. When he finally decided to retire, he would have a severance package the size of Stan's entire life-time earnings.

"You hear from Vic or Jeremiah yet?" Stan asked.

"I got a text message from one of Jeremiah's 'people' this morning. He's running behind schedule, but we're still on his calendar."

Stan winced. "Must be a tough life when you have to schedule in a beer with your buddies."

Malcolm had used this rendezvous as an excuse to try out his new thirty-five-foot Catalina. He and his wife Audrey were delighted with an excuse to take the single-masted sloop for its maiden voyage from its berth in Milwaukee, north along Wisconsin's Lake Michigan coast, through the canal at Sturgeon Bay, into Green Bay, and up into the harbor at Fish Creek.

Stan and Malcolm saw each other only once or twice a year and when they did get together, they relished every minute of reminiscing they could manage. And tonight there would be all four guys—the *Fractious Four*, as they used to call themselves.

Stan was looking forward to dinner up in Sister Bay with his three buddies and the three wives. But even more, he was looking forward to the time after dinner when the women would more than happily say their good-nights and leave the men to wander until they found a bar that would let them be as raucous as they wanted, telling their stories and laughing over jokes that nobody but they thought were funny.

"You're looking good," Stan observed. And he meant it. Malcolm's dark brown skin glowed. His belt showed no sign of bulging and his course black, short cropped hair was only beginning to show signs of gray.

Malcolm's chuckle quickly turned into a deep throaty cough. Maybe looks were deceiving, Stan thought. Malcolm quickly produced a handkerchief and coughed into it.

"The doctor says it's just sinus drainage. But Audrey's been bugging me to get a chest x-ray."

"Why don't you?" Stan asked, sipping at his drink. "I ignored that heartburn for too long. Look where it got me. I ended up with a triple bypass."

Malcolm coughed again, then put his handkerchief away. "I've been coughing this way since college."

"Snored a lot, too, as I recall. Was that due to sinus drainage?"

Malcolm grinned. "Most likely. That and the six-packs we used to down."

Stan and Malcolm had been the most unlikely of roommates, thrown together by luck of the draw. Malcolm, a starting running back for the Wisconsin Badgers, was one of the few Black students on the team back then, recruited for his size and speed. Stan, on the other hand, preferred to spend his nights at the library. It wasn't so much that he enjoyed studying, but his penchant for research was in high gear even way back then.

By their sophomore year, however, Malcolm had gotten kicked off the football team for taking part in anti-war protests with Stan, Jeremiah and Vic.

"There she is." Malcolm pointed as Emily came in through the door. "Pretty as the day she first arrested you."

Stan looked up and smiled at the sight of his wife. At fifty-seven, she was even prettier to him than she was the day they had first met. Her strawberry blonde hair seemed to be getting blonder as she got older. Or was it just that the gray highlights favored the short-cropped style with just enough curl that it never lay flat? Stan delighted in Emily's frustration with the stubborn locks that sprung out in unexpected ways.

At 5'6 she was still fit, her frame not giving much credence to the extra twenty pounds that she always complained about. And then there was the tattoo, in a place only she and Stan knew about. Just thinking about the little rose caused him to blush.

"She didn't arrest me. She just processed my arrest," he said with a grin.

"And I'd do it again in a minute." Emily kissed Stan and hugged Malcolm. "Need a designated driver?"

When lunch was over, Stan and Malcolm hauled their golf bags to where Emily had parked the RV. She opened the door to the neat little storage compartment under the main body of the motor home, and the men hefted their bags inside.

"So this is how you plan to spend your retirement." Malcolm's voice was ripe with skepticism as he eyed the massive vehicle.

"The open road. A ribbon of highway. And no motel bills." Stan patted the front fender. He tap-danced to avoid the sprinkler system that a groundskeeper had just turned on. "We're heading out to Boston first thing in the morning. Catch the I90 down near Chicago, and it's non-stop from there to the Boston Tea Party."

"Non-stop except for a little diversion at Niagara Falls perhaps?" Malcolm winked at Emily.

"Hey!"

All three spun around to look at the grungy groundskeeper who was glaring at them. "You can't park that thing here. You gotta move it." He sniffed and rubbed his hand across his nose.

"We're going. We're going." Emily scowled at him, held up her keys as evidence. She followed Stan and Malcolm into the RV.

The men settled themselves into the recliners Stan had insisted on installing before they left. Emily eased herself into the captain's seat, checked her mirrors, and then slowly rolled the Winnebago out of the parking lot.

"Hey, Em," Stan asked. "What was that up on top?"

"I picked up a carpet this morning. To put under the awning. I think you'll like it."

Stan grinned at Malcolm. "Oh, I thought maybe you picked it up to roll around on. Make a little whoopee on."

"In your dreams, mister." And Emily stomped on the gas, causing the rig to lurch.

They dropped Malcolm off at the Fish Creek marina. Audrey stepped out onto the deck of the sailboat to greet them.

"Any luck this morning?" Audrey asked.

Emily pointed to the top of the RV. "I got a great deal on a Persian carpet!"

Audrey glanced up and frowned. "You bought a used rug?"

"Twenty bucks. It'll be perfect for under the awning. Portable, too."

"Quite the deal," Audrey said. But it was obvious to Emily she disapproved. Audrey was a woman who bought her carpeting only at the most elegant of establishments. "We'll meet you here at sixish?"

"We'll be here," Stan said.

They waved their goodbyes and Stan and Emily headed back to the campground, leaving Malcolm and Audrey to spend the rest of the afternoon napping on their boat.

Emily glanced over at her husband. "You're looking forward to tonight, aren't you?"

Stan smiled an impish smile. "It'll be nice to see Glenna again," he said.

"Glenna? You mean Jeremiah's wife?" Emily asked. "You're not serious."

"Hell yeah. She's young. And pretty. And..."

"And...?"

"Smart?"

"How would you know that? We spoke to her for all of five minutes at their wedding. And with that dress she was wearing, I'm sure you didn't listen to a word she said."

"I don't remember she was wearing a dress."

"I'll bet you don't!" Emily reached over and shoved at his shoulder playfully.

Stan held up his hands as if to ward her off. "Hands on the wheel, if you please."

Emily checked her outside mirror, watched as a sporty little Jeep hustled up behind her.

"It's been a long time since you've seen any of the others." She maneuvered the RV into the busy traffic of the highway. At a break in the oncoming traffic, the Jeep zipped around them on the left. "It was nice that Vic thought of getting you guys together."

"Yeah, well, Vic's that kind of a guy."

"You said he was working on some sort of a book?"

"His memoirs. I'm sure he's got a story or two to tell."

Father Victor Virchow, a Catholic priest, was on leave from his diocesan duties and was using the time to write his much-sought-after memoirs about his controversial work as a social activist. He'd been in touch with Stan by phone and by email a lot recently while he worked on the chapter about their college days.

Vic wanted to milk the "Fractious Four" for their memories to fill in some of the details. Malcolm was game. Pinning Jeremiah down had been a bit trickier. Stan was certainly willing—more than willing. He loved nothing more than reminiscing about the '60s. And he never backed down from a good political debate, a real likelihood since Jeremiah Douglas, currently serving in the State Senate, was in the middle of a rancorous campaign for governor. Somehow he'd gone through the same coming-of-age experiences in the same civil rights and Vietnam war protest days as Stan, Malcolm and Vic, but Jeremiah had emerged as a Republican. It made Stan reach for his blood pressure medicine just thinking about it. To Stan's chagrin, it was looking like Jeremiah had a good chance of upsetting the reigning Democrat and taking the governor's mansion for himself. The problem was, his campaign schedule was so tight he couldn't pin down a date to get together with his old buddies without the press and his whole campaign crew tagging along.

Finally, after much prodding from Malcolm, Jeremiah had cleared his schedule for one evening. The politician agreed to join them in Wisconsin's Door County, where he owned a summer home. Vic was subbing for an ill priest up in Ellison Bay, a small community north of Stan and Emily's campground, so meeting up in "The Door" was a natural. As for Malcolm, Stan guessed, he was happy for any excuse to take his new sailboat for a cruise.

Stan looked forward to an evening of drink and debate with The Fractious Four.

CHAPTER 4

Stan put his arm around Emily's waist and pulled her closer to him as they stood at the starboard rail of *Audrey's Dream*, watching the bluffs sail by. The evening was still warm and surprisingly balmy, the water calm as the setting sun took on a soft golden glow. The short trip from Fish Creek to Sister Bay lulled them into a feeling of serenity. Emily squeezed his hand and Stan leaned over to brush his lips across her forehead.

They'd gone back to the Winnie that afternoon and rediscovered the old intimacy they'd thought they'd left behind in their marriage. They had always joked that retirement was going to be a time of renewed vigor. But it was surprising how busy their lives could get, even when they weren't working. Stan was glad for this road trip, glad for some time alone with Emily. Glad for the soft rays of the setting sun that backlit the woman he loved and brought out the beauty that she'd never lost but that he had to admit he sometimes took for granted.

A little later, Stan and Emily returned to the dock where Malcolm and Audrey's sailboat was moored. Malcolm had offered him and Emily "a ride" to the restaurant, suggesting they motor by water from the Fish Creek harbor up around the bluffs to Sister Bay. They would moor at the Sister Bay Harbor and from there it would be just a short walk to the restaurant where they were to meet the others. Stan was grateful for the offer. It would certainly be easier than fighting to negotiate the RV into a non-existent parking space around the popular dining establishment.

"Would you look at that?" Malcolm pointed to an old lighthouse sitting up on the bluff. The rays of the setting sun bounced off its glass chamber, lighting it up.

"That's the Moose's Leap lighthouse," Stan said.

"We toured it yesterday. You'd probably enjoy it," Emily offered.

"It dates from the 1850's," Stan said. "The interior's been remodeled. It's pretty authentic looking."

"Being a lighthouse keeper's wife couldn't have been much fun in those days," Emily observed.

"No, it was a pretty isolated lifestyle back then."

"All those windows to wash!" Audrey exclaimed. "I absolutely do not do windows!"

Emily and Stan laughed.

"Well, lucky for me she's not a lighthouse keeper's wife." Malcolm winked. "It would cost me a fortune in maid service!"

Moments later, he pulled the boat around and into the small harbor at Sister Bay and eased up to the pier. Stan and Emily helped him secure the vessel; then the four of them walked the ten minute jaunt up to the restaurant.

Emily looked down over the choir loft rail and watched Jeremiah Douglas and his wife Glenna work the crowd as they made their way through the throng of diners. Tall, handsome, his dark hair only just beginning to show gray highlights on the edges, he was obviously a man whose face was well known in the community, a man in the midst of an active campaign. A woman that Emily didn't know followed at a respectful distance as Jeremiah shook hands with a couple at one table, slapping the back of a man at another, greeting people by name, introducing himself to others, his smile captivating. Glenna, a stiff smile plastered on her face, spoke to those she knew and waited rather impatiently to be introduced to those she didn't. At one point, she glanced up to where Emily, Stan and the Hoovers were laughing over drinks, and sent a calculated smile up their way. Emily didn't envy the woman her role as the wife of a man determined to be the next governor of the state.

Emily's first reaction when they'd arrived at the restaurant was that she was horribly underdressed. Her summer blazer and slacks seemed suddenly shabby next to Audrey's chic, short-waisted red leather jacket and capri pants. Why do we women care? Emily wondered. But, much to her chagrin, she found that she did. And watching Glenna greet potential constituents in a low-cut, sleeveless, sequined cocktail dress wasn't helping to assuage her sense of personal fashion failure. She herself would never wear chiffon, but she did like the champagne color of the dress. And those strappy high-heeled shoes! Emily glanced down at her own practical sandals and sighed. She'd never make it in Glenna's fashion world.

The restaurant—aptly named The Pulpit—was an upscale dinner club housed in a hundred-and-fifty-year-old renovated church. The stained-glass windows that decorated the walls, while not the originals, gave the dining room a charming ambience. When they'd first entered, the sprightly young woman stationed at an old pulpit converted into a hostess podium asked if they had reservations.

"I believe they're under Jeremiah Douglas's name," Malcolm told her.

"Of course. Follow me." The hostess wound her way through the crush of patrons waiting for tables. Even though the peak summer season had passed, the post-Labor Day crowd swelled on the weekends until the weather turned bitter. The fall colors and harvest festivals were a big draw to city dwellers wanting to get away for a relaxing weekend.

She led the small group through the noisy main dining room with tables elegantly covered with white tablecloths, and past a row of old church pews converted into roomy booths.

At the back of the dining room, she disappeared around a corner. Malcolm gave the others a quizzical look as they followed her. They found themselves at the bottom of a small spiral staircase. The hostess led them up the stairs and into what had obviously once been the choir loft of the old church. A dozen tables were set in the loft, but except for their party, it was empty.

"Well! It looks like we get our pick of tables," Audrey exclaimed.

"Oh, Mr. Douglas likes to seat his guests near the rail," the hostess said. "You won't have to worry about noise. Mr. Douglas prefers exclusive use of the loft when he's here."

"Oh, he does, does he?" said Emily. Stan poked her in the rib with his elbow. "Well, I'm sure we'll enjoy the view."

"Mr. Douglas said to go ahead and order drinks right away. He'll join you shortly. Sondra will be your hostess for the evening."

Malcolm nodded at the young woman and thanked her. As they pulled out their chairs, Emily noticed that the table was set for eight. She wondered who was rounding out their party. Sondra appeared moments later. Stan asked for his usual brandy manhattan. Malcolm ordered bourbon—Jack Daniels—for himself and a key lime martini for Audrey. "A vodka and tonic, with a twist of lime," Emily ordered when the waitress got around to her.

Jeremiah, Glenna, and their guest had entered the restaurant just as the drinks were being served. Emily noticed three extra drinks on the waitress' tray, and surmised that Sondra had anticipated the needs of their host and his wife, as well as that of the mystery guest. Sure enough, they appeared in the choir loft just moments after the waitress.

"Stan! Malcolm!" Jeremiah gave the men hearty handshakes. Then he hugged the women. "Emily, you look as young as ever. And Audrey...ravishing! You remember Glenna." The women gave Glenna quick cheek hugs. Sondra unobtrusively slid the drinks in front of the newcomers and disappeared.

Jeremiah turned to include the second woman. "And this is Shannon, Shannon Lambert, the most determined campaign manager you will ever meet."

Shannon reached out to shake hands all around, repeating each person's name as she went. She wore a sea-green, fitted, linen suit, heels, and a studied lack of suntan. "I hope you don't mind my joining you," she said.

"Any friend of Jeremiah's..." Malcolm replied, holding out a chair for the younger woman.

Emily guessed the campaign manager to be in her early to mid-thirties. She wore her hair in a short, pert cut. And she exuded a captivating energy despite the dark puffiness under her eyes.

"Got caught up in a last minute news conference," Jeremiah said by way of apology for being late. "Some reporter trying to make an issue out of hot air. Where's Vic?"

Stan glanced at his watch. "I would have thought he'd be warming the bar stool long before any of us. Guess he got held up, too."

"That man needs a job with regular hours," Malcolm observed.

Jeremiah laughed and swirled his drink. "Yeah, well, we could all use jobs with regular hours. I vote we order now. I'm hungry and I'm on a tight schedule. Vic can catch up when he gets here." He beckoned the waitress with a smile.

Emily watched as Glenna downed her martini. She noticed that while Jeremiah held his drink, stirred the ice, shook it, brought it close to his lips, stirred it again, he really drank very little of it. She suspected it was a strategy he'd developed to allow him to look like he was being sociable but to always be in control of his wits, something she thought more politicians ought to model.

Just as Glenna finished the last of her drink, Sondra appeared with another, ready to take their orders.

Emily perused the menu. Should she order the bacon-wrapped pork chops marinated and stuffed with Boursin cheese, spinach, roasted red peppers, and mushrooms? Or the grilled, wild Alaskan salmon, accompanied by seasoned mashed sweet potatoes and sautéed vegetables? She decided on the salmon, marveling that Sondra was able to keep track of their entire order without writing anything down.

"Ooh, that sounds good," Audrey gushed, pushing her pink cat's-eyes reading glasses up into her hair, where she left them nestled among the tight black curls before closing the menu with a snap. "I'll have what she's having, but no potatoes. You can double up on the veggies."

"I'd like the spinach and artichoke salad, dressing on the side," Shannon requested, quickly setting aside her menu.

Stan and Malcolm both asked for the rack of lamb, served with Lyonnaise potatoes and sautéed carrots. Jeremiah simply said, "I'll have the steak." Sondra didn't ask how he wanted it done or what kind of potatoes or salad dressing. She'd obviously waited on him enough to know already.

Without even looking at the menu, Glenna said tightly, "Give me what she's having." She nodded at Shannon. "And another of these." She held up her half-finished martini glass, then announced that she needed to use "the little girls' room." As she stood, she wobbled momentarily. Jeremiah frowned, waited until she'd turned her back to the table, then waved his hand unobtrusively over the martini glass, signaling to Sondra that Glenna was finished.

"Listen, guys, I'm going to have to apologize," Jeremiah said. Acknowledging their looks of consternation, he continued quickly, holding his hands palms out as if to quell their protests. "I know. I know. I promised I would go out tonight and do the Fractious Four thing. But..."

"But the work never stops for a governor wannabe," Malcolm drawled with a wink toward Stan.

Jeremiah gave Malcolm a reproachful grin, "I do have a jam-packed schedule and I have to get up mighty early in the morning."

"It's my fault," Shannon offered as mitigation. "Clearly I've overbooked the Senator's schedule."

"Not to mention he has an image to maintain. And an all-night drunken eulogy to our youth at the local watering hole likely wouldn't go over well with the press or the electorate." Stan grinned to show there were no hard feelings.

"Look, when I get to the governor's mansion, I'll have you all over. Dinner. Maybe even a sleepover. I hear the mansion has lots of guest rooms."

"A slumber party?!" Emily laughed.

"With jammies and dancing?" Audrey added to the fun.

"More like a barbeque. With plenty of libations and no need to drive home afterwards."

"To a winning campaign, barbeques, and pajama parties!" Stan toasted, holding his drink glass. The others followed suit, toasting the candidate.

Glenna made her way back to the table just as they were setting their glasses down. Nevertheless, she picked hers up, raised it in a quasi toast of her own. "To my husband." She downed a large gulp.

"So what are you thinking?" Stan asked Jeremiah. "You gonna pull this one off? Become the dairy state's fearless leader?"

Jeremiah shrugged, deferred to Shannon. "Guess you'll have to ask *my* fearless leader. She seems to think we're polling pretty well."

"Jeremiah's polling at fifty-one percent, which isn't bad coming into the final four weeks. Clearly he's got the people's attention. I think we can win this one with a comfortable margin."

"Kind of tough going against an incumbent, isn't it," Audrey asked.

"You know, the interesting thing is," Shannon asserted, "every race Jeremiah has run and won has been against an incumbent."

"Really?" Stan asked. "I guess I hadn't kept track."

"He has a knack for being the right guy at the right time when people are ready for new blood in their government."

"New blood!" Glenna said, raising her glass again, then drinking a long draught.

Shannon politely ignored her. "I have to tell you, a couple of terms as governor, and this man will be ready to unseat any opposition party that might be inhabiting the White House."

"The presidency?" Audrey seemed incredulous. "You're looking that far ahead?"

"It's not out of the realm of possibility."

"My husband the president!" Another toast, another drink. "Maybe then he'll be able to afford the payments on that stupid yacht he bought last year. *The Jerry Rig.* Of all the stupid names."

"Well, now," Jeremiah interjected, discretely moving the water glass closer to his wife. "One race at a time. What I'm interested in right now is what's right for the people of Wisconsin. Whatever the future holds, we'll just have to wait and see."

The salads arrived, but Father Vic still hadn't made an appearance.

"How odd that he should be so late," Emily said. "I don't remember him having trouble with schedules."

"He was the only one who ever made it on time to class!" Malcolm said. "Remember the time you slept through that final?" He pointed his glass at Stan. "You were about fit to be tied. Came up with some lame excuse about a rash."

"It was poison ivy! You conned the prof into believing you'd gotten into some poison ivy the night before, and she took pity on you. Let you take a make-up exam." Jeremiah bellowed his laughter.

"You had calamine lotion daubed all over your body to make it look more realistic!" Malcolm laughed, too.

"Hey, I eventually got an A on that test," Stan defended himself.

"What subject was it?" Audrey asked.

"Philosophy. 'Ethics and the Value of Honesty in an Enlightened Society!'" Everyone at the table laughed loudly.

"Emily, do you have Vic's new number in your cell phone?" Stan asked. "I left mine in the Winnie." Emily shook her head and sighed.

"I have it," Malcolm said, pulling out his phone and punching numbers. Malcolm growled into the rectory's answering machine, "If you're there, Padre, you're late for the service. And we've got a lot to confess, so you'd better hurry. We're up in the choir loft at the Pulpit." He clicked off and winked at the others. "Wouldn't want the housekeeper to get suspicious." Audrey giggled, took a delicate sip from her martini.

"It must be hard being on call twenty-four seven," Stan observed. "I don't think priests get paid enough."

"Probably one of the old geezers in his parish decided tonight was the night to meet the Old Man at the Pearly Gates." Malcolm suggested. "Or maybe a winsome widow felt the need to unburden her soul before taking up with the gentleman next door."

"Oh, Malcolm!" Audrey swatted him lightly on the arm. "Don't be disrespectful."

"Well, what else could it be that would keep old Vic from a night of good food, good booze, and even better company with the Fractious Four?" Malcolm asked.

As if on cue, the "good food" was served and Emily marveled at how different wild Alaskan salmon tasted from the farm bred variety she bought at the grocery store.

At the end of the meal, Jeremiah ordered cognacs all around and a variety of cheesecakes to share. Emily noticed that Shannon only took one bite. The young campaign manager let Jeremiah finish about a third of his drink, then glanced at her watch.

"Senator Douglas, Glenna," Shannon said to the couple. "I'm so sorry to do this to you. But you promised the Thompsons you'd drop by their condo before you left town tonight. They've got a small group of supporters with checkbooks just itching to be tapped into." She smiled apologetically, but her tone was firm. Jeremiah Douglas, the politician, needed to move on to his next campaign event.

Jeremiah nodded, picked up the dinner bill that the waitress had left. "The tab's on me," he said, pulling out his wallet. "We'll chalk it up as a campaign expense."

"Oh, you don't have to do that," Emily chided.

"He can't do that. It would be buying votes. We'll each pay for our own," Malcolm said.

The three men threw their money on the table and the party pushed back their chairs.

CHAPTER 5

"Say," Emily said.

"Say what?" Stan tickled her shoulder with his fingers and pulled her a little closer as he leaned back and gazed up at the hazy swath of stars splayed across the night sky. He lifted his glass, feeling the smooth tingle of the cognac against his lips. The gentle bobbing of the boat made him horny again in a sleepy kind of way. The waning autumn moon smiled down on them.

After their evening at the Pulpit, they had motored the Catalina back around the bluffs to the small harbor nestled next to Moose's Leap Campground. Malcolm pulled out some deck chairs and a bottle of cognac.

"Emily, dear, I just have to show you the latest grandbaby!" Audrey's heels clip-clopped as she ducked back into the cabin. A moment later, she emerged with a silver-filigreed framed photo in one hand and a martini glass and stainless steel shaker in the other. Handing the photo over, she plucked her reading glasses from her hair and perched them on her nose so she could peer over Emily's shoulder.

"Looks like his grandfather," Emily said with a smile.

Audrey thrust the frame in front of Stan.

"Good looking little fella," Stan said, giving the photo a perfunctory glance.

"He has my smile," Audrey declared. "And his mother's eyes." She pushed her glasses up into her hair and stroked the photo with a soft sigh.

"What a glorious night!" Emily leaned back, staring up into the sky. "A shooting star!"

She pointed and the three others turned their heads just in time to see the glow of light as it burned its way across the sky.

"Wow, you don't see one that lasts that long very often," Stan said.

"It's a sign," Malcolm declared. "Good times ahead."

"Speaking of signs," Audrey said, "Emily, did you see the sign for that darling little art nouveau gallery just across from the restaurant? Maybe we could go up there tomorrow."

"I'm sorry. We're leaving in the morning."

"Oh, well. That's too bad. This community is just rife with artists and galleries. Why, just this morning I discovered the most tantalizing little shop with a piece of sculpture that would be perfect for the front foyer."

Malcolm raised an eyebrow at her.

"I admit, it was a bit pricey," she said.

He coughed.

"All right, it was way overpriced. Still it was a perfect treasure." She looked at him disparagingly. "I *didn't* buy it!" Stan winked at Emily.

"At least I didn't spend the morning rummaging through other people's junk." Audrey elbowed Emily good-naturedly.

"Hey, to each her own treasures," Emily replied.

Audrey giggled, noticed her glass was empty, waved it at Malcolm and giggled some more.

Malcolm reached for the martini shaker and poured her another drink.

"Speaking of treasures, that Persian rug I bought," Emily said. "It's up on top of the Winnie. Maybe Malcolm could help you get it down. I'd like to spread it under the awning."

"Tonight?" Stan asked.

"I'm anxious to see how it looks," Emily replied.

"Previously owned art. How quaint," Audrey said. Then she hiccupped. "I want to see it. Let's do go see it, Malcolm. Right now."

"Sure, why not?" But he made no effort to move from the lawn chair perched on the deck of the Catalina. He tilted his glass to his lips.

"No, really. I think we should go," Audrey persisted. "I can't imagine what it could be like to live in a mobile home. I want to see that, too. Now."

"It's an RV," Malcolm corrected her. "A motor home."

"Isn't that what I said?"

"You said a mobile home. A mobile home stays parked in one spot. In a mobile home park."

"Then why on earth do they call it mobile if it doesn't move? Your mobile home moves, doesn't it, Emily?"

"Yes, Audrey." Emily smiled in the dark. "My motor home is very mobile." She reached up and tickled the fingers that were tickling her shoulders. Stan gave her hand a squeeze, sharing her amusement.

"Well, then, let's get mobile and go see it." Audrey stood up sloshing her martini. She drained what was left in the glass and set it on the gunwale.

Malcolm got up with a sigh and offered his hand to Emily. The quartet clambered off the boat and on to the dock, then stumbled along the darkened road toward the campground.

"Damn good thing we're not driving," Malcolm pronounced as he reached for Audrey's elbow to keep her upright.

"Damn good thing," Stan echoed. "Need one hell of a big car to fit all four of us in the front seat. Evening, folks!" He waved at a couple stoking a campfire next to their vintage Airstream.

A round of jovial greetings filled the night air. The campground, which had been all but deserted two nights before when Stan and Emily had first pulled in with their own Winnebago, was now ablaze with party lights and campfires.

"Looks like our neighborhood at Christmastime," Emily observed as they wove their way through the campground.

"It's a party!" Audrey tittered. "I've never been to a trailer park party. How quaint."

"It's a state park, dear, not a trailer park," Malcolm chided his wife as they trailed the Remingtons into a secluded little cul-de-sac.

The Remington's RV had been backed into a small copse of mixed maples, beech, and white birch. A striped awning stretched out over the doorway. A lone wood picnic table sat near an empty fire pit.

"Here we are. Home sweet home away from home." Emily waved her arm with a flourish. "Can we give you a tour?"

Stan pulled a ring of keys from his pocket and thrust one into the lock of the oversized vehicle. Fumbling his hand along the inside wall for the switch, he flipped on the light and invited them in.

"It's like a teeny tiny housh...house!" Audrey stumbled through the door.

Emily mimicked her friend's reaction. "It is a *housh*," she said. "A *housh* on wheelszh. We take it with us where ever we go."

"Kind of like a *shnail?*" Malcolm reached out to steady his wife.

"A shnail on rollershkates!" Audrey hiccupped.

"Shall we commence the tour?" Stan bowed, waving one arm. "What you've got here is your conventional class A motor home."

"What's a class A motor home?" Audrey asked.

"Hell if I know," Stan said.

"A gently used class A motor home," Emily clarified. "It's got ten years of living and traveling on it already."

"You mean you got it at one of your garage sales?" Audrey asked. She spun around.

Stan and Malcolm both grabbed for her to keep her from falling over.

"Must have been some garage." Malcolm said.

"A really loooong garage." Audrey flung her arms out wide.

Stan jumped back to avoid getting hit. "Here you have the cockpit," he said, pointing at the driver's seat.

"A chauvinistic misnomer if there ever was one," Emily quipped.

"And here we have the living room, the kitchen and the dining room, all rolled into one." Stan indicated the interior of the rig.

"It's so cute!" Audrey said.

"Well, I don't know about cute," Emily responded. "But it's certainly serviceable."

"And down this hallway is the bathroom and the master bedroom. And there you have it. A mansion on a chassis."

Stan turned around abruptly to find them all wedged in the hallway leading to the sleeping area.

"I do believe we're *shtuck*!" Audrey announced.

Emily started to laugh at the ridiculous situation. And of course, the laughter was infectious. The harder they all laughed, the tighter they became wedged. Malcolm fell into a paroxysm of coughing, so that Stan had to slap him hard on the back, causing him to cough even harder. Finally Stan decided to take command of the situation.

"Okay. One at a time. Audrey, you go first. Back out. No, no, that way, honey." He grabbed her by the shoulders and turned her around. With lots of giggling and playful poking, they edged out of the hallway and out of the RV.

"Emily, what say you and Audrey build the fire?" Stan suggested. "Malcolm and I will climb up top and fetch that rug you've been clamoring for."

CHAPTER 6

Audrey's scream shattered the tranquility of the campground.

Malcolm grabbed her and pulled her to his chest. The motion muffled her cry which turned into a series of fitful sobs.

Emily grabbed a flashlight and squatted next to the body that had rolled out of the rug.

"Stan, call 911," she ordered.

Stan jammed his hand into his pocket, suddenly sobered. The evening's hilarity had morphed into panic.

"My cell phone? Where is it?" he shouted.

"I don't know. Your golf bag?"

He ran to the RV, unlocked the storage bin over the back wheel, dragged the golf bag out, and rummaged frantically for his phone. In frustration he up-ended the entire thing, scattering clubs and balls onto the hard-packed dirt.

"Here it is!" He reached down and snatched the small phone from under a putter, punched in 911. Nothing happened.

"It's dead!" he shouted in a panic.

"Stan! Here." Malcolm tossed him his Blackberry. Stan punched numbers again.

"We need an ambulance! Hurry!" he shouted into the gadget.

Emily shook her head. "The coroner." Her voice was matter-of-fact, authoritative. "Tell them to send the coroner."

She aimed her flashlight at the head. The body was lying face down. This one was definitely not a candidate for CPR. The skin was cold to the touch. She peered closer at a blood-stained spot on the back of the man's shirt. A bullet-hole?

"The campground," Stan was shouting into the small phone. "Moose's Leap. You know, the one in Fish Creek. Hurry!"

Emily stood up and glanced around the campsite. "Don't touch anything," she started to say. But it was too late. Malcolm had approached the body, grabbed it by the shoulder and rolled it over.

"My god! It's Vic!" Malcolm said, choking on his words.

Stan stood frozen, eyes wide and horrified, the phone forgotten as he, too, recognized the man. Emily gently took the phone from his hand, spoke into it in a business-like tone.

"This is retired Michigan police officer Emily Remington. My location is the Moose's Leap Campground on Highway 42. Site thirty three. We need a police squad and a coroner's unit. We have a dead body here." Emily listened for a moment. Then, "Negative. This one's definitely deceased. Appears to have been shot."

Behind her, Audrey began to sob again.

It took the local police officer seven minutes to arrive at the campground and locate their site. It took other campers at Moose's Leap just a minute and fifteen seconds, by Emily's calculation, to gather and gawk from the moment the squad car made its appearance, siren wailing, lights flashing. There really wasn't any need for that, Emily thought, but she knew she would have done the same. Standard procedure.

In the minutes between the 911 call and the officer's arrival, Stan had announced in a shaky voice, "I need a drink. Anyone else?" Without waiting for an answer, he headed into the RV.

"Don't touch anything!" Emily blurted out again. "You could destroy evidence."

Stan paused with the door half open, looked at her. "Our fingerprints are all over everything around here. I don't think a few more on the Jim Beam bottle are going to make a difference either way." And he disappeared inside. Moments later he came out with a small tray and four drinks. Bourbon. Doubles. Straight up. Malcolm and Audrey eagerly reached for theirs. They were huddled together at the edge of the campsite, as far away from Vic's body as they could manage. Even with the new drinks, everyone had sobered up quickly.

When Stan had offered the tray with the last drink to Emily, she passed. She was on the job now, even if she wasn't officially "on the job." He handed her a pen and notebook, one of his yellow legal pads, not the little pocket-sized kind that police officers usually used. She nodded at him appreciatively and began writing notes as she examined the campsite and the RV. When the local police officer arrived, she went over and greeted him.

"The sheriff's on his way," the young officer told her as he climbed out of his vehicle. "Let's see what ya got."

He had turned off his siren, but left the red and blue lights flashing to invite and welcome the recreational gawkers and sight-seers.

Not long after, the County Sheriff arrived, his tires crunching the gravel on the edge of the road. He frowned at the crowd as he stepped out of his vehicle. He stood a moment, hitched up the police belt around his stocky girth, observing the situation.

The younger officer hurried over.

"Sheriff Pelletier, I've secured this crime scene, sir. The body's over there on the alleged rug. These are the perps that found it."

"Perps?"

"Witnesses, sir."

"Terry, shut off those lights."

Officer Terry quickly obeyed orders.

Emily blinked a couple times to adjust her eyes to the darkness, then she looked up into the frowning eyes of Sheriff Fred Pelletier.

"I'm Emily Remington. I'm the one who called it in."

He looked past her to the men hovering around Audrey.

"She claims she's a police officer, sir," Officer Terry said.

"Retired. From the Escanaba, Michigan Public Safety department," Emily corrected the younger officer.

"Uh huh." The sheriff grunted, and without looking at her, strode over to where Vic's body lay on the rug. He glanced down. "Yup. He's a goner."

He turned finally to Emily. "Don't s'pose there's any chance you knew the victim?"

"Actually, yes," Emily replied.

Pelletier raised an eyebrow.

"His name is—was—Father Victor Virchow. He's a—was—a Catholic priest. He was working up at St. Theresa's in Ellison Bay."

"I thought Father Gannon was the pastor up there," Pelletier said.

"Gannon's apparently on sick leave. Vic—Father Virchow—was subbing for him."

Pelletier nodded, turned to the other officer. "You writing this down, son?"

Emily watched, bemused, as the young man frantically patted his pockets for a notebook and pen.

"So, I take it he's not from this area?" Pelletier asked Emily.

"No, I think his official diocese is Madison. But he's been living with his sister in Green Bay for the past year."

"You got a name for this sister?"

"No, but Stan will have. He and Stan were good friends."

"Stan being...?"

"My husband. Stanford Remington."

"And Mr. Remington was the one who found the body?" Pelletier asked.

"Well, we all did. Stan and Malcolm pushed it off the roof of the RV, but we were all standing here when they unrolled it."

"The body was up on the RV?" Pelletier glanced up at the roof of the massive vehicle, then at the bent, ripped awning.

"It was rolled up inside that rug I bought this morning over at Bailey's Harbor. I had the men tie it onto the roof because I wasn't sure how clean it was and I didn't want it in the RV until I could clean it."

"Shit!" Audrey exclaimed, "Do you know how much it's going to cost to get blood stains out of a carpet?"

Pelletier swung in her direction.

"And you would be...?"

Audrey, horrified at having brought attention to herself, shrunk back against Malcolm.

"This is Audrey Hoover," Emily explained. "And her husband, Malcolm. They're from Milwaukee."

"I think they can speak for themselves."

"We're here for a reunion," Malcolm interjected, seeing the color rise in Emily's cheeks.

The sheriff gave him and Audrey a quick appraisal, then glanced over to make sure the other officer was writing down the information. Then he turned back to Emily.

"I think you all have some explaining to do."

Emily took a deep breath and began recounting the events of the day as they had begun earlier that morning. "After I dropped Stan and Malcolm off at the golf course, I took the RV by myself looking for garage sales..."

CHAPTER 7

"And now, young lady. Do you have the names of these men?"

Emily fought the anger rising in her. "Men?"

"The ones you supposedly bought the rug from."

"Oh." Emily shook her head. Negative.

"An address where you bought it?"

Emily shook her head again. "But I could find it. In the daylight."

"I'm going to have a lot more questions. But for now I'd like to talk with the others," Pelletier said, glancing down at the body again. "Terry, you got an ETA for the coroner?" he asked the local cop.

"Dispatch said a half hour. He was over to Bailey's Harbor, at a fish boil. Should be here any minute."

Pelletier nodded. "Why don't you get the camera out of my car and start taking some shots."

"I'm on it, sir!"

The young police officer sprinted over to the command vehicle and Pelletier turned to Stan.

In answer to the sheriff's question, Stan explained, "We had planned on meeting him. He was supposed to have joined us for dinner this evening. But he never showed up."

"Did you have contact with him recently? Maybe in the past forty-eight hours? Earlier this week?" Pelletier asked.

"No. As far as I know, none of us talked with him in the last couple of days."

"Anyone else at that dinner?" Pelletier prodded.

"Well, yeah. There were several of us. Besides me and Emily and the Hoovers, there was Jeremiah Douglas and his wife."

"*The* Jeremiah Douglas?"

Stan nodded. "And another woman. His campaign manager."

"You know her name?"

"Shannon. Shannon Lambert."

Stan jumped at a sudden flash of light. He turned to see the younger officer taking pictures of Vic's body. "I can't believe this happened to him. How could he have gotten into that carpet?"

"That's what we're going to find out." Pelletier was momentarily distracted by a succession of flashes. He grimaced then glanced down at the glass in Stan's hand.

"You've had a couple of drinks tonight?"

"Oh, this. Cripes! It was such a shock. Needed something to steady the nerves. And, well, yeah, we had a couple at dinner." When Pelletier didn't comment or say anything further, Stan blurted out, "And we had a nightcap on Malcolm's boat." At Pelletier's raised eyebrows, "It was moored then. We had a couple of drinks on the boat and then walked here so Emily could show off the rug. There was no driving involved, if that's what you're worried about. And Emily, she never drinks when she's on the job, so once we found the body, she hasn't had a drop since."

Stan suddenly realized he was blathering. He snapped his mouth shut. As a flash highlighted Vic's body again, he took another long gulp of his Jim Beam.

"I'll get back to you." Sheriff Pelletier strode off to meet the coroner whose van was just edging its way through the crowd clustered around the campsite. The flashing from the camera was nearly constant now.

"Terry! Get rid of these people!" Pelletier shouted.

The officer threw the camera down onto the hood of the patrol car and ran toward the crowd, arms flailing. "Okay, people! Back off! Back off! Nothing to see here!"

Stan wandered over to where Malcolm and a teary-eyed Audrey were sitting on a picnic table.

Emily watched Sheriff Fred Pelletier lead the coroner to Vic's body and converse with him in hushed tones. Pelletier slapped the coroner on the shoulder jovially and headed over to the small group now sitting at the picnic table. Emily couldn't hear what Pelletier was saying, but Malcolm and Stan moved away, reluctantly leaving the sobbing Audrey with the sheriff. It would be a long night of interviewing and questioning.

Emily generally preferred to reserve judgment about people, especially on the first meeting. But Pelletier rubbed her the wrong way. She couldn't fault his investigative style. If Pelletier was any good at his job, Emily knew, they'd each be telling their stories to him again before the night was over. Tedious, repetitive, exhausting, but necessary. It was standard procedure and good police work. But his patronizing attitude rankled her. Emily decided to blow it off and walked over to where Stan and Malcolm had parked themselves in a couple of lawn chairs to watch the activity with dismay.

It was several hours later before the coroner took Vic's body away. Emily held Stan's hand as Officer Terry helped the coroner slide Vic into the long, black body bag and zip it shut. Stan was trembling.

Emily recognized that in their long years of marriage, Stan had never been exposed to this violent a tragedy, and now one so personal. She understood how hard this must be for him. He and Vic had been close friends since college. By the time Stan and Emily had started dating, Vic had already left school for the seminary. Emily had only really known him from their once-or-twice-a-year visits and the stories Stan loved to tell.

Emily wondered how best to help Stan with his grief. But even more than that, she wondered who had killed Vic. And why?

As Officer Terry tacked the yellow crime scene ribbon from tree to tree around the Remington's campsite, Pelletier turned to Emily and Stan. "I can't let you stay in the RV tonight." No apology. It was just the way things were. Emily nodded.

"Can we pack a few things?" Stan asked.

"Sorry, it's a crime scene," Pelletier said.

"Any idea where we can stay tonight?" Emily asked.

"My cousin owns a small motel in town," the younger policeman offered. "I'll see if she can work something out for you."

Emily watched in dismay as he strung the last of the yellow tape across the door of the Winnebago.

CHAPTER 8

"You threw him off the roof?"

"I didn't know he was in the rug," Stan had protested in answer to Sheriff Pelletier's question.

"Well, it certainly wasn't the fall that killed him." But the county sheriff's skeptical look had belied his words.

Stan was mortified remembering their earlier conversation. He felt as if he had indeed killed his good friend. *How could I have been so cavalier up there on the roof? How could I have been so drunk? My God, what have I done?*

Regardless of how much Emily tried to tell him—with her no nonsense police attitude—that he wasn't responsible for Vic's death, that in fact Vic had been dead for several hours, perhaps even a day, still Stan couldn't shake his guilt.

"Who do you think killed him?" Stan asked when they were alone later that night. "Why did they roll him up in that rug? Why did they put him up on our Winnebago? *Why* would they kill him?" The questions were coming fast and furious. "My god! If this is someone's idea of a joke..."

"...it's cruel and despicable," Emily finished his thought. She handed him a strong cup of coffee, then poured herself one from the small coffee maker provided in the motel room. They moved out onto the tiny balcony. Even though the night was chilly, they both preferred it to the stuffiness of the room.

"And that sheriff! Emily, I can't believe he declared the Winnebago a crime scene!"

"It's standard procedure, hon." She sipped at the steaming mug.

"It's as if he thinks we killed Vic. Right there. In our... our..."

"He thinks no such thing. He simply has to preserve evidence."

"You don't think the murderer was inside our motor home, do you?" Stan shuddered.

"I doubt it. The door showed no evidence of tampering," Emily offered. She rubbed the palms of her hands slowly along the warmth of the coffee cup. "When I think about it, I bet I only met Vic a dozen times in all the years we've been married," she mused.

"Well, yeah, he'd left for the seminary before you and I started dating. I think that was just a couple of months after the bombing."

"Oh, god. The bombing." Emily closed her eyes against the memory.

"Sometimes I still have nightmares about it," Stan said softly. "I dream that you're in a squad car parked in front of the building, getting ready to check it out, and I'm trying to reach you to tell you to get out of there."

"I wasn't doing car patrol in Madison back then. That was before they let women do anything but dispatch and process. I was on foot patrol that night only because they were short-handed."

"Well, dreams have their own time line, I guess. I can remember the sound of it. What was it, something like three or four in the morning? The concussion hit my apartment building like an earthquake and just about knocked me out of bed."

"Did the bombing have something to do with why Vic went into the seminary? I don't remember you ever mentioning it," Emily said.

"You know, he was sort of a perennial student back then. Thrived on campus life. And not particularly religious, although I knew he was a Catholic. I just don't even remember him going to Mass during any of those days. He was sort of the undeclared ring-leader of our Fractious Four. He was the one who always found the next protest, the next sit-in. I mean, Malcolm and I believed fervently in every protest we took part in. Even Jeremiah, in his own way. But Victor. Vic's belief in the greater good was always more intense, more profound. It was like he lived and breathed it." Stan sipped at his coffee, let the hot liquid rest against his tongue for a moment. "It seemed like he never outgrew the sixties the way the rest of us did."

Emily sat quietly. She knew from long experience it was better just to let him ramble with his thoughts. The story of Vic would emerge if she didn't interrupt.

"I remember how shocked I was that afternoon—it must have been early October, just a month or so after the bombing. Vic asked me if I wanted to go get a beer. After we'd had three or four, he announced he was going into the seminary. I thought it was a big joke. Toasted his insanity and ordered another round. But he was dead sober serious. I could have spit my beer right then and there. I reminded him that he hadn't been inside a church since before I'd met him."

Stan shook his head at the memory.

"He said the very fact that he'd lost his religion during those years was all the more reason he knew his calling was the real thing. 'God is never obvious in his invitations.' That's what he said. 'And he doesn't always call those already in the choir.' I thought he was nuts."

Stan got up, took Emily's cup and went inside to pour them each another cupful of coffee. When he returned and handed it back to her, he sat for a long time saying nothing. After a while he simply repeated, "I thought he was nuts."

They watched as the sliver of moon kissed the tops of a stand of cedars.

"The thing about Vic was, he believed that everything he did—fighting for the end of the war, for civil rights, for human rights—had all been God's work. He truly believed that. He told me that he just hadn't realized it until that awful day of the bombing.

"I'd noticed a change in him, of course. He'd gone into a deep depression. I didn't understand it at the time. I mean, he didn't have anything to do with what happened. But what he told me was that for weeks afterward—I suppose just because of the horror of it—he'd just sort of lost his moral compass. He didn't know anymore what was up and what was down in the world. All he knew, he said, was that innocent souls were dead. He went into seclusion. He avoided me, Malcolm, everyone. He stopped going to classes. He told me that day that he'd spent two weeks wandering the streets at night and weeping uncontrollably.

"Finally he went and sought out an old friend of his father's, a Capuchin priest. He said he confessed four and half years worth of sins, then bared his soul of all his moral conflicts and confusions—those were his words. I remember them clearly. 'Moral conflicts and confusions' about everything he'd ever done during his protests against the war. Made me feel like shit, because I wasn't particularly conflicted or confused. And then he said—get this—he said he confessed his ambivalence about the bombing. Apparently the priest was a good listener. Never judged Vic. Never put him down for four years of living in apparent sin. All he said to Vic was, 'When God speaks, it's important to listen.'"

"Did Victor think God was speaking to him by letting a bunch of crazies bomb a building and kill innocent people?" Emily was incredulous.

"Well, that's the thing. That's apparently what Vic had accused this Capuchin of implying. But that wasn't what the old man was saying at all. The priest had simply told him, 'What I am telling you is God had been speaking to you for four years before that bombing. The bombing—an unfortunate, horrific coincidence—somehow has managed to open your ears.'"

The moon was now half sunk into the cedar stand. It lit up a small cloud passing over it.

"So that's when Victor decided to become a priest?"

"Not that very day. But not long after. By the time he and I talked, he'd made up his mind. He told me that if he was going to make a difference in the world, doing it as God's work was the best route for him. So that's what he did. He graduated as a political science major and a week later entered the seminary."

The moon was gone. The sky looked suddenly empty and desolate.

"I think I need to go to bed," Stan said.

Emily nodded, took their coffee cups and went inside. Stan stood up as well, but leaned against the rail for a long time, gazing out at the moonless sky. Finally he heaved a jagged sigh and shuffled back into the stuffy warmth of the motel room where Emily was almost asleep on the bed.

"His sister," Stan said.

"What?" Emily asked. "Who?"

"Vic's sister. I suppose I should call her in the morning."

51

CHAPTER 9

Emily stood in the shower, feeling the hot water cascade over her head and shoulders and down her back. The spray was forceful, and there were times she felt she had to emerge for air. She was hoping the water would wash away the awful memories from the night before. If she closed her eyes, she still saw the stiff body roll out of the carpet like a prize in a macabre competition.

But something was nagging at the back of her brain; something wasn't right. She reviewed the crime scene. A shiver ran down her back, despite the hot water. The crime scene was their Winnebago, their home away from home. And the victim was her husband's good friend. She forced herself to set her emotional involvement aside for the moment and look at the situation with the practiced eye of a police officer who'd surveyed many crime scenes. Something seemed out of place, out of sorts. She shook her head, causing spray to hit the shower curtain. If only she could put a finger on it. Maybe later in the day. She certainly wanted to go back to the campsite and look at it more thoroughly and in the daylight. And with the vantage point of caffeine in her system, rather than alcohol.

The heat of the shower felt less intense now; perhaps she had run the hot water tank empty. Turning the faucet to the off position, she parted the shower curtain, reached for the stiff white towel hanging from a rod next to the tub, and wrapped it around herself. She used a second towel to tousle her wet hair. After running a comb through the soft curls, she slipped into the bra and panties she'd worn the day before. She hoped they'd be able get back into the Winnie for fresh clothes soon.

Memories of the night's flurry of activities still lingered. The initial stunned silence as the four friends realized what lay before them on the darkened earth. Malcolm reaching for the body and turning it face up before she could stop him. The hasty 911 call. The strangled wailing from Audrey. The startled voice of Malcolm shouting, "My god, it's Vic!" The lights flashing from the police cars and the coroner's van. The hushed murmurs from the crowd of campers that had gathered to watch and speculate. The sheriff's cynical questions put to the tipsy foursome, shocked out of their alcohol induced states by the sight before them.

The sheriff. What a jerk. Emily had known cops like this all her working life. They had started their careers with perhaps an altruistic goal, helping the community be safe and secure. But years of run-ins with sassy kids, drunk community leaders, petty crooks and liars, frequent calls at the same addresses for domestic violence had rendered them with a perverse, cynical view of the people they served. These cops didn't believe anyone, didn't like anyone. Cops like Pelletier treated everyone with the same arrogant attitude, except for an occasional slip when they took pity on a homeless teenager and found her a safe home or rescued a little old lady from a peculiar traffic offense.

Pelletier had been rude and offensive, talking down to Emily specifically, since she had taken the lead in describing the situation and providing information about how and what. But Emily had learned to shrug off cops like him. There was no point in letting him bother her. This might not be her beat, but she wasn't about to back down when it came to investigating a crime that hit so close to the heart.

She opened the bathroom door, checking to make sure the curtain was closed before coming out into the room in her undies. Stan sat on the edge of the bed staring at the TV set. *NEWS BREAK!* banners flashed across the screen. A local anchor was describing the events of the night before.

"...police have not yet confirmed the identity of the homicide victim found last night at Moose's Leap Campground. However, our Eye-On-The-Scene reporter is interviewing witnesses at the campground."

The scene switched to the reporter, the yellow-taped RV behind her. "What can you tell me about last night?" she asked as she thrust the microphone into the face of a man in a Packers cap.

"It was gruesome," the camper exclaimed. "Blood all over. I know I heard those shots. I remember tellin' my wife. 'Didn't that sound like a gun shot?' People ain't safe around here—"

Emily stepped between Stan and the TV. "You said last night that you wanted to call Vic's sister." She grabbed her wrinkled slacks and blouse from where they lay on the bed and pulled them on.

Stan hit the OFF button on the remote.

"Yeah, I'm trying to remember her name. Begins with a B. Beth, maybe. Belinda. Betty. Beverly. That's it. Beverly." Stan was already rummaging in his pocket for his cell phone.

He dreaded this call, dreaded the words that would have to somehow leap from cell tower to cell tower all the way from Fish Creek past Sturgeon Bay to the city of Green Bay to tell a woman that her brother, someone she had loved since childhood, was dead. Murdered. Stan tried to power on the phone. No juice. Damn. One of these days he'd learn to keep it charged, he chided himself.

"Do you have a power cord in your purse?"

Emily rolled her eyes. She dug into the one bag the sheriff had let them keep and pulled out her power cord. She also produced an extra pair of reading glasses. "You might need these, too," she said.

"Thanks. But what the hell am I going to read? That sheriff wouldn't let me take my laptop or even a book. What did he think? That I hollowed out my favorite annotated copy of *Poor Richard's Almanac* and hid the murder weapon in it?"

Stan jammed the power cord into the small portable phone and then into the wall, thus eliminating the portability that was the reason he'd bought the damn thing in the first place. He punched the numbers for directory assistance. Then he punched in the sequence the computerized voice had given him for Beverly Thayer. The phone rang three times before Beverly picked up.

"Hello?"

"Beverly?"

"Yes?"

"It's Stan. Stan Remington."

Emily signaled that she was stepping outside onto the balcony. Stan waved his thanks and turned away, focusing on the woman on the phone.

"Stan! Oh, it's so good to hear your voice. The bishop just called. Vic's..." A sob rose in her throat, breaking off her words. "Vic's been...murdered."

"Yes. Yes. I know." Stan suddenly wished he was doing this in person. "Oh Beverly, I'm so sorry. This must be very hard on you." Stan wiped his nose with his handkerchief. He sat down heavily onto the room's floral couch. "I'd, I'd like to help. In any way I can."

"Stan." Her voice was still shaky, but more in control now. "Who could have killed Vic? He was such an honest soul."

"I agree. No one I knew had more integrity." Stan started as a sudden sharp rap sounded on the motel door.

Emily hurried in through the balcony doors. "I'll get it."

Sheriff Fred Pelletier stood outside their room, his right hand rocking the handle of the pistol at his hip. "Mornin'. I have some more questions. For each of you. Alone."

"Stan's on the phone right now. Why don't you and I go out to the court yard?" Stan watched appreciatively as Emily reached for her gray sweatshirt on a hook by the door and stepped out of the room, shutting the door behind her.

He fingered the phone cord as Beverly's voice came through the tiny appliance.

"The sheriff," she said. "I think he told me he was from Sturgeon Bay. He called right after I talked to the bishop. He was asking me lots of questions about Vic. About you and Malcolm, too. Why? He doesn't think you...?"

"Unfortunately, Malcolm and I found him." Relieved that Emily had taken the sheriff outside, Stan didn't have the heart to tell Beverly how they had dumped his body off the top of the motor home. "I'm sure the sheriff just wants to know who we are and what we might know about why Vic was killed." Stan's voice sounded more confident than he really felt. Why would the sheriff be asking questions about *them*? He should be looking for the murderer.

"You saw his body? How was he...? How did he look?" Beverly's voice was a whisper of pain now.

Stain took a deep breath. The images started flashing in his mind again. "It was rough, Beverly. Seeing my friend, seeing Vic that way. But he... he looked like it must have been sudden. You know. Like he didn't suffer. There was a bullet hole. But I didn't see any bruises."

Stan could hear her weeping now, quietly, on the other end of the line. "Is there anything I can do for you, Beverly?"

"Thanks, Stan. The bishop's office will help me plan the funeral. Father Rydelle, the bishop's representative, is here right now. But, yes. There is something you can do for me."

"Sure, what is it?"

There was a pause. "I have this idea, but I can't talk about it now. The sheriff wants me to go up to the morgue in Sturgeon Bay to...to...to identify Vic. I also need to go to St. Theresa's rectory up in Ellison Bay to get Vic's stuff. I don't think there's much. I'll call you when I'm on my way back and we can meet to discuss it."

"Okay. I'm at a motel called Jessie's Nest in Fish Creek. Right on 42. I'll wait for your call. Let me give you my cell phone number."

Stan told her once again how sorry he was about Vic, and they said their goodbyes. He clicked off and set the phone down on the desk to finish charging.

CHAPTER 10

Emily and Sheriff Pelletier sat across from each other in the white-washed gazebo that dominated the small, well-tended courtyard of the motel. Beds of marigolds and chrysanthemums flanked the outside of the structure. Emily had positioned herself on one of the three benches surrounding a green wood-slatted table, which provided space for guests to enjoy an ice cream cone, play cards, or smoke away from the non-smoking rooms.

She folded her hands together on top of the table to steady herself. She wasn't particularly nervous, but the intensity of emotions from the night before had thrown her off kilter. She had a sudden flash of sympathy for the many "persons of interest" she'd interviewed in her own long years of law enforcement. She appreciated, perhaps for the first time, the anxiety displayed by those whom she questioned about things as simple as traffic accidents or home invasions.

Pelletier took off his wide-brimmed hat and placed it on the table between them. There was a period of protracted silence as the sheriff fumbled with the button of his shirt pocket, pulled out a small tattered spiral notebook and a Bic pen and set them on the table.

He removed his dark tinted sunglasses and rubbed his eyes. Emily suspected he'd been up most of the night. When he looked up, his blue eyes stared at her with a hint of cynicism. After a moment he slid the sunglasses back onto his nose, which gave him a decided advantage when it came to non-verbal sparring. Emily could no longer read the intensity of his gaze, or even whether it was directed at her or somewhere over her shoulder. As most police officers do, he waited for her to speak first.

She fought the urge to smirk. That was her own m.o. Old habits die hard, and she wasn't any more inclined to initiate the conversation than he was.

Sheriff Pelletier's face was pocked by the scars of adolescent acne. He flexed his fat, stubby fingers with the nails bitten to the quick. A few wisps of blonde hair topped his head but he had made no attempt to grow the side hair long to comb over the bare spot. He smelled faintly of Old Spice and pipe tobacco. A Good Ol' Boy, Emily thought.

Emily won the stand off.

"Tell me again how you found the body of..." he consulted the open notebook. The black scratchings on the page were so disjointed Emily wondered if he could read his own handwriting. "...of Father Victor Virchow."

"The rug was up on the roof of the Winnie. Stan and Malcolm rolled it off the roof and untied it. The body was there. In the rug." Emily furrowed her brow at the memory. Something was nagging her about that sight.

"How do you suppose it got there?"

Emily shrugged. "Haven't a clue."

"But you know the guy, right?"

"A little. Actually he was an old friend of my husband's. I'd only met him a few times."

"How did he get into the rug?"

Emily just shook her head and brushed away a fly buzzing in front of her face. She fought the urge to make his work harder by answering as briefly as possible. Was this really how others felt being questioned? After all, she did want Vic's murderer found, didn't she?

The sheriff tapped his pen impatiently on the table. "When did you last see the good padre?"

"I hadn't seen him in several years. He was supposed to meet us for dinner and we were surprised when he didn't show up."

"Tell me about the dinner."

"It was supposed to be a reunion."

The sheriff jotted down a few more incomprehensible scratchings. "The restaurant...?"

"The Pulpit. In Sister Bay."

Pelletier nodded his head. "Can you go over that guest list again?"

"Besides us—that is, Stan and me—there was Malcolm and Audrey, Jeremiah Douglas and his wife, Glenna, and his campaign manager, Shannon Lambert." Emily was silent a moment.

"Vic should have been there." Emily was surprised to find her eyes tearing up and quickly blinked away the tear. "As I said, it was a reunion of old college friends. But he never arrived."

"How often did they get together?"

"Well, Malcolm and Stan see one another occasionally— maybe a couple of times a year. Stan and Vic kept in touch quite frequently, I think. E-mail and phone calls mostly. For several years after college, all four used to get together frequently, but after a while..." she shrugged. "Well, you know how it is. The visits got more and more infrequent. I would guess the last time they were all together was, oh, five, six years ago."

When Emily stopped, the sheriff looked at her waiting for more. When she didn't offer more he said, "Just trying to see the big picture. Who arranged this dinner last night?"

"Malcolm, I think. Maybe Vic." She shrugged. "Actually I only became aware of it once the date was set."

"Any idea who might want the good padre dead?"

"Not a clue." Emily shifted her weight on the bench and stretched her back. She was getting stiff.

"Now about this rug. Tell me again how the body came to be in there." His pen was poised in the air in anticipation of scrawling down her response.

"I told you, I don't know. I was as surprised as anyone." For heaven sakes, did he really think she'd put it there? "I bought the rug at a garage sale yesterday morning. And last night, when we took—when Malcolm and Stan pushed it off the top of the RV and unrolled it—there was Vic. Dead." Emily felt a warm flush course through her body. She was sure her face was beet red.

"A garage sale, huh? Tell me more about that. Where? What time exactly?" The pen was poised above the notebook again and Pelletier was watching her closely.

"About eleven a.m. I remember checking the time on the dash. Bailey's Harbor. There was a neighborhood sale—eight or nine families on the same street."

"Did *you* put the rug up on the roof?" His voice indicated disbelief.

A small bead of sweat formed on her upper lip. Shit! "Of course not." She swiped at her lips with the back of her hand. The heat was rising inside her. "Two guys from the house where I bought it rolled it up and hauled it up top." Suddenly she stood up and ripped at her sweatshirt, unzipping it part way but pulling it over her head before she could finish, fighting to keep her blouse from riding up with it. Then she sat back down and calmly folded the sweatshirt, setting it on the bench next to her.

The sheriff stared at her, at a loss for words.

"Hot flash," Emily said with a smile.

Pelletier was off his beat. "I, uh, I take it there was no body in the rug then?"

"As a matter of fact, I didn't check. I didn't actually see them put it up there. I was at another house. The rug was there, all tied up and fastened to the RV when I got back."

Pelletier glanced over at the neatly folded sweatshirt, then took a deep breath. "Where was your husband all this time?"

"At the golf course—the State Park course—with Malcolm. I picked them up around one. I'm afraid I was a bit late, but they were happy enough at the 19th hole. I drove Malcolm back to his boat down at Fish Creek Harbor and then Stan and I went for lunch."

"The rug was on the roof the whole time?"

She nodded. "We didn't try to take it down until last night when we found the body."

Pelletier flipped to a new page in the notebook. A yellow butterfly landed on the table between them and then flitted off. The morning sun had now risen enough that the gazebo was in complete shade. Emily was grateful, for the day was promising to be warm and humid. She wished she had a tall glass of iced tea about now.

"Mrs. Remington! Mrs. Remington, I'm so glad I caught you." Jessie, the inn's proprietor, a petite woman with short, tousled hair, walked purposely toward them. "Do you know how long you and your husband will be staying?"

Emily looked at the sheriff, who shook his head.

"For a few days anyway. Why? Is there a problem?"

"I'm wondering if I could move you from room eighteen to room thirteen. A returning customer will be arriving this afternoon, and she always asks specifically for eighteen. Fact is, she's had it reserved for months."

"Oh, sure. I'll let Stan know. We can be out of the room in a half-hour or so." She and the sheriff watched Jessie go back to the café.

"Just a couple more questions. Where were you and the RV the rest of the afternoon?"

"After lunch we drove to our campsite. We, uh, took a nap." Emily blushed, remembering their lovemaking.

"A nap? For how long?"

"Well, you know. The whole afternoon."

"You napped the entire afternoon?"

"Well, not the *entire* afternoon."

"Then, what did you—?"

Emily couldn't make herself look him in the eye.

"I assure you, we were in the RV the whole time."

"Is there anyone who can verif—" The sheriff suddenly seemed to get it.

"Of course not," she snapped.

There was an awkward silence as Pelletier tried to figure out what to ask next. "About what time did you leave the RV?"

"About six. After we showered and dressed for dinner."

Pelletier changed the subject. "Did the padre have anything with him that was valuable?"

"When he died?"

"I mean when he came up to sub at St. Theresa's."

"I don't know," said Emily. "He was a priest. What would he have that would be of value to anyone else?"

"Some priests have expensive chalices. Gifts from parishioners. Things like that."

"I guess you'd have to ask Stan. I'm certainly not aware of anything." She looked at him curiously. "Why?"

"Just trying to determine motive." Pelletier folded his notebook and put it and the pen back in his shirt pocket, buttoning the flap securely. "I think that's about it for now. Stick around will you? After I talk to your husband, I think we should go for a drive to find that garage sale."

Emily nodded her agreement. "I'll wander over to the café for a cup of coffee while you chat with Stan."

"I appreciate that," Pelletier said. Emily watched as he lumbered back to the room where Stan was just finishing up his phone conversation with Vic's sister.

Emily stood up and stretched her back. She was turning toward the café when a woman called her name. It was Shannon Lambert, getting out of a new silver Lexus in the parking lot. Emily was impressed that the woman was driving a hybrid. She had pulled in next to Pelletier's empty squad car.

"Do you know where the sheriff is?" Shannon asked, walking briskly toward her.

"He's with my husband, Stan."

"I need to see him right away."

"I don't think he wants to be interrupted right now. Why don't you come have a cup of coffee with me?"

A shadow of impatience flicked across the woman's face. But she smiled. "I'm dying for a cup of coffee."

Over steaming mugs Shannon reached for Emily's hand. "This is so shocking. How horrible it must have been for you to find Father Virchow's body."

"It's upsetting for everyone. How's Jeremiah?"

"Totally devastated. I've cancelled all his appointments for today. Clearly he needs time to grieve over his friend."

"I take it he spoke with the sheriff?"

"They met early this morning. Emily, is there anything I can do? Has the media been a problem? I have contacts if you need me to—"

"We're fine. We just want to find out what happened to Vic."

"Of course. I'll make a few phone calls—make sure the local police have all the resources they need." She handed Emily her business card. "If you or Stan need anything."

Emily took the campaign manager's card, not sure what exactly she or Jeremiah's office could do that wasn't already being done. But she was grateful for the offer.

Stan sat hugging the edge of the sofa, hands between his knees. Pelletier had pulled up a straight-back chair to sit facing him. After the usual questions about what they'd been doing the night before, where and when things happened—the same questions he'd asked Emily, Stan assumed—Pelletier switched subjects.

"Tell me about this friend of yours," Pelletier said. "The padre."

"Vic? Vic was..." Stan thought for a moment, framing his answer. There were so many things he could say. How Vic was a phenomenal priest, one who really cared about people, who modeled his life truly on the teachings of his savior. He could tell him how Vic had been there for him when Stan's father died suddenly of a heart attack while Stan was still in college. How Vic had counseled him during tough spots in his marriage. "Vic broke a lot of hearts when he went into the seminary," he finally blurted out.

Pelletier raised an eyebrow at this.

"He was the kind of guy women loved to love," Stan went on. "They loved talking to him. Maybe because he was such a good listener. Maybe for the very attribute that made him such a good priest." Stan laughed as he remembered, "And they didn't stop loving him just because he had a collar on."

Pelletier seemed nonplussed. Stan grinned.

"I can't tell you how many times, in how many parishes he found himself fending off a woman who was obsessed with trying to seduce him. One nutcase even took her shirt and bra off in the confessional! Bless me, Father, for I am sinning as we speak." Stan was laughing now. "I thought Vic would bust a gut telling me that story! Oh, I know, he wasn't supposed to reveal what people told him under the seal of confession. But this woman wasn't confessing, she was stripping!"

By now Pelletier could no longer suppress his own grin.

"I don't suppose you have a name for this woman? Know what parish she was at?"

Stan just shook his head no.

"Anyone else stand out?" Pelletier asked. "Anyone who might have taken his rejection of her personally? I mean, even though he was a priest?"

"Gee, not that I can think of. I mean, there was one woman who kept moving from parish to parish, every time he'd get transferred. She was pretty much a nuisance. I think at one point he even got a restraining order against her. I suppose you could find out from the bishop."

Pelletier nodded and added a note to his list.

"The padre ever get any gifts from his admirers—women or otherwise—that might be considered expensive?"

"He showed me a crucifix he'd gotten once. From a parish council as a thank you gift when he'd gotten transferred. It was gold plated and had diamonds on it. I dunno. I suspect that cost a pretty penny."

"Would he have had it with him up in Ellison Bay?"

"Hard to say. I suppose it's possible."

"Anything else?"

"I don't know. Parishioners gave him gifts all the time. It actually sort of bothered him. But what he might have carried with him, I can't say."

The sheriff shifted in his chair.

"Tell me about Mr. Hoover."

"Malcolm? What about him?"

"What was his relationship with the padre like?"

"They were friends. We're all friends. What are you getting at?"

"Just gotta ask. He ever take exception to any of those fanatical movements the padre got himself involved in?"

"You mean Vic's work organizing protests against racial injustice? His efforts to get the government to take a stand on eliminating poverty? Hell, Malcolm was usually standing right there next to Vic at the front of the rally."

"His wife one of those who found the padre attractive?"

Stan's jaw dropped. He just stared at the lawman. Finally, he collected his wits. "I guess you'd have to ask her."

"I will," Pelletier said. And he stood up to end the interview.

CHAPTER 11

An hour later, Emily climbed into the passenger side of Sheriff Fred Pelletier's Chevy Tahoe. The big man had yet to smile.

"Got a cousin works for the Gladstone police up near you," Pelletier said as he eased the vehicle out onto Highway 42 heading north. "Maybe you know him? Name's Cal LeBlanc."

"Cal? Yeah, I know Cal. He's been with the Gladstone force for years," Emily said. A quick picture of Calvin LeBlanc flashed into her head; he was just about the exact opposite of Fred Pelletier. Where Pelletier was stocky and solid, Cal was tall and wiry. She thought they likely were about the same age, just shy of fifty.

A quarter mile from the motel, the sheriff turned onto County Trunk F and barreled east across the peninsula. Emily guessed that there was more to Pelletier's casual mention of his cousin than just a conversation starter. More than likely he had already contacted Cal to find out what he knew about Emily and Stan. That was just good police work, and Emily would have done the same if the tables had been turned.

Thank goodness Cal knew both of them. The Gladstone police officer had taken some courses at the college in Escanaba a few years back and had Stan as an instructor for a U.S. history course. And of course he and Emily knew each other from law enforcement seminars, social events, and the occasional professional cooperation that went on between the two police departments. She was confident that Cal would give her a good report.

Emily gazed out at the countryside. She'd been down this road just twenty-four hours earlier. But then she had been behind the wheel, focusing on locating the numerous garage sales listed in the local classifieds. Now she was free to take notice of the abundant cherry orchards and the scattered dairy farms. Emily remembered Stan telling her about World War II German prisoners of war being put to work picking cherries from the orchards up this way. She wondered if they appreciated how different their experience was from that of most prisoners of war. Likely they did. Stan had said that some of them had chosen to stay in America when the war ended.

The day had started out bitingly cool, as early autumn days often did in this part of the country. But, as those same autumn days often did, the air was quickly growing warm, the sun burning off the last of the ground fog that had settled over the farm fields during the night.

Emily could smell the lingering odor of spent bonfires and burning leaves, a smell she remembered from her childhood. She gazed at the old farm buildings that would have been abandoned and left to rot in any other part of the country, but here were almost all given over to art galleries and gift shops or renovated retirement homes. Halloween came early to these parts with pumpkins taking over front lawns, ghosts hanging from trees, and raggedy gravestones popping up in unlikely places.

As the cruiser sped through the intersection of two quiet country roads, Emily's eye was caught by a rustic looking art gallery that she decided was likely a reincarnated crossroads general store. Pelletier slowed the car to avoid a flock of wild turkeys taking their time crossing the road. An osprey flew overhead, circling its nest in a cell tower. Emily was amazed at how different this backroads area looked from the ones she was used to traversing in Michigan's Upper Peninsula and even in the northern counties of Wisconsin. If there was poverty on this peninsula, it was well disguised by pride of ownership. Even the occasional trailer home had a manicured lawn and variegated garden.

"You said earlier this was your first time over at Moose's Leap," Pelletier observed.

"It's a nice campground. Wish we could have stayed longer," Emily said ruefully.

The officer nodded his head. "You know why they call it Moose's Leap, don't ya?"

Emily looked at the sheriff with a curious smile. "Tell me," she said.

"Had to do with an old Indian rite-of-passage ceremony. The Winnebagos, I think it was. Or maybe the Potawatomis. Anyway, when their boys reached the age of puberty, they had to prove their manhood to all the young Indian maidens. So the elders would round up all the moose in the area. And the young men—just teenagers, really—would jump on the moose's backs and race them to the edge of the bluff. They were supposed to jump off just before the moose leaped to their death into the bay. The brave that came the closest to the edge of the bluff before jumping off got to have his pick of all the fair maidens. Thus, Moose's Leap."

"Well! That's a new version," Emily exclaimed. "The only problem with it is, there are no moose on this peninsula."

"Yeah, them Indians. It was real rough on the herd."

Emily stared at Pelletier. He didn't take his eyes off the road. He didn't smile. He didn't wink. But there was a twitch at the corner of his lips that betrayed him.

"I think maybe you people on this side of the bay drink a bit too much moose juice," Emily observed.

The trip across the peninsula had taken no more than twenty minutes. As they approached the end of County Trunk F in the middle of Bailey's Harbor, Emily could see the waters of Lake Michigan. The mood of the lake was certainly different from that of the Green Bay side of the peninsula. Here the water was rougher, more expansive, like looking out over the ocean. Ore ships traversed these waters, ships as big as some ocean freighters.

At the T in the road, the sheriff turned the car south onto State Highway 57, the main thoroughfare of the small fishing town. Emily directed him into the neighborhood of ranch-style and older two-story, middle-class homes.

"I parked the Winnebago here," she said, pointing out the spot just to the left of a utility pole where she had worked so hard to fit the oversized vehicle the day before.

Pelletier pulled the police cruiser into the same spot. Emily got out and looked around. "It was a neighborhood sale. I must have stopped at ten houses. But the one I bought the rug from was that brown and white clapboard house with the porch."

"You stay here, by the car."

Emily frowned. "So, what happened to professional courtesy? Doesn't count this side of the bay?"

Pelletier gave her a sidelong glance. He grunted once and Emily took that to mean she was invited along on the interview after all. She fell into step behind him as he walked down the block. They climbed the porch steps and Pelletier rapped loudly on the front door.

The teenage girl with the wad of gum in her mouth answered the door. She chewed for a moment before acknowledging them. "Yeah?" She chewed some more. Emily wondered if it was the same piece from yesterday or if she had bothered to start the day with a fresh stick.

"Your parents home?" the sheriff asked.

"Yeah." She turned her head into the room. "Ma!" She chewed while she waited for her mother to come to the door.

"Yes?" the mother said. She was a slight woman, not much bigger than her daughter, and with the same dishwater blonde hair. Neither of them seemed to have spent much time brushing it that morning. "Is there a problem?"

"I'm Sheriff Fred Pelletier, Ma'am. I have a few questions I'd like to ask you about your garage sale."

"My garage sale? Why? I didn't break any laws. You don't need a permit to hold a garage sale, do you?"

"No, Ma'am."

"Look, if you think I was selling stolen goods..."

"No, Ma'am. That's not the issue. Do you mind telling me your name?" Pelletier asked.

"Do I have to?" the woman grew nervous.

"No, Ma'am. I could call in your address and we could find out your name that way. But I'm a busy man, and that would just serve to irritate me, and I don't think we want to start our conversation out with me being irritated."

"Oh. No. Of course not. I'm Cindy Lowden. This is my daughter Amy."

Amy blew a bubble with her gum and popped it. Cindy looked at Emily curiously.

"She was here yesterday," Amy said. "Bought that ugly rug." Then she blew another bubble.

"This is retired police officer Emily Remington," Sheriff Pelletier said. "We have a couple of questions about that rug. May we come in?"

Cindy opened the door reluctantly and they squeezed past.

"That rug was ours free and clear to sell. And all sales are final. You're not complaining we charged too much, are you? There's no restrictions on what you can price things at a garage sale."

"I'm happy with the price I paid for the rug," Emily offered.

"We didn't steal that rug. Are you saying we stole it?"

"No, Ma'am," the sheriff said. "There've been no complaints against your garage sale."

"Did my son do something? Did Mikey steal something from you?" the woman asked, her voice rising. "Mikey! Mikey!!"

"Ma'am," Emily said, "when I bought that rug, a very nice man rolled it up for me."

Cindy looked confused.

"Dad." Amy snapped another bubble.

"Todd. That would have been Todd. He do something?"

"And there was another man that helped him carry it to my RV. Maybe a brother?" Emily asked.

"Uncle Ted."

"He—your husband—told me the funniest story about Moose's Leap."

Pelletier looked at Emily, chagrined.

"Yeah, that's Todd, all right," Cindy said, relaxing a bit. "He's always tellin' that story."

"Are they around?" Emily glanced over at Pelletier, afraid she was overstepping her bounds, but he nodded and gestured for her to continue. "We need to ask them a couple of questions about the rug and how they got it up onto the RV," Emily said.

"Yeah, sure. Well, Todd is. He's out back working on the lawn mower. Ted's likely down at the harbor. He runs a charter fishing boat. Amy, go get your father."

Amy rolled her eyes and slunk out of the room. "Dad!!" She yelled as she walked through the back of the house.

Emily looked around the living room as they waited. There was very little furniture left in the room. Boxes were stacked against one wall.

"Are you moving?" she asked.

"We found a place north, just off 57. This was a rental. I got some money when my dad died last year, so we wanted a place of our own," Cindy was getting chatty now. That was good. That meant she was relaxing.

73

Todd came in from the kitchen, wiping his hands on an already dirty dish towel.

"There a problem?" he asked.

"They're here about that rug you sold her yesterday," Cindy explained.

"If it was a lemon, ain't my problem."

Emily grimaced. "Not so much a lemon." She stopped herself there.

"Cindy here says your brother helped you put the rug up on the RV?" the sheriff asked.

"Yeah?" Todd tossed the dirty rag onto the couch.

"Anyone else around when you put it up there?"

"Lotsa people. The place was crawlin' with garage salers. You missin' something from that camper? Cause if you think I went inside..."

"No," Emily intervened. "We're just wondering if you noticed anything odd about the rug?"

"Had a stain on it. But you musta saw that before you bought it. Look, lady, if you want your money back..." Todd was definitely not happy about the situation.

"No. I paid a fair price. We're just wondering if maybe you left the rug alone at anytime after you rolled it. Could somebody have gotten at it?" Emily suggested.

"What? And like put something in it? You mean like a prank?" Todd scratched his head. "Nope. Ted and I didn't roll it until just before we put it up on your rig. You were there when we were coming down. You saw us."

Emily nodded her head.

"Look, if someone snuck somethin' disgusting into that rug, I'm real sorry. But if it was somethin' valuable, well I might have some owner's rights."

After a few more routine questions, the sheriff thanked Todd and Cindy for their cooperation. He nodded toward the door and Emily started out. As she reached for the screen door handle she heard a loud POP! She turned quickly. Amy leaned against the doorframe, licking a burst of sticky pink off her lips.

"Well, Ms. Marple, I think our next stop is the harbor. I'm thinking Uncle Ted will be expecting us."

Emily nodded. *Ms. Marple?* she thought. She opened the door of the SUV and climbed in.

"By the way," the sheriff said as he buckled his seatbelt across his broad chest. "I appreciate your discretion."

Emily looked at him.

"I've got guys on my force would've given the game away." Pelletier started the engine. "I appreciate working with someone who knows the drill." He pulled the car out into the street.

"I don't think we're going to hear anything different from Ted," Emily ventured.

"Likely not."

They found Ted Lowden on the pier, loading fishing gear into a small outboard that looked like it had seen better days. He wasn't at all surprised to see them.

"Sheriff Pelletier, I take it?" he said, ignoring Emily.

"Yes, sir. I understand you helped your brother Todd put a roll of carpeting up on Mrs. Remington's RV."

"There was nothing wrong with that carpeting when we put it up there. I watched Todd roll it up. We tied it with twine. And the lady there saw us up on top. Todd was concerned maybe you think we took something from the RV?"

"No," Emily said. "Nothing was stolen."

"Then what's the problem?"

"No problem," Pelletier said. "We're just asking questions. Do you remember anyone unusual around about that time?"

"Shit, it was a neighborhood garage sale. There was weirdoes roaming all over the place. Todd even had to chase some nutcase from his bathroom. Guy just took it upon himself to help himself to Todd's private facilities. But no one who looked suspicious or nothin'."

"Do you happen to know Victor Virchow? Father Virchow?" the sheriff asked.

Ted scratched his head in the same way Todd had. "He a priest? I'm not Catholic."

Pelletier nodded.

"There's a Catholic church on practically every damn corner up in these parts. Sorry, Ma'am," Ted said. "Your man from one of those?"

"We just wondered if you knew him," Pelletier said. "I appreciate you helping us out."

Ted hopped onto the boat. "No problem." He pulled a cooler off the dock and heaved it onto the deck. "Ever decide you wanna go fishing sometime, gimme a call. Lowden Charter Service. I can give you a law enforcement discount."

"Thanks. I'll keep that in mind."

Emily led the way down the pier and back to the dock.

"Well, Ms. Marple. What's your take on our boy Ted?"

"If he has something to hide, he's pretty damn slick about it."

On the road back to Fish Creek, Emily was quiet as she gazed out the window. She was trying to piece together how Victor's body had gotten into that rug if Todd and Ted hadn't put him there. And chances of their being able to do something like that were pretty slim. As Ted had said, there were far too many people around for them to have done anything. Though it wasn't impossible. But neither of the men had seemed to have a clue as to what she or the sheriff were fishing for. And there was still something about the rug that was bothering her.

Todd had mentioned a stain. Emily remembered the stain. It was likely spilled soda or a food product that hadn't been sponged out, she'd thought at the time. And judging by the way Cindy and Todd seemed to keep house, Emily decided that was a likely scenario. The stain hadn't bothered her. For twenty bucks, she could spend a few minutes and some spot remover cleaning it up. In fact, she had planned to shampoo the rug the first chance she got. But now, Emily knew she would never be able to shampoo out her memory of Vic lying bloody on her rug.

"You get to a fish boil yet, Ms. Marple?" Pelletier broke the silence. Emily turned to him as if coming out of a fog.

"A fish boil?"

"Unique to the Door."

"Stan and I did go to one—must have been an eon ago—when our daughter Megan was a little girl. She thought it was pretty yucky."

"Sounds like a kid."

But Emily remembered that she and Stan had enjoyed the experience. Fish boils were usually held outdoors, in backyards or courtyards of the local taverns. A huge pot or tub was filled with salted water and heated over an open fire. Once the water was boiling, the cook would dump in potatoes and onions. It was all in the timing: moments before the vegetables were done, the master boiler, as the cook was called, added chunks of fresh whitefish. Then at just the right moment, when the fish was deemed to be finished cooking, the master boiler poured kerosene onto the fire, causing it to flare up and the water to boil over. They claimed this method causes the fish oils that rise to the top to boil away. Whatever it was that did it, the fish tasted great. Served with butter, coleslaw, bread and draughts of cold Wisconsin beer, the fish boil was a dinner not to be forgotten.

Emily sighed. Although she and Stan would were likely to still be around for the next few days, it was unlikely that they would be in the mood for the music, laughter, and mugs of beer that always surrounded a fish boil. It was not the kind of event one felt like attending right after discovering a friend had been murdered.

"So, what is this Ms. Marple business?" Emily asked, suddenly feeling irritated. "Do you even know who she is?"

"Agatha Christie," Pelletier said, tossing the word around like a light salad.

"You've read Agatha Christie?" This was a side of him Emily hadn't expected.

"*Murder on the Orient Express.* You think we don't read this side of the bay?" He gave a sidewise look that Emily had trouble interpreting.

"Miss Marple's not in *Murder on The Orient Express,*" Emily informed him matter-of-factly.

"Just testin' ya." Pelletier winked. "Let me see... you ever read *A Pocket Full of Rye*? Maybe *Murder At The Vicarage*?"

He had made his point.

"You *have* read Agatha Christie."

"The libraries this side of the bay are a bit limited in their selection." He offered a hint of a smile. About the most Emily expected she'd ever get from this guy under the circumstances.

As he dropped her off at the motel, she turned to him. "Thanks for including me on the investigation, Sheriff Pelletier."

"Fred, to you."

CHAPTER 12

Stan's conversation with the sheriff still rankled as he walked toward the marina at Fish Creek. Emily was right. The man was a jerk. Trying to pull all that stuff out of him about those crazy women who followed Vic around, tempting him to forsake his calling. And on top of it, pairing Audrey with that crowd of nutcases!

Stan took a deep breath and looked out over the array of watercraft that floated in the small harbor. A half dozen fisherman in small boats puttered out toward open water, idling past the small "no wake" buoys that would allow them to crank up the motor, their bows rising into the air, as they shot out into the bay. He spotted Malcolm's single-masted sloop moored to a slip at the end of the dock. Malcolm, his jaw set grim and taut, coiled the docking lines ready to cast off from the dock.

"Looking to take on a first mate?" Stan asked.

Malcolm looked up, shading his eyes from the late morning sun. "Can always use an extra hand." He offered his own hand to steady Stan as he clambered aboard.

"You look like you didn't sleep last night," Stan observed.

"You saying you did?"

Stan shook his head, ran his hand across the chin he'd forgotten to shave that morning. "I feel like I haven't slept in a month."

Malcolm started the engine. "Grab those stern lines. You can put them in the locker there." He loosened the bow lines and pulled them into the boat.

Stan pushed off from the dock with his foot, then steadied himself as Malcolm gave the motor just enough juice to put it in reverse, setting the vessel into motion. After a moment Malcolm slid the engine into neutral, letting the vessel drift until they were clear of the slip. Then he pushed the throttle into gear. The boat surged forward. Stan felt the sudden drop in air temperature as the craft motored out of the small harbor and into the deeper water.

A few minutes later Malcolm slipped the engine into neutral again and hoisted the sails. Once he knew he had the sailboat under control, he cut the engine. Without a word the two men rode the waves, tacking to catch the slight breeze. The sun warmed their faces despite the chill.

After a half hour or so, they lost what little wind there was. With Stan's help, Malcolm lowered the sails and steered the vessel toward a tree-rimmed alcove at the mouth of a creek.

Stan watched a dozen feet of chain snake out of the bow, and the small anchor settled into the sand below. Malcolm shut the engine down and fetched two fishing poles and a can of bait from one of the lockers. Wordlessly the men dropped their lines over the edge and settled themselves down for a long, languid wait. The air was warming up again. Malcolm opened a small cooler and pulled out two cans of Leinenkugel.

"Kind of early in the day for that, isn't it?" Stan inquired. Malcolm just shrugged, popped open his can. He was about to return the other to the cooler when Stan said, "What the hell. Gimme one of those Leinies." He was surprised at how good it tasted so early in the day. Likely the effects of the sun, the wind, and the water. Not to mention the mournful camaraderie. He looked toward the shore and spotted an egret stalking the shallows among the reeds.

Malcolm finished the first can of beer, crushed it with one hand, and tossed it through the open hatch door. It rattled lifelessly before coming to rest somewhere in the cabin. Stan suspected Audrey would not be pleased to find her home away from home littered with empty beer cans.

"Hell of a thing." Malcolm's voice was a deep rumble.

Stan thought he saw his friend swipe quickly at a moist eye before bending and reaching for another beer. Malcolm took a long slug from the fresh can, but a coughing fit interrupted him.

"It'll ease up after the first good frost," he promised as he regained his breath. "Allergies. Wreaks havoc with my sinuses." He took another slug of beer. "Man, I remember how I used to have to badger you to go to my football games."

"Yeah, we made that stupid deal. I go to your games on Saturday, you go with me to the library on Sunday."

"I had you fooled into thinking I was flunking that history class." Malcolm's attempt at a laugh turned into a wheeze.

"Like you would have flunked anything. On the Dean's list every single semester. That was a real con job you did on me."

"Hey, you needed to get a life. I did that for you."

Stan grunted. He reached for another beer, popped it open, and slowly savored the first draught.

"Remember that day in the Chancellor's office?" Malcolm finally asked.

Stan nodded his head and smiled despite himself. How could he forget any of those heady times? He and Malcolm had been pretty naïve about a lot of things. They didn't have a clue how nasty things were going to get during this particular sit-in. All they knew was that they were passionately against

U.S. involvement in Vietnam, and they were outraged that the university was allowing chemical weapons research to be conducted on *their* campus. And to top it off, a major chemical company was on campus recruiting employees for their part in the war effort.

"That whole day would have been a fiasco if it weren't for Vic," Malcolm said.

Stan remembered the scene vividly. The air in the Chancellor's office had been electric. The students crowded the floor, sitting knee to knee, arms locked in solidarity. If the police had the notion to remove one of them, they would have to remove all of them. What the protesters hadn't counted on was the tear gas. Stan's eyes watered at the memory. The stinging. The panic that spread through the crowd.

"God, yes. When the police arrived with the tear gas, I thought it was all over right then and there," Stan said, "But Vic, he just walked around with that calm voice of his and kept all of us from doing anything stupid."

A week later, when Vic had appeared in the open doorway of Stan and Malcolm's dorm room, it hadn't occurred to either of them to do anything but join him. "There's a meeting. Tonight. In the commons. Get as many people as you can and be there."

When Stan and Malcolm stepped into the commons, there were already at least a hundred people present and more streaming in. A speaker stood at the front of the room, shaking his fist as he ranted.

"Do we want our university to be the source of horrific death and destruction? Can we continue to permit our research centers to be used to create chemical weapons?"

"The vice-president will be on campus tomorrow," Vic leaned over and told them. "We're organizing a rally."

Stan and Malcolm quickly volunteered to help. They joined a work group and produced several dozen anti-war placards.

While they were working, one of the frat boys stopped by. He was wearing a red and white cardigan and dark slacks, his hair neatly trimmed in contrast to Stan's locks that hadn't seen a barber since sometime sophomore year. Stan had seen this guy a few times in classes but didn't know his name.

"Jeremiah Douglas," the young man said, extending his hand. Instead of shaking Jeremiah's hand, Stan plopped an industrial stapler into it. Jeremiah quickly got to work fastening the signs to the shafts. Despite their rather off-key beginnings, Jeremiah quickly hit it off with Stan, Malcolm and Vic. Stan was never sure why. But he suspected that each of the four had personality traits that complemented the others, regardless of how dissident the relationships seemed on the surface. In fact, Vic had been the first to warm up to this gregarious young man who was looking for a way to fit in. He quickly spotted the potential for leadership and maneuvered Jeremiah into situations where his gift for calling people to action was put to good use.

"Vic was so passionate about what we were doing. So committed. I gotta admit, I was pretty much in it because it was the thing to do," Malcolm said, slurping down another beer.

"I think it was that way for a lot of us," Stan agreed. "Vic, he stayed the course. He held onto that passion all his life."

"The voice of reason when the rest of the world has gone insane. Here we go..." Malcolm stood up suddenly and yanked on his fiberglass rod. His thumb and forefinger worked the small handle as he reeled in a ten-inch smallmouth bass. He took the golden brown fish with the milky underside off the hook and held it up for Stan's inspection. "Yup. He's the one should be alive today." And he tossed the wriggling fish back into the water.

They fished and drank beer until the sun was so high in the sky they could feel its scorching breath on their necks.

"I talked with Beverly this morning," Malcolm said. "Broke my heart."

"Yeah. I spoke with her, too. She's a strong woman, though."

"She say anything to you about that book Vic was working on?" Malcolm stowed the fishing poles.

"No. Why?"

"Just wondering. You ever talk to him about it?" He pulled in the anchor.

"We chatted a couple of times," Stan offered. "He was pretty passionate about wanting to get his story out there."

"I dunno." Malcolm started the motor. "Just opening up a can of worms, that book." He turned the sloop out into the bay.

Stan looked at his friend quizzically, but Malcolm didn't pursue the conversation any further.

As they approached the marina, Stan could see Audrey striding up the wooden pier, shopping bags in hand. It was hard to make out her expression because of the oversized sunglasses she wore. He gathered the docking lines in his hands, and glanced up. Audrey stood at the end of the dock, tight-lipped, as Malcolm threw the engine into reverse to slow the boat down then maneuvered the craft into position parallel to the dock.

"Hello, Audrey," Stan said. It was evident she wasn't about to wait for the boat to be secured before boarding, so he held out a hand to help her with her step.

"Stanford." She accepted his hand and stepped over the side, but as soon as her feet touched the deck she let go, almost as if burnt.

Oh, Christ, Stan thought, *she doesn't blame me for all this, does she?* The petite woman disappeared quickly down the companionway.

Stan hopped up onto the pier with the docking lines in hand. He wrapped the stern line around a wooden piling first, then secured the bow line to an iron cleat. After tying the sails, Malcolm joined Stan on the dock. The rattle of beer cans slamming into a garbage container caught their attention.

"The sheriff quizzed us again this morning. Audrey was pretty upset by the end of it." Malcolm hesitated a moment before adding, "Thing is, he asked an awful lot of questions about you." He looked over at his friend. "Do you, you know, maybe...get the feeling he's pegged you as a suspect?"

Stan rubbed his sunburned forehead. "I gotta tell you, from the questions he kept throwing at me, I was thinking maybe he had designs on you."

"Bullshit" Malcolm exploded, jerking the knot so tight Stan was fearful it could never be undone again. "One of my best friends is dead! All I can think about is how awful he looked rolling out of that damned rug. And now this goofball of a sheriff thinks one of us did it? He can go to hell."

CHAPTER 13

It was one of those days when Emily couldn't decide whether she was hot or cold or just right. The humidity likely had something to do with it. And the thick, passing clouds that plunged the earth into swaths of shadow for brief moments at a time. And, she supposed, those irritating hot flashes didn't help.

After lunch, she and Stan strolled down the main road into the State Park, having decided to walk off some of last night's dinner, stress and restlessness, not to mention the horror of the sight of Vic's dead body rolling out of the rug. She also just wanted to be with Stan—alone—for a while. The warmth of his hand in hers was comforting. They walked for a long time without speaking, nodding cordially to others passing by: a young father sporting his little girl in a backpack, an elderly couple dressed alike in yellow shirts and navy pants out for a brisk walk, a family of five on bicycles. Traffic was surprisingly heavy with cars pulling tent campers, RV's and pickups towing fifth wheels or motorboats—all on their way out of the park, heading home after a weekend of camping.

The warmth of the sun brought sweat to her brow. Flies buzzed around her head and she slapped at her ankle where one bit. They passed a marshy area, where red-winged blackbirds perched precariously atop cat-tails and long grasses. Crickets chirped and crackled. The lake sparkled through the trees. A small clearing revealed a grassy beach, and they noticed a blue heron posing for them, its profile clearly etched against the background of grass and water.

"I don't suppose you have the camera with you," Stan whispered. "That would be a great shot."

"It's in the Winnie. I had to leave it behind last night."

Last night? Was it really only last night? It seemed much longer since their campfire party had turned into a crime scene. The sheriff's questions echoed in her mind. How did Father Vic's body end up in the rug? Who put it there? Most importantly, who killed him and why? And what was it that was nagging her about the rug? She glanced at her husband walking beside her. His face was relaxed, perhaps for the first time since they had unrolled the rug. She didn't want to break this moment of calm for him so did not speak the words running through her head.

They stood quietly for a few moments until the heron turned his head the other way and eventually disappeared into the deeper grass. Monarch butterflies flittered around the late-blooming goldenrod and asters. A cooling breeze from off the lake had refreshed them, but now, as they resumed their walk down the road, a stand of red oak and sugar maples again blocked the view—and the breeze. Emily wished they had thought to bring a bottle of water.

A few moments later they came upon a narrow road branching off from the main one and leading into a small campsite.

"There's probably a drinking fountain outside the restrooms over there," Stan suggested.

"Good, I'm thirsty, too." She wiped the sweat from her brow.

They walked past a couple of dusty RV's and a tent camper clustered around a brown wooden building. After several gulps of water cooled deep in the ground, Emily told Stan she wanted to use the facilities and walked around the building to the women's room. When she emerged from the stall, she approached the line of sinks and turned on the tap water.

"Hello," she said to a little girl in a red checked shirt and dirty white shorts washing and washing and washing her hands, soap lathered up to her elbows.

"Have you seen the murderer?" The girl peered at Emily through her bright blue sunglasses. "My mommy said not to talk to any stranger because they could be the murderer. Did you know there was a murderer in the park last night? My daddy said somebody killed somebody. And I'm not supposed to go very far from camp because there's probably a murderer around. I've been looking and looking, but I haven't seen anybody that looks like a murderer. Have you?" She paused to bring wet soapy hands up to scrub her face.

"No, I haven't seen any murderer either." Emily shook the excess water from her hands, and wiped them dry on her jeans because a sign taped to the blow dryer said it was out of order. She was not surprised that the story of the body being found was circulating around the campground—even to this small cluster of sites a mile away from where the Remington's motor home was parked. "But then, I haven't been looking." That's a lie, she thought with surprise; she *was* looking. Curious about exactly what story was being told, she asked, "Tell me what happened."

"Well, a guy dressed like the Terminator came into the campground on his motorcycle, shooting and shooting and shooting. Then—BANG!—somebody got shot and fell to the ground like this." The girl clutched her heart, soapy lather spreading on her shirt, twirled around three times and dropped to the cement floor with a big "UUUGH." She opened up one eye to look at Emily. "Then he was dead. And the police came in their cars with the sirens going 'EEEEOOOOO EEEEOOOOO' but the Terminator guy was too smart for them and he hid in the trees and waited 'til past midnight when everybody was in bed and then he got back on his motorcycle and VROOOMed out of the park."

"Wow," said Emily. "Just like in the movies."

"Angie! Angie! Where are you?" a woman's impatient voice called from outside.

"Gotta go." Angie jumped up, wiped more soap onto her shorts and ran out the door.

Emily joined Stan, who was sitting in the sun on a rough-hewn bench. She pointed in the direction where Angie and her mother were climbing into their camper.

"She asked me if I'd seen the murderer."

"Did you tell her 'No, but the cops think my husband did it?'"

"Stan! It was quite the story, but apparently the whole campground knows about Vic." As she related Angie's version to her husband, Emily slipped her hand into his. They stood and walked toward a fishing pier jutting out into the lake. "How did your session with Fred go?"

"Fred? Oh, you mean the sheriff? First name basis now, eh? Just as well get on his good side. I think he suspects me and Malcolm. He asked all sorts of questions about how we knew Vic, where we were earlier in the day, when we had seen him last; you know the drill. Felt like I was on a witness stand."

"He's just trying to get all the facts. And until he finds them and starts making connections and seeing a pattern, he'll keep asking them. He's looking for two things in particular—motive and opportunity. Who would want to kill Vic and why. Who has unaccounted time, access to the weapon, and the strength to get his body up onto the Winnebago."

"He was pretty heavy-handed with the questions about Malcolm."

"Again, he's got to look at all the angles."

"Come on! It's Malcolm we're talking about here. He was as close to Vic as I was. Your *Fred* even implied Audrey might have been chasing Vic. If that had been the case, I can see where Malcolm would have been pissed enough to do something crazy. But, come on..."

Emily saw the conflict in his face. "Stan, Malcolm's not a suspect." But she wasn't sure she was telling the truth.

They had wandered down a black-topped path to the end of the pier and stared out across the bay to the harbor in Fish Creek. Despite the humidity, the air was clear, and cottony white clouds drifted overhead in a bright blue sky. A thin veil of haze made the shore on the other side of the bay look farther away than it really was. A small sailboat bobbed in a cove off to their left.

Dangling his feet over the edge of the pier, a boy of about nine held fishing pole and played with it, bobbing it up and down slowly to attract fish. His father stood over him sliding a wriggling worm onto a hook.

"How's the fishin'?" Stan asked the boy.

"Great! Lookit here!" the boy held up a stringer with five or six small perch and then dropped it back into a pool of water between some large rocks.

"Jason, don't keep taking the fish out of the water. We need to keep them fresh." His mother glanced up from her task of slathering a younger sister in sunscreen.

Emily and Stan sat down on a bench at the end of the pier and watched seagulls crying and gliding over the choppy waters of the bay. The breeze was cooler here and now Emily wished she had her sweatshirt with her, or at least a long sleeved shirt. Then she wished she could make up her mind about whether she was hot or cold. Stan's face, shaded by the straw hat he wore to protect his balding head, was beaded with sweat, and damp circles had appeared on his blue golf shirt, but he said nothing about feeling warm. She didn't mention her discomfort; he'd only tease her about acting like

Goldilocks. Everything was too hot, too cold and never just right.

"You and *Fred* find anything out at Bailey's Harbor?" Stan asked breaking the tension.

"Not much. The people we talked to weren't very helpful."

"Your sheriff doesn't seem like much of a detective to me."

"He's smarter than he looks. He's checked us out already. Called Cal LeBlanc up in Gladstone."

"He say if he checked out Malcolm and Audrey, too?"

"He didn't say. But I would assume so."

"Malcolm's pretty put out by all these questions, I gotta tell ya."

"You saw Malcolm today?"

"Spent a couple hours fishing with him while you were with *Fred*." Stan picked up a stone and threw it into the water.

Emily glanced at her husband, brows furrowed, as he watched the ripples grow into ever larger rings, splashing into the pier.

"Did Malcolm say how Audrey's doing? She was pretty freaked out last night."

"It's been tough for her. She's angry." He tossed another, bigger stone into the lake. "Malcolm said something odd."

Emily raised an eyebrow.

"About Vic's memoir. Said Vic was opening a can of worms with it. Those were his words. Opening a can of worms."

He was quiet for a while. Then Emily asked softly, "What are you thinking, Stan?"

"I don't know what I'm thinking," he said. "I don't what I think about any of this."

A tinny trill broke the silence of the scene. Stan's cell phone. Emily was impressed that for once he had it on and charged. Stan fumbled with it for a moment before getting it settled comfortably near his ear.

"Hello?" Stan listened a moment and then looked at his watch. "Yes. I know the place. I'll see you in an hour." He pushed the off button and turned to Emily. "Beverly wants to meet me at the Sundrop Cafe."

"Beverly? Vic's sister? Why?"

"Oh. I forgot—I never had a chance to tell you about my conversation with her. She asked if I'd help her with something, and wants to discuss it with me in person."

"What does she want you to do?" asked Emily.

Stan shrugged. "Probably help go through some of Vic's stuff, I'm thinking." They stood up and began walking back to the main road.

"You go ahead back to the motel," Emily said. "I want to go check out the Winnie. Something's bugging me and I can't put my finger on it. Perhaps another look at the scene will jog my memory."

"Do you think you could grab some clean underwear for me while you're there?"

"Yeah, I'm going to need some, too."

After exchanging a quick kiss, he loped up the road toward the park entrance and the motel. Emily turned down a side road that would take her to the Remington's campsite.

CHAPTER 14

Emily walked briskly along the shoulder of the quiet park road. A sudden rumbling behind her sent her scuttling into the tall grass as a shiny new five-wheeler pulling a trailer loaded with jet skis tore past, kicking up dust in its wake. She watched it lurch around a bend, then brushed herself off and stepped back onto the road. She shook her head remembering the bickering that had accompanied their own arrival at the park just three days before.

Stan had pulled into the campground early in the afternoon after paying the weekend fee. It was early enough in the day that there were still plenty of empty spaces. "Tell me when you see a good spot."

"Oh just park anywhere. It really doesn't matter."

Stan had slowed down from 15 mph to 5. "How about this?"

"No. Too close to the bathrooms."

"How about that one?" He'd gestured toward a spot next to the playground.

"Not enough shade. It'll get too hot. Besides, we'll have kids running through our lot the whole time."

After a bit, he'd stopped at a site at the end of the road. "Plenty of shade here. Plus you'll never see the neighbors. Trees all around."

"It's perfect, but..."

"But...?"

"Well, come on. You'll never get this baby under that tree. Not with that big branch sticking out."

Stan shoved the shift lever into reverse. Emily groaned. She realized she'd just issued a challenge. There was no way Stan would pick another spot now. Resignedly, she climbed out of the big vehicle to direct him. Emily remembered watching in amazement as the Winnebago smoothly slid into the spot brushing only a few leafy branches.

The tinny notes of a far away sounding rendition of *Für Elise* broke her reverie. It was her cell phone.

"Hey, Mom! So how's the road adventure going?" Megan's voice always felt like a bit of sunshine to Emily.

"Well, it's been a bit more adventuresome than we thought it was going to be. It's looking like we're not going to get to Boston right on schedule."

"Why? Having mechanical problems?"

"Not exactly." Emily hesitated. She hated to worry her daughter, but then she was never one to withhold information from family members. "There's been a death."

"What? Are you and Dad okay?"

"Yes, we're fine. It was Father Vic, your dad's old college buddy. Remember him?"

"The one I was a flower girl for when I was little? Did he have a heart attack or a car accident? When? You sound out of breath. Are you sure you're ok?"

"It was his first Mass. You were four." Emily sidestepped her daughter's questions.

"So tell me how he died," Megan persisted.

Emily hesitated again. She'd come to the head of one of the park's many hiking trails. Was this the shortcut to their campground? She wished she had picked up the camp map at the gate when they walked in.

"Mom? Mom?" A note of panic in Megan's voice brought Emily back to the phone conversation.

"I'm ok. I'm hiking in the park and I'm trying to get my bearings. How are the kids?"

"Mom. Tell me about Father Vic. What happened?"

So much for trying to change the subject. Emily waved her hand to brush away a sweat bee buzzing around her face.

"Someone apparently shot him. The police are conducting an investigation, and nobody knows yet exactly what happened." She decided to avoid mentioning that Vic's body had been found rolled in a rug on top of their Winnebago. It was one thing to discuss the death of an old college buddy; it was another to bring it that close to home.

"Weren't you and Dad going to meet with him and Uncle Malcolm and Aunt Audrey and those other guys?"

"That was the plan. But he never showed up."

"Let me talk to Dad. Is he very upset?"

"Dad's not here. He walked back to the motel." Oops! Emily made a face. Too late now. Megan was sharp and she'd pick that up right away.

"Motel? What motel? Why aren't you in your motor home? Mom, what is going on?"

"All right. All right. I didn't want to worry you for nothing. Father Vic's body was found, uh, near our Winnie. The sheriff asked that we stay in a motel for a few days while he conducts his inquiries. Now, tell me what the kids are up to." Emily said this last in the firmest mother's voice she could summon.

Megan surrendered. "The big news is that Wynter won her first swim meet; she was the anchor in a relay and won with her famous backstroke."

"That's great! Tell Wynter I'm very proud of her."

"Bad news is, I promised her she could get her ears pierced if she took first place."

"Oh, Megan, you didn't."

"Mom, I didn't seriously think she had a chance to even be in the top three."

"So what are you going to do? What does Philip say?"

"That's the problem. I haven't told him yet."

"Well, good luck there. So how are the twins?"

"They're fine. Oh, shoot! One of them just tipped over the juice bottle. I gotta go, Mom. When do you think you'll get here?"

"I don't know, honey. I'll call in a couple of days."

"Okay. Take care. And give my love to Dad!"

Emily put her phone away and focused on finding her way to the campsite.

Stan walked into the village of Fish Creek dodging traffic that was still heavy with weekend tourists. By the time he reached the Sundrop Café, he had worked up a bit of a sweat. He paused in front of the restaurant to catch his breath. The diet starts right now, he thought, chagrined.

He took off his sunglasses as he entered, blinking into the darkness to find Beverly. Until this moment, he hadn't realized that he probably wouldn't recognize her. Although they had seen one another frequently when he and Vic were close friends in college, he hadn't really seen her since. The woman he had in mind was still a twenty-two year old with wire-rimmed glasses and long straight hair parted in the middle and held in place by a beaded headband.

"Stan!"

A plumpish woman with short, frosted hair approached him and hesitated before giving him a quick hug.

"Beverly. I'm so glad to see you. And I am so sorry." Stan studied her for a moment. She had aged pretty well but bore little resemblance to the college student he remembered. Her plump face smoothed out wrinkles that would have graced her face had she been thinner. Large owl-like red frames swallowed her face. The lenses were thick, giving one the impression that her dark brown eyes were twice their size. He grasped her hand and she pulled him over to a corner table where she had been sitting.

"You look great! I recognized you the minute you walked in," she declared.

"You haven't changed a bit since the last time I saw you. When was that?" Stan smiled at her. They both knew they were both lying.

"Vic's first Mass, I think. If I remember correctly, your daughter was a flower girl. Vic had a picture of her on his living room wall. Did you know that? She was licking cake frosting from her fingers and wearing a pale pink dress. The wreath of flowers in her hair had slid over one eye. It gave her such a cockeyed, impish look. How old was she then? About three?"

Stan nodded uncertainly. Actually, he hadn't remembered Megan's role in the ceremony. It was touching to think that his old friend had kept her picture around. He wiggled on the wicker chair and glanced around the restaurant, feeling a bit uncomfortable in the fussy decor. Definitely a feminine place—pink and purple sprays of dried flowers on the wall, figurines of fairies and wide-eyed animals, a hint of fragranced candles hanging in the air. Even Emily would think it a bit much, he mused.

"I'm starving!" Beverly announced, a false note of enthusiasm in her voice. Stan felt she was trying very hard to keep things ordinary, as if this was just a social visit between two old friends. "What are you going to order?"

Stan watched wistfully as the waitress, balancing plates of cherry pie mounded with ice cream, hurried past their table. He pushed the menu aside. "I honestly don't have much of an appetite," he said.

Beverly set her menu on top of his. "To tell you the truth, I can't stomach the thought of healthy food right now, either.

But, Vic loved cherry pie. Why don't we share a piece in his memory?"

Stan smiled. "Let's do it."

"Bring me a raspberry lemonade, please. And a piece of cherry pie and two forks," Beverly told the waitress when she returned to their table.

"With ice cream," Stan added. "And coffee for me."

"I'll be right back with the coffee."

As the waitress hustled off, the cheerfulness left Beverly's face and a tear slid down her cheek. Digging in her purse for a tissue, she sighed. No more pretense.

"Stan, I still can't believe it. I dread the thought of seeing him lying there in that funeral home. You said you found him. Tell me what happened. Everything. Please."

"We—that is Malcolm and I—found him, uh, near my Winnebago." Stan reached across the table and took her hand. "Look. I don't want to upset you. Let's just leave it at that."

"No! I want to know. Please tell me everything. Please." Her voice dropped to a determined whisper. "I need to know, no matter how disturbing it may be. If I have to imagine, I'll never be able to let it go."

Stan nodded. The waitress returned to the table with the pink colored lemonade in a tall frosty glass and his coffee in a dainty cup and saucer splashed with pink and purple flowers. She set a plate with a large piece of warm cherry pie, ice cream melting over the top, between them. She handed them each a fork. Stan picked the coffee cup up, pinching the handle between his thumb and forefinger. His little finger pointed awkwardly toward the ceiling.

"I can't tell you how awful I feel about this." He picked up the fork and played with the pie. "When we found him, Vic was rolled up in a rug Emily had gotten at a rummage sale. It, the rug, was on top of the RV. We'd been imbibing a bit. A bit too much, in fact. And Emily wanted to show off her find, so Malcolm and I...we pushed it off the roof. It was heavy, you see."

Stan put the tiny cup down with a faint clatter as it met the saucer. He looked at the woman sitting across from him.

"When we untied the rug and unrolled it, out came Vic."

He flushed with embarrassment and babbled apologetically. "I'm so sorry. We didn't know he was in it. If we did, we surely wouldn't have just dumped it off the roof like that."

He was surprised to hear Beverly giggle. "Actually, if it weren't so horrible, it would be funny. Vic would have appreciated the humor in it." She blew her nose delicately.

Stan reached across the table and took her hand. "I am so sorry."

"You know, Jeremiah Douglas called me this morning. What a nice man! He's got to be so busy with his campaign. To make the time to pay his condolences. And Malcolm, too, of course. I always liked him."

"Beverly, tell me what I can do for you."

Beverly stuffed the wad of tissue into her handbag and nodded toward a small wheeled suitcase which had been tucked in the corner behind her chair. "Vic's papers. Did you know he was writing his memoirs?"

"We'd been in touch about it in the past couple of months. I was helping him with some of the research. Especially the era of the late 60's early 70's."

"He was involved in all those war protests. The civil rights demonstrations. Living conditions for migrant workers. It's really an important bit of history about what the church calls the social justice movement. But of course it wasn't always popular with the bishops and other higher ups. I know how much you like research, and I was wondering if you'd finish his book for him."

"Me? Gosh, Beverly, I don't know. I mean, I've got several projects of my own going right now."

"Did you know Malcolm tried to talk him out of writing it?"

"Malcolm?"

"Vic never said why. Please, Stan, at least take a look at his papers."

"Yeah, sure, of course. I can do that."

"Thank you. I have to be honest. It makes me nervous the thought of keeping those papers around. I know they'll be safe in your hands."

"Safe?"

"Stan, yesterday Father Rydelle didn't just come to offer the bishop's condolences; he wanted Vic's papers. In fact, he was pretty insistent about it. He made me uncomfortable. I told him I didn't know where they were, sort of hinted that Vic had taken them with him last week when he went to sub for the priest in Ellison Bay. But of course, the only things he took with him were a couple of books he was reading. When I get to the rectory, I'll pick them up."

"What does the bishop want with Vic's stuff? Surely he's not planning to finish the book?"

"More likely he wants to dispose of them. You know that Vic and he were not on the best of terms. In fact the bishop had recently removed Vic from his last parish because he was getting involved in the local politics, trying to save an immigrant Mexican neighborhood from being demolished to build a new high class condo complex. They put him on 'indefinite sabbatical.' That's why he was subbing for other priests. But he didn't complain. It gave him time to write. He came to spend some time with me after my divorce, and that's how the Green Bay bishop knew he was available to sub when that priest got sick up north. You know that Harvey and I broke up?"

"Vic mentioned something about it. I'm so sorry."

"Don't be. The reality is, I kicked the bastard out. But it was tough going for awhile, and Vic, he was so wonderful. He stood by me and was there when I needed him." Beverly's eyes filled with tears again, and Stan reached out to touch her hand, give it a gentle squeeze. She sniffed a bit, then patted his hand in return. "I really appreciate you seeing me on such short notice. I've been in such a quandary over Vic's papers."

"Beverly, did you tell the sheriff about Vic's memoirs?" Stan asked.

"Only that he was writing them."

"Have you thought that maybe you should give Vic's notes to the sheriff rather than to me? Maybe it could help in the investigation."

Beverly pleaded with Stan. "You're the only one I trust them with. How do I know that the bishop won't find a way to get them from the sheriff? Some sort of legal wrangling. That priest did claim they belong to the Chancery, after all. But I don't believe that for a minute. The problem is I can't afford the kind of high powered attorneys the Church has working for it if my claim to Vic's work is challenged."

Stan sipped at his cooling coffee thoughtfully. "I could look them over. I might be able to determine if there's anything of value that could help the investigation. I'd have Emily to advise me. You remember my wife, Emily? She's a police officer. Well, was. She's retired now. But she's an experienced investigator."

Beverly's eyes lit up with hope. She gripped his hands. "Stan, I trust you. I trust you to do what's right with Vic's work. If there's anything the sheriff should know about, by all means, bring it to his attention. Just, please, please don't let these papers out of your sight. I want Vic's book to get published. Maybe you're the one to finish it. Maybe you'll decide not to. But I believe God's hand is guiding this, and that one way or another, Vic will get his chance to speak about all those things that were so important to him."

Stan was too moved by her outburst to do anything but nod.

Beverly pushed her fork and napkin away without ever having tasted the pie. Stan dipped his fork into the plump cherries. The sweet tingling on his tongue reminded him of the reality of the living.

CHAPTER 15

Emily stood and surveyed the campsite, which was haphazardly decorated with yellow police tape. She felt her stomach tighten as she approached the Winnebago. It reminded her of that time she'd been involved in a hostage situation out on a county road not far from Escanaba. A rundown mobile home nestled in the woods provided the backdrop for a horrific triple murder and hostage taking. When it was all over, she remembered, she had slumped against the back bumper of an ambulance, watching as a junior officer draped the scene with yellow tape.

Shrugging off the memory, she carefully stepped over yellow tape and approached the fire pit, where half-burnt logs lay in muddied ashes. Who had put the fire out? She couldn't remember doing it. The deputy, she supposed. Or the park ranger? She picked up a stick lying nearby and poked through the ashes a moment, before deciding there was nothing to be found there. Striped navy and white canvas lawn chairs, the kind that hugged your body and were hard to get out of, sat near the fire pit, where they had been left the night before. Their drink glasses remained on the table. Of course, no one had really been there to clean up. The rug was gone, as were the ropes that had bound it, having been taken as evidence by the police. She closed her eyes to remember the sight of the night before, but opened them quickly when an unsettling feeling hit her stomach.

She walked to the rear of the RV, which was hidden in a copse of trees, out of sight of casual passersby. The darkness and isolation of their campsite would have helped to conceal any activity back here. She checked the sandy ground for footprints, for signs of disturbance. Of course, Stan and Malcolm had caused most of it themselves as they struggled up the ladder and pushed the rug off the roof. She climbed the ladder herself, only as far as needed to see the roof. Nothing there. She hadn't expected to see anything. Any evidence would have been taken by the police the night before.

As she clambered back down the ladder and completed her circuit of the vehicle, a young man in a park service uniform drove up, got out of his truck and walked to the garbage can nearby. He lifted the lid, poked his head in, and then put the lid back. When he saw Emily, he called out to her.

"Hey. Waddya doin' in there? Can't you see the police got it roped off?"

"I'm assisting the police," Emily stated. Well it wasn't a lie really; she just had no jurisdiction here. She stepped back over the tape and approached his truck. "Can I ask you a couple of questions?"

"I dint see nottin'. Wasn't even here last night. Was home." The man raised a trembling hand to ward off a mosquito buzzing in front of his baggy eyes. "I don't even work around here usually."

Now that she was closer, Emily could see how nervous he seemed. Both his hands were trembling, his eyes bloodshot, his breath coming in wheezes. He was definitely high on something. She realized that he was the same man who had chastised her at the golf course parking lot the day before.

"Then what are you doing here now?"

He shrugged. "I just wanted ta see."

Emily watched him climb back into his truck, start it up and drive away a little too fast for the campground road.

Emily unlocked the door to the motor home. Things inside looked pretty much as they had the night before, except for the fingerprint dust that left a film over counters and doors. Careful not to touch anything, she went through a mental inventory of everything in the motor home, checking to see if anything was obviously out of place. But other than what the crime scene investigators had stirred up, nothing seemed particularly amiss. With a sigh, she headed back into the bedroom. She slipped a couple of pair of undies for each of them into her pocket. She was tempted to grab another sweater for herself and Stan's navy windbreaker and a baseball cap hanging on a hook behind the bedroom door, but she knew she was pushing it with the undies. Stepping back outside, she locked the door and murmured, "Don't give up hope, Winnie. We'll be back. I promise."

She turned to begin the long walk back toward the park entrance. As she rounded the bend near a fork in the road, a gray Ford Focus with a TV-5 CBS logo emblazoned on its side pulled up to her. The driver's window whirred down and a blonde kid no more than twenty stuck his head out. "Hey, lady! Do you know where they found that body last night?"

"Yeah. But you're in the wrong campground. It's on the main park road about two miles up that way." She pointed in the opposite direction.

"Thanks!" The reporter deftly backed up, turned around and headed for the main artery.

Emily knew he'd discover he'd been duped eventually, but for now the press had been kept at bay.

CHAPTER 16

"We can't stay here cooped up in this motel room all day."

Emily gazed over the top of the blue ceramic mug containing her third cup of decaf coffee. "I'll go nuts." After a breakfast of veggie omelets at the motel's café, they had returned to their room toting a pot of fresh coffee, two mugs, and a copy of the Green Bay Press Gazette. She and Stan had both been tempted by the tray of pastries—cinnamon rolls, large blueberry or banana nut muffins, freshly made donuts and scones—that their waiter had brought to the table. But they resisted.

Stan sat on the couch clipping his fingernails onto the newspaper. "I think I'll stay here today and go through Vic's papers."

Emily's face lit up. "Of course! Maybe we'll find something I can take to Sheriff Pelletier."

"Em..." Stan dumped his clippings into the garbage and neatly folded the newspaper. Emily looked up at him. Stan was never neat with anything. He seemed unsure how to say what he wanted to say.

"Would you like me to wait and go over them with you after you've had a chance to, you know, revisit...?"

Stan nodded. Emily understood his feelings. Reading through these papers which represented Vic's life would help Stan grieve the loss of his friend. The investigation could wait. Maybe later that day she'd have a look.

"I'm sure I can find something to keep myself busy," she said.

"Well, don't go to anymore rummage sales. I'm not sure I can take another surprise." Stan caught himself. "God, how can I joke about such a thing?" His voice felt suddenly thick and he swiped at his eyes.

Emily sat next to him and took his hand in hers. "What I really want to do is find out more about Vic's murder."

"No, you're going to keep out of this investigation. It is not your jurisdiction. Hell, what am I talking about? This is not even your job anymore."

"But you know, a fresh eye never hurts."

"Look, you'll just get in the way and contaminate the evidence. Your friend Fred has been pretty accommodating, but don't push him too far."

"Well, I have to tell you, the thought of traipsing around cutesy little gift shops with Audrey fills me with dread." She stood and stretched. "Maybe a walk would do me good. You want to go?"

Stan slid his hand onto her thigh, squeezing tentatively. "I can think of something I'd rather do than go for a walk."

"Now?"

"We're retired. We have no obligations. We're—"

A scream filled the air.

Stan sat up startled. Emily was already off the couch and out the door.

"—alone." Stan finished to the empty room.

Emily rushed out the motel room door to find one of the young cleaning crew, in her motel uniform of jeans and a yellow t-shirt, standing near the gazebo and sobbing into her hands.

"What's wrong?" Emily asked. But the teenager was too hysterical to answer. Emily took her by the wrists and forced the girl to look at her. "Calm down. I can't help you unless you talk to me."

The girl took a deep breath, then in halting English said, "The lady. The lady. She full of blood. Maybe, maybe dead!" She started to sob again.

"What's wrong?" Stan asked, stepping up behind Emily.

"Stay with the girl," Emily said to Stan. She cautiously entered the open door next to the linens cart.

Emily's eyes took just a moment to adjust to the comparative darkness of the room. In that moment she took in the chaos of upended furniture and an overturned mattress—a sure sign of a struggle—and the woman's body lying bloodied and at an awkward angle on the floor near the television. There was no way this body was still alive, but Emily felt the neck for a pulse anyway, confirming what she already knew.

"Oh, my god!" It was Stan. Emily looked up. He was ashen, his eyes wide.

"Call 911," Emily ordered. "No, not this phone," she said as he reached automatically for the phone in the room. "Get the cell phone. Then find Jessie. But whatever you do, don't let her into the room."

Stan nodded and disappeared.

Taking the few moments of quiet that she knew would end when the police arrived, Emily surveyed the room and the body. The victim appeared to be middle-aged with short graying hair. She wore a pale green pant suit with a flowered blouse. She lay on her back, her brown eyes staring lifelessly up at the ceiling. The mattress lay half off the bed at a cockeyed angle, but the bed had not been slept in. Since the maid was preparing to make up the bed for the day, Emily surmised that the murder had taken place the night before.

Perhaps the woman had been surprised and then struggled with her assailant.

An opened suitcase lay next to the suitcase stand, white cotton panties, athletic socks, navy shorts and an assortment of colorful t-shirts strewn about the floor. The wastebasket was upended, with tissues and advertising circulars scattered. A can of Diet Pepsi had spilled over the desk and onto the floor.

Emily stepped carefully over the debris and into the bathroom where a cosmetic case had been tossed about, its bottles of lotion, lipstick, and hair products littered around the sink. Green gelatinous liquid slowly seeped from the bottle of herbal shampoo lying on its side. She edged the bathroom door with her foot, just enough to make sure there was no one lurking. When she turned back into the room, she realized that what she had first thought was a struggle now appeared to have been a frantic search for something. Why else would the stuff be disturbed in the bathroom? That also explained the mattress askew on the bed, which would be hard to do in a struggle.

She turned her attention back to the woman lying on the floor. Blood congealed into a small pool under her head and soaked into her hair.

The sound of a police siren alerted Emily to the need to exit the premises. She knew Fred would not be happy to find her in the presence of yet another dead body.

Emily was standing at the open door of the motel room speaking with Jessie when the sheriff's black and white Chevy Tahoe pulled into the motel parking lot, blocking in several patrons.

Pelletier surveyed the exterior of the motel with one sweep of his eyes, then nodded curtly to Emily as she stepped aside to let him enter the room. She knew better than to follow him in at this point. She let him make his own visual assessment of the crime scene, knowing full well that he'd call her in when he was ready. She hoped he appreciated that she knew not to contaminate evidence.

Less than five minutes later she heard his deep voice from within the room. "Mrs. Remington." Emily went inside to join the police officer.

"So. What's your story this time?"

Emily explained how she'd heard the maid scream and then found the body lying in the room.

"I assume you didn't touch anything?"

"I checked for a pulse. Nothing else."

"I assume you made sure the perpetrator was no longer on the premises?" the sheriff questioned.

"The bathroom was empty. No sign of anyone lingering."

"Where's the girl who found her?"

"Oh my god!" A voice from the doorway. Jessie, the motel owner, stood transfixed at the scene before her.

"Ma'am, I'm sorry, but you have to stay out of here. Mrs. Remington," again the formal attribution from the sheriff. "Please take her and the girl to the motel office and wait for me there."

"Of course." Emily steered Jessie, who was now softly moaning, out to the motel courtyard. By now a small gathering of people clustered around the shaken housekeeper, murmuring words of comfort. Some were other motel employees, notable in their yellow t-shirts, others probably guests or patrons of the café.

Emily pushed through the crowd. She nodded grimly at Stan and took the girl's arm. "Come with me. You too, please," she said to the hotel owner. She led them both to the motel lobby, leaving Stan behind. Jessie pointed to a door behind the desk. They entered a small neatly organized office. Both women were in a state of shock. Emily sat them down on the couch opposite the desk. "Perhaps you'd like me to get you some tea or something?"

Jessie, relieved to have something to do, said, "I'll get it." She walked out into the reception area and returned a few moments later with a tray laden with a steaming teapot and three cups. As she poured the tea, Emily asked the girl, who was still sitting on the couch staring into her hands, what her name was.

"Olga."

Emily waited.

"Olga Zhirinovsky."

"Where are you from, Olga?"

When the girl did not answer, Jessie said, "Olga's from Russia. Vladivostok. I employ a number of students for the summer who are internationals. They're hard workers, and usually less demanding than American students who always want time off or don't show up for the breakfast shift because they had a hot date the night before."

Emily nodded. She had noticed that most of the wait staff, despite impeccable English, had accents. She sipped her hot peppermint tea, at a loss for words. What she really wanted to do was question them, but she felt it inappropriate. She knew the sheriff would want to question them himself. However, Jessie was eager to talk.

"Her name is—was—Letitia Gardiner. She is a customer who has come here for the last—oh, fifteen years or so. She always wanted the same room on the same days in October, the one she and her husband shared the first time they were here. He died suddenly a week after they checked out. I think it helps her grief to relive that time. Now they're both gone." Jessie stopped her monologue long enough to grab a tissue from the box on the desk and blow her nose quietly.

"She's from the Chicago area. Owns a business, a flooring store, I believe. Pretty successful. I mean, I think she had quite a bit of money. Who would want to kill her?"

Emily shrugged. Jessie was talking to relieve her nervous tension. She answered many of the questions Emily would have asked without any encouragement.

"I don't know. The police will find out what happened."

The girl Olga sat numbly, holding her cup of tea, but Emily noticed she had yet to take a sip. She was short and slight of build, with medium-length dark blonde hair. Her facial features reminded Emily of one of the Russian Olympic figure skaters, Tatiana something, or that gymnast Olga Korbut. This Olga must have sensed Emily's appraisal, for her brown eyes which had been sightlessly staring down into the cup of tea, now rose and looked into Emily's eyes.

"My papers. I have a work visa. The police..." She stopped, taking a deep breath, and her eyes darted wildly from Jessie to Emily.

"Oh, Olga, you're not going to be sent away. Your papers are all in order," Jessie reassured her. Turning to Emily, she explained, "I spend a great deal of time making sure all my workers are here in the States legally by verifying their visas or green card status."

Emily nodded and said to Olga, "The police will just want to hear what you saw when you went into that woman's room. They probably won't even ask you for your papers, just your name and where you live."

She stood and walked over to the small window at the rear of the office. It faced away from the courtyard where the rooms were and toward the entrance road to the park. Had the medical examiner arrived? Part of her knew it had only been fifteen or twenty minutes since she escorted the other women to the office, but she was frustrated to be stuck in this room and not at the scene of the crime. What was Fred finding out that she had missed on her cursory examination of the room?

A soft knock on the door made the two women with her jump. Emily opened the door to a young officer.

"The sheriff would like to speak with you, ma'am," he said. "I'm to stay with these two ladies here."

CHAPTER 17

Stan stood quietly in the refuge of his motel doorway. He was shaken, but mostly because the eerie scene reminded him of the incident at the campground a couple of nights earlier. Stan was relieved that, at least this time, there was no connection with him and Emily. Except, there was Emily, in the center of things, having taken charge of the crime scene until the sheriff arrived.

Stan turned and stepped into their motel room, a safe haven from all the commotion outside. Feeling slightly nauseous, he went into the bathroom. He took several deep breaths. His face in the mirror looked tired and wrinkled. He had never thought of himself as wrinkled before. He splashed cold water on his face and reached for one of the scratchy white towels.

Wandering back into the living area, he was at a loss as to what to do, what to think. He sank into the over-stuffed sofa and picked up the remote control. Flicking on the TV, he let his thumb do the walking, aimlessly surfing channels, knowing that it could be a long while before his wife returned. He watched the Weather Channel long enough to see that the local forecast was for sunny skies and temperatures in the low 70's. A perfect day for him and Emily to—Dang it! Why was she there anyway? She was retired and she was supposed to be with him. A few more channel stops convinced him, not for the first time, that the more channels, the less there was to watch. Even the History Channel, his favorite, was doing a purely speculative piece on the Mayan ruins and their connection to crop circles and ancient astronauts. Hitting the power button, he let the screen go blank.

He looked around for his book, the one about Door County shipwrecks Emily had picked up for him at the garage sale. *Where did I put it?* he wondered. The bedroom. Maybe on the nightstand. As he walked toward the bed—Ow! Damn!— his toe caught the end of a small piece of luggage. Sitting hard on the bed, he rubbed the sore toe and stared at Vic's suitcase. That's when he remembered his book was still in the RV.

He cursed again as he hobbled back into the living area, pulling the carry-on behind him. He hefted it onto the time-worn coffee table and pulled the zipper open. Inside were a couple of spiral bound notebooks, several brown, accordion-style pocket folders stuffed full with papers and news clippings, several bulging three-ring binders, and two leather-bound journals.

Reaching for the top journal, he slid the strap through the loop holding it shut and let the book fall open to a page at random. Vic's tight, precise handwriting filled the page. The words suddenly blurred. Stan fought the tears welling in his eyes. He just couldn't look at this now. It was too personal. Too private. Snapping the book shut, he replaced the small strap and put the journal back into the suitcase. Perhaps the pocket folders.

He picked up one labeled "Greenbriar Housing Restoration Project." Another read "Political Asylum," a third, "Liberation Theology," a fourth simply, "Peace." The last pocket folder was labeled "Bishop Metzler, Madison Diocese." The bishop! He remembered Beverly saying that a priest from the bishop's office had wanted desperately to get his hands on this suitcase. Was this the reason?

Stan eagerly dove into this last pocket folder. Inside, several manila folders organized the contents. He pulled out the first, labeled "Correspondence," from the bigger pocket.

Sitting back on the couch, he propped his feet up on the coffee table, opened the folder and quickly scanned the top letter, dated some three weeks ago. It was written on official diocesan stationery with what Stan remembered as the seal of the Catholic Church in the top right hand corner. Bishop Henry Metzler's elaborate but illegible signature in dark black ink dominated the lower half of the page. A quick scan revealed the letter to be confirmation of a temporary assignment for Father Vic to substitute for Father Richard Hanauer at St. Theresa's parish in Ellison Bay, at the request of His Excellency the Most Reverend James R. Cassell, Bishop of the Diocese of Green Bay.

Stan paged through more letters, scanning their contents. Most appeared to be rather mundane correspondence— assignments, approval for vacation time, parish finances. He paused for a longer letter—one in which Bishop Metzler chastised Vic for participating in a protest at the state capital over a proposed cut in food stamps for the working poor. "Political protest is not your calling; please confine yourself to your pastoral duties." Other letters indicated transfers of various priests from one parish to another.

Stan noted that the letters had been systematically arranged by date, the most recent on the top and the oldest, dated some ten years earlier on the bottom. He paged through the communiqués quickly, scanning them for—he wasn't sure what. He *was* intrigued by the number of times Vic had been reprimanded for taking a stand for the poor, the handicapped, the unwanted, the beleaguered. One letter, in contrast, thanked the priest for his efforts in placing a refugee family from Bosnia.

Nestled deep in the pile were a collection of newspaper clippings with notes in Vic's handwriting. The articles referred to priests transferred "effective immediately" from a parish to an administrative position in a diocesan office. Vic's notes included comments about the re-assignment of these priests to new parishes six months or so later, on the other side of the diocese.

One clipping concerned the allegations by two altar boys of inappropriate conduct by their parish priest. Vic had recorded the gist of a conversation with a parishioner whose cousin's child had claimed his priest had touched him in an uncomfortable way. The allegation was vague, but disturbing nonetheless. There was a copy of a letter from Vic to the bishop expressing concern about these rumors and suggesting that the bishop investigate them. A brief, unofficial, handwritten reply from the bishop politely told Vic to mind his own business.

Stan also found interesting a letter strongly advising Vic to refrain from making undue accusations, even those in private to the bishop. Another dated just two months prior told Vic that since he had chosen to ignore "my counsel," he was being removed from his pastoral duties in an inner city parish in Milwaukee and placed on "administrative leave."

A knock on the door startled him.

"Just a moment!"

Stan hurriedly placed the manila folder back into the accordion-style file, making sure all the folders were in their original order. He quickly stuffed the pocket folder back into the suitcase, closed it and pushed it up against the wall next to the couch where it was out of sight.

At the door, he peered through the peephole. Not the sheriff or a deputy. He was surprised at his relief. Why was he behaving as if he had something to hide from them? He told himself he was just relieved that the police didn't seem to be interested in his account of the incident in the room several doors down.

"Yes?" He opened the door just a few inches. An eager young woman flashed an ID card in his face.

"TV 5 news. May I ask you a few questions?"

"I don't know anything about the woman they found this morning. Sorry, I can't help you."

"Actually, I wanted to ask you about Father Victor Virchow. I understand you were—"

Stan quickly recovered his poise. "I have no comment. Leave me alone."

He shut the door firmly in her face. For a moment he resisted the urge to peer back through the peephole, but his resistance quickly broke down and he looked long enough to see that the stoop was empty.

He grabbed the thermal pot left over from their breakfast and poured himself another cup of coffee. It wasn't very hot, but palatable enough. Pulling out the suitcase again, he pulled out another folder.

The sudden jangling of the room phone caused him to jump. The phone was as unnerving as it was insistent. Stan put the file down with a sigh and crossed the room to the desk. He picked up the phone's receiver.

"Yes?"

"Is this Stan Remington?" The line crackled.

"Who's calling, please?"

"My name is Father Paul Rydelle. From the Chancery Office in Madison." When Stan didn't respond, the priest added, "Bishop Metzler's office."

"Yes, I know who you are."

"Mr. Remington, I understand that you were a personal friend of Father Virchow."

"Yes." Stan decided to be cautious. He knew from years of experience with Emily that sometimes it was better to answer only the question at hand, not to elaborate unnecessarily.

"I'd like to express my condolences." There was that crackle again. "It must be very hard to lose a close friend like Father Virchow."

"Thank you." Stan's radar was on full force. The guy was suddenly sounding like a telemarketer. Pleasant, but with an undercurrent that there was something he wanted. And it wasn't to make a sale.

"It's a difficult time for me as well," the priest said.

"You were friends?"

"Associates." *Well, at least he's honest,* Stan thought. "We often worked together. In the priesthood we are all brothers, cut from the same cloth, so to speak." *Can you lay it on any thicker?* "And of course the bishop is mourning the loss of one of his sons." *Oh, now that's a good twist.*

"It's been hard for everyone," Stan offered.

"Mr. Remington, let me get right to the point of my call." *Yes, please do,* Stan thought. "Father Virchow had some papers—"

"What kind of papers?" Stan asked him, eyeing the folder on the table. *I can play this game, too.*

"He was working on a book. About…" the priest seemed to hesitate here, "about the work of the Catholic church in the Midwest."

"Oh, is that right?" Stan was beginning to enjoy the conversation now. "Is this something he was doing alone? Sounds like a lot of work involved. Who was helping him with the research for this book?"

The priest hesitated again. "I was." *Oh boy,* thought Stan. *That's one for the confessional. Two Hail Mary's, please.* "The point is," the priest went on, "now that Father Virchow is deceased, his estate belongs to the diocese. That includes any work he'd already accomplished on his book and any and all notes, papers, etcetera."

The guy had actually said *etcetera.* Stan came from an academic community and he'd never known anyone to actually use the word *etcetera* in conversation.

"Is that right?"

"We thought that maybe Father Virchow had given you some of his writings and notes."

"Why would you think that?"

"I spoke with his sister yesterday, Beverly Thayer. She claims she has no knowledge of where his papers might be."

Stan chose not to respond.

"Mr. Remington, it's important that I recover those papers."

I'll bet it is, Stan thought. "Have you tried the sheriff's office?" he voiced.

"Of course I did." The man sounded irritated.

"Well, sorry I can't help." Stan was feeling pretty proud of himself that he'd gotten through the conversation without having to offer up any Hail Mary's of his own. Well, maybe a Glory Be or two for the lies of omission.

"Listen, I'm on my way to Fish Creek right now."

That's why the connection crackled. Rydelle was on the road, using his cell phone. Now that Stan realized it, he could hear the occasional rush of air when a truck passed by on the two lane road.

"I've just come from St. Theresa's. Why don't I stop by your motel? We can talk more. I'm maybe twenty minutes away."

Shit! Stan panicked.

"No. This, uh, this isn't a good time. Sorry, I have to go now." He slammed the phone before the priest had time to say anything more.

Twenty minutes! Stan knew he had to get out of the motel. He needed to find somewhere where Father Paul Rydelle from the Chancery Office in Madison could not find him—or Vic's papers. But where could he go? He pulled aside the gauzy curtain and peeked out the front window. The parking lot was filled with police and emergency vehicles. Damn! Why wasn't Emily here to tell him what to do?

Stan grabbed the suitcase, but the lid flopped open and pocket folders and papers spilled to the floor. *Shit! Shit! Shit!* He scooped the files and papers up and stuffed them haphazardly back into the suitcase. He shut it and jerked at the zipper. He glanced up at the door. The library! Fish Creek's small community library was just up the block. Who would look for him there? He could walk there in less than ten minutes. He headed out the door.

The sunlight hit him square in the eyes. His sunglasses. Stan turned around, wheeling the suitcase behind him and searched the dresser for his sunglasses. Where were they? He looked on the side table. Nope. The nightstand! He rushed toward the bedroom. Ow! Damn! This time he cracked his shin against the coffee table. He hobbled into the bedroom, grabbed his sunglasses, then hustled back out the door.

CHAPTER 18

Standing on the threshold of the dead woman's room, Fred looked grim as Emily approached. He folded his tiny notebook and tucked it into his shirt pocket. She glanced over at the ambulance as it pulled away. No sirens, no red lights.

"Thought maybe you'd take a look," he said as Emily stepped over the yellow police tape that cordoned off a portion of the courtyard and followed him into the room.

"Want to venture a scenario?" he asked.

Emily stepped out of the way of a deputy dusting furniture for fingerprints. Nothing had been moved, except for the body.

"My first thought was that there was a struggle between the attacker and the woman. Her name, by the way, was Letitia Gardiner. But looking at the mess in the bathroom, I'm inclined to think that the perpetrator was searching for something and she surprised him. Or her. But I don't think the bed had been slept in. The contents of her suitcase and toiletries bag were on the floor, again indicating a search."

Fred nodded, agreeing with her assessment, but offered no comment in return. Emily was again acutely aware of the tenuous nature of her situation here. He was using her and her abilities, but whether he had exonerated her culpability in Vic's murder was not clear.

"Did you find out anything from the owner and the girl?" Pelletier asked.

Emily was not sure whether he had expected her to question them or to keep her ears open to any conversation that may have occurred between them. She suspected the latter. "The girl's name is Olga Zhirinovsky. She's an international student from Russia and not very trusting of police. I'd handle her with care if I were you. She'll probably clam up out of fear that you'll deport her or imprison her. I think she was just unfortunate enough to be the one to happen upon the body. According to Jessie, Mrs. Gardiner was a regular guest who always reserved the same room; in fact—."

Emily hesitated. It had occurred to her earlier that room eighteen was where she and Stan had stayed the first night after Father Vic's body was found. Jessie had asked them to move yesterday morning. Was the search intended for their room?

"In fact, what?"

"In fact, she...she had just arrived yesterday." Emily wasn't ready to share that bit of information with the sheriff yet.

"In fact, wasn't this the room you and Mr. Remington occupied the night you found your padre?"

Emily feigned surprise. "Why yes. Yes, I do believe you're right!" She bit her tongue. Anymore disbelief and he'd know for sure she had already known this fact. She wondered again, for probably the tenth time in two days, why she felt the need to hide things from him.

The radio clipped to Pelletier's belt squawked. He pulled it out, turned away and spoke briefly into it. When he was finished he turned back to Emily.

"I'd like you with me as I talk to those two ladies, if you don't mind, Ms. Marple."

Emily nodded.

As they entered the office, the deputy rose from the chair beside the desk and Fred motioned for him to leave. Jessie and Olga were still sitting on the couch where Emily had left them, Jessie holding one of Olga's hands. Olga had calmed down considerably, but her face was still a pasty white and her eyes darted nervously from Emily to the uniformed officer. Emily sat in the deputy's chair. Fred took the chair from behind the desk and positioned himself near the two women.

Emily listened to his questions and the women's answers with only part of her brain. He was covering the same ground she had learned by just listening to them a little while ago. Fred had hardly glanced in her direction since they had entered the room. She figured he wanted her there more to calm the nerves of the young Russian woman.

Emily was more concerned right now about her realization that the woman was killed in the room that she and Stan had occupied the night Father Vic's body was found. Could it be that the search was really intended for their room? Why? What could someone be looking for? In fact, who knew they were staying at Jessie's motel anyway? Well, Malcolm and Audrey and the sheriff and his deputy. But anyone else would have figured that they were just tourists, come to spend a few days in this beautiful area. She didn't even think that anyone except Pelletier and his deputy even knew that they had a connection to the body found in the state park.

It seemed too much a coincidence for two murders to happen in the same area in such a short amount of time. She knew that Fred had probably thought of that also. She glanced at the sheriff sitting in front of the couch. He was leaning toward the women and had reached out a hand to calm the younger one. His voice was quieter and more intimate than Emily had heard before. Soothing.

He turned to Emily. "Mrs. Remington, do you have any questions for either of these ladies?"

"Jessie, who else besides you would have known that my husband and I had been in room eighteen the night before last?"

Pelletier's eyebrows rose briefly. He studied the woman's face as she answered.

"No one except me and my cleaning crew."

Once they were outside again, Pelletier said, "Thanks, Ms. Marple. You've been a big help."

"I'll bet you say that to all the girls."

He grinned, and clearly dismissing her, turned to re-enter the building. "I'll just see if I can use that office to make a few phone calls. You're free to go back to your room, but—"

"Don't leave town," she finished for him.

As Emily headed back to her motel room, she noticed a woman with a news camera talking with one of the deputies; he pointed in Emily's direction. She groaned inwardly; but she wasn't quick enough to alter her route and avoid the woman striding determinedly in her direction.

"Mrs. Remington!"

Emily waited for the woman to draw nearer. If there was no escaping, maybe she could keep the conversation a little more private.

"I understand you were in the party that discovered the priest's body."

Emily nodded.

She aimed the camera in Emily's direction. "Tell me how horrific that was!"

Emily stared at the red blinking light on the camera. "I really can't comment."

The woman frowned. "Then how about the rectory? Do you have a reaction to what happened there?"

"The rectory?"

"The break-in."

Emily was caught off guard. Fred hadn't mentioned anything about a break-in. "At St. Theresa's, you mean? What do you already know about it?"

"Well, so far, everything's off the record. The police are being pretty tight-lipped. In fact, they haven't made a public announcement about it yet." The woman seemed eager to be getting a scoop.

"Then how do you know about the break-in?" Emily asked.

"My mother's boyfriend's aunt is the housekeeper."

Emily's eyebrows went up; but the woman seemed pretty proud of her investigative skills.

"And what did your mother's boyfriend's aunt say about the break-in?"

"The place was trashed!" the woman blurted out. "Mrs. Curtin was the one who discovered it. The police told her she wasn't to talk to the media, but her nephew called me."

"When did she discover the break-in?"

"Yesterday morning. She was distraught about what happened to that poor priest, and she'd gone in to make sure everything was all right."

"Did Mrs. Curtin notice if anything was missing?"

"Apparently nothing, as far as she could tell."

Emily smiled into the camera. "Thank you very much for your time." She turned and walked briskly away, leaving the chagrined reporter fumbling to shut off her camera.

Emily's smile faded as soon as her back was turned. This was an unsettling turn of events. Despite Pelletier's recent camaraderie, she was still an outsider to the investigation. And perhaps even a suspect. At the same time, she was grateful he included her in anything at all. She fully understood why he hadn't told her about the rectory being ransacked, but still it irritated her.

"Stan!" she called as she opened the door to their room. No answer. The bathroom and bedroom doors of the small suite were open. No Stan. His cell phone was plugged into the outlet next to the bed stand. At least he remembered to charge it! But a lot of good it did here. He likely went for a walk, she thought, but he should have left a note.

Her cell phone went off, a muffled *Für Elise* and a vibration in her pocket. *Well, it can't be Stan.* She checked the LCD readout. Audrey. That surprised her.

"Hello?"

"Emily? This is Audrey Hoover."

"Hi, Audrey. How are you doing? How's Malcolm?"

"I'm not afraid to say that this is the crappiest vacation we've ever had. All I want to do is go home, and the police won't let us."

Emily wondered if she had run out of stores to shop in. "Is there anything I can do to help?" she asked, knowing instantly she'd regret the offer.

"Do you have a magic wand that can make this whole thing go away? Oh, I know that sounds callous, and don't think I don't feel for poor Vic. But honestly, they are treating my Malcolm as if he was a suspect. He's a nervous wreck. I can't imagine Stan is faring any better."

"Not much," Emily admitted.

"Emily, the reason I'm calling is that I've lost my reading glasses."

"The pink ones? That look like cat's eyes?"

"Well, yes, I suppose you could describe them that way. They're Giorgio Armani and incredibly expensive. I have looked absolutely everywhere. The only thing I can think is that I dropped them when we were touring your recreation vehicle."

"I've been there, Audrey. And I don't remember seeing them."

"Well, could we go and look again? Together?"

"Audrey, it's a crime scene."

"Oh! Don't remind me. I shudder every time I think of it."

"Well, then—"

"But I am absolutely frantic to find those glasses. I have a car. A cute little Mustang convertible that I rented. I'll pick you up. Tell me you can be ready in twenty minutes."

I can be ready in five, Emily thought. But do I want to?

"Please!"

"Okay, Audrey. Twenty minutes."

Twenty minutes later, Audrey drove up in a bright red Mustang with the top down. Emily climbed in and directed her to the campground and the RV. As she shut the engine off, Audrey sat with her hands rigidly gripping the steering wheel. She shuddered visibly. Emily looked over at the bits and pieces of yellow crime scene tape wafting in the light breeze.

"I can go in by myself," she said.

Audrey took a deep, dramatic breath.

"No. I must face my fears."

She climbed out of the car, strode determinedly ahead of Emily toward the big vehicle. At the bottom step she stopped and shuddered again.

"I've got the key," Emily said gently, stepping in front of the other woman to climb the steps and unlock the door.

Emily blinked against the darkness of the interior and waited for her eyes to adjust to the dimmer light. When they did, what she saw sent a sinking feeling to the pit of her stomach.

CHAPTER 19

Stan trudged up the sidewalk past a rainbow of gingerbread houses. The black suitcase bumped over the cracks in the walk behind him. Breathing heavily, he regretted his lack of regular exercise. The hill was steeper than he'd thought it would be. The idea that he could drop dead of a heart attack right here and now nagged at him. He patted his shirt pocket. Yup, the diminutive vial of nitro was there, just in case. He lumbered on.

At the village hall which housed the library, he struggled to get the suitcase through the automatic door that shut too quickly behind him. Stan muttered under his breath. A young woman, whining toddler in arm, grabbed the door and held it for him.

"Thanks," Stan mumbled. "Cute kid." But the kid wasn't cute at all. His diaper sagged and he had a nose that desperately needed wiping. The kid stopped whining a moment to look at Stan. The he set up an even louder howl.

Sweat trickled down Stan's face and stung his eyes. He spotted the men's room door and hurried toward it. He stopped at the drinking fountain and slurped eagerly at the weak stream of water. Then he ducked into the men's room long enough to splash his face with cold water and towel it dry. He checked the top of his balding head for signs of sunburn. He'd forgotten a hat and knew that Emily would chastise him later when she saw the red.

Refreshed, his breathing again slowed to normal, he pulled the suitcase down the hallway. Glass doors on his left led to the small, one-room library. A teenager with spiked blonde hair and a silver hoop through her nose frowned at him from behind the circulation desk and asked if he needed help.

"Just a quiet space to review some papers," Stan replied in a voice louder than he intended. An older man reading a newspaper at the reference table put it down long enough to glare in his direction. A child's giggle floated from the storybook section.

"Over there." The librarian's nasal voice was equally as loud as Stan's, causing him to cringe. She pointed to the back corner of the room.

"Thanks."

A bay window looked out over a small garden dotted with wildflowers and a surprisingly clean bird bath. The sun in the morning must make this corner pretty warm, but now in the afternoon, the corner was full of diffuse light. Two overstuffed leather chairs filled the space of the bay. There was even a footstool, Stan noted with relief.

Settled in, Stan laid the suitcase on the floor beside him out of the way of traffic and opened it up. After a quick shuffle through the folders, Stan picked up the three binders and put his feet up on the stool. One labeled "Bombing" caught his eye. The bombing. He closed his eyes. In an instant he was back in 1969.

He and his friends—Malcolm, Vic, and Jeremiah—had been active in the Vietnam anti-war movement while they attended UW-Madison. They had attended a number of protest rallies and had even been arrested for a sit-down strike once. In fact, that's how Stan and Emily first met. She had processed his arrest and he was immediately smitten with the strawberry blonde beauty who fingerprinted him. He tried flirting with her and asked her to dinner. But she rebuffed him politely and moved on to the next protester. After his arraignment, he was let go on his own recognizance, but a few days later he returned to the police station to seek her out. She was surprised to see him again. This time she flushed with embarrassment as he apologized for his earlier behavior. She consented to meet him for dinner the following weekend. And the rest, as they say, was history.

Stan opened the binder and thumbed through the index tabs. A flood of memories overwhelmed him. His parents waving good-bye from their Chevy station wagon as they left the curb outside his dorm. "Remember to write!" his mother called as the car pulled away from the curb and he blew her a kiss. Stan remembered the high of anticipation mixed with a sudden bout of anxiety. He was eighteen and on his own for the first time in his life.

Stan's folks had been taken aback when they found out Malcolm, his new roommate, was Black; but Stan thought it was cool that he was among the few white students on campus to have a black roommate. It suited his liberal, egalitarian philosophy.

Stan recalled that within a few days, he and Malcolm had explored a number of the students' groups whose booths had popped up on campus. They filled out interest cards at recruitment meetings for the student newspaper, student government, chess club, drama group, fraternities and sororities (of course Malcolm and Stan had only girl-watched prospective members at that table). Within a week, they and others in their hall had received phone calls asking for volunteers from an anti-Vietnam War group. Stan and Malcolm didn't remember filling out that particular card, but were game for anything that involved girls.

So one evening they found themselves at an off-campus apartment on Johnson Street with a couple dozen other students. Stan didn't remember much of the conversation, except that it was very philosophical and left wing. Mostly he remembered the smell of tobacco smoke and the beer which flowed freely. Bags of Fritos and potato chips were passed around the group and most people grabbed a handful to shove in their mouths before passing the bag on. He had joined in the drinking but was careful to nurse the one can in his hand. Later that evening, he watched with amazement as a man in a long pony-tail pulled out a cigarette paper and a bag of what Stan first thought was tobacco. The man rolled the paper into a tube, patted in some tobacco, licked the edge of the paper and twisted the ends. As he lit the cigarette, a flame flared up, lighting his face. He took a puff, inhaling deeply, making a whistling sound as he drew in air. A sweet fragrant smell filled the room. Stan was amused now to remember how startled he had been when he realized that it was grass—marijuana. Stan refused the joint when it was passed his way. He had been more interested in seeing what people looked like when they got high than in getting high himself. Several months later, Stan finally tried his first joint.

Stan did remember that he and Malcolm first met Vic at this gathering. An intensely passionate young man, Vic drew people to him. Some were just lost souls who attached themselves to anyone. Despite his slight build, wire-rimmed glasses, and long dark curly hair—or maybe because of it—girls were constantly falling in love with him, but he didn't seem to notice. Even the guys who seemed to hate everything and everybody were drawn to Vic. Other camp followers were interested in politics, particularly socialism or Marxism; but Vic, although he had socialist leanings, could not abide being labeled.

Vic had managed to accommodate all these disparate people into his life. He enjoyed their company, treated them all with respect and kindness, yet was firm with them when they disagreed with him. Actually, if it weren't for his inherent sense of morality, Vic could have been a very dangerous kind of demigod, using the people who trusted and loved him to his own ends. But he was humble and righteous and never took advantage of the power he had over people.

Not that he was a saint, mind you. Stan recalled a particular party when Vic had gotten royally drunk. When the host took issue with Vic's ever louder political rantings, Vic took a swing at him, but lost his balance and knocked himself out cold on the edge of the coffee table. Stan and Malcolm had to carry him home that night.

Their junior year found Vic on academic probation. He had pissed off one too many professors.

Vic's wardrobe consisted of two favorite t-shirts and a pair of gray flannel slacks, shiny in the knees and the seat, that he'd picked up at a nearby thrift shop. One dark gray sweater must have been his favorite; it had a hole in the shoulder seam and the cuffs on the sleeves were ragged. Vic would play with a piece of loose yarn, poking it back into the ribbing and knotting it on itself to prevent further unraveling. He never got around to going to the barber and cut his hair himself, so it was often choppy and stuck out in the oddest places.

Stan remembered the moment of the bombing, like he remembered where he was when he heard Kennedy was shot, when the Challenger exploded, and when the Twin Towers were hit. Stan, who was sleeping soundly after pulling an all-nighter studying for a big test in his Theories of Western Civilization class, was rocked in his bed by the concussion. Dazed and disoriented, he rolled onto the floor. Malcolm burst in disheveled and distraught. He obviously hadn't been to bed yet. "Oh, my god, they did it!"

"Wah? Who?" Stan shook his fuzzy brain and eyed Malcolm through bleary eyes. "What time is it anyway?"

"Four-thirty. Listen. They've really done it now!"

"Done what? Damn it, Malcolm, be specific."

"Killed people."

"Who?"

"Some grad students working at the chem lab. Geez." Malcolm suddenly sat down on the edge of the bed, gasping for breath. "I...can't believe...I could've...oh, my god! The party! A bomb blast!"

"Take a deep breath. Just tell me what happened." Stan sat up and put his arm over the shoulder of his visibly shaken roommate.

Malcolm's voice wavered. "Someone planted a bomb in the chem lab. It went off and they say it killed a couple of students working there. Oh, god. It could've been me."

"Do you know who planted it?"

Malcolm shook his head.

"What do you mean it could have been you?" Stan persisted. But Malcolm remained silent. A rap on the door was followed by Vic's voice.

"Are you guys in there! It's me. Vic. Let me in!"

"Mommm! Charlie won't give me back my book!" The whining child yanked Stan from his reverie. He sat up suddenly, spilling the binder and its contents onto the floor.

CHAPTER 20

Emily took a step back landing squarely on Audrey's red leather boots.

"Ouch! What did you do that for?" Audrey shoved her forward and into the RV, following close behind.

"Oh, my god!" Audrey tugged at her friend's sleeve frantically. "What happened here?" She now clutched Emily in a death grip.

Emily pried herself free. "I need to take a look."

"I don't think we should be here."

Emily agreed with her friend, but her curiosity won out over protocol. "You stay outside. I'll only be a moment."

Audrey retreated to the picnic table and paced until Emily's return.

Emily surveyed the damage. Cooking utensils, plates and glasses were pulled out of cupboards and thrown to the floor. Emily was grateful that the dishes she had chosen for the motor home were a set of green Morning Wisp Corel she had bought at a rummage sale; at least none appeared to be broken. Stan's penchant for plastic glasses had saved the tumblers strewn about. What food had been in the compact refrigerator was now scattered across the floor and the door swung open. Ants swarmed the sugar spilled near the entry and Emily's steps squawked on the tiny crystals.

Emily bent to pick up her favorite white sweatshirt which was now stained by raspberry jam from a broken jar. One of Stan's books also lay in the spilled jam.

"Emily, come on! Somebody could be hiding in there," Audrey called.

Emily stepped outside to join her. As much as she wanted to investigate more, she realized she needed to call the sheriff. She fumbled through her purse looking for the card Pelletier had given her and dialed his cell.

"Pelletier, here."

"Fred, this is Emily Remington."

"What's up, Ms. Marple?"

"Our RV has been broken into."

"Anything missing?"

"Not that I could see from a quick look. I thought I ought to call you first."

"Say! What are you doing there anyway? The place was cordoned off."

Emily groaned. She knew he'd challenge her presence eventually.

"I'm here with Audrey—Mrs. Hoover. She lost her glasses and thought maybe she'd—"

He cut her apology short. "I'll send someone right out. We'll have to establish a time frame."

"It likely happened since sometime yesterday afternoon."

"How so?"

"I came here yesterday afternoon to get some clean underwear," Emily confessed. "It was fine then." She heard him sniff in disgust on the other end of the line.

"Probably connected to the attack in room eighteen," she continued.

"Well, that makes three break-ins in forty-eight hours."

Emily feigned ignorance. "Three?"

"The rectory, up at Ellison Bay. The housekeeper reported a break in. Sometime on Saturday as near as we can figure. Must be looking for something."

Emily's breath caught in her throat. Vic's suitcase. Had Stan left it in their room? Or had he taken it with him, where ever it was he'd gone? Emily experienced a moment of panic. Stan. She had to find him.

"You still there, Ms. Marple?"

"Yeah. I was just thinking. Listen, I gotta go." And she hung up before he could tell her to wait for the deputy to arrive.

"Stan?" Emily rushed into the motel room as Audrey roared off in the Mustang. "Stan!" No answer. Where was he? She dialed his cell and heard the ring on the other side of the bed where he had left his phone.

Angry, she shouted at his voice mail, "Why don't you have your phone with you? Where are you?" She blinked away tears of frustration. The suitcase. She looked in the corner of the bedroom and then in the small closet by the door. It was not there. Stan must have taken it with him. But where? Emily whirled around and looked at the room again. Something wasn't right about it. She went to the closet again. Someone had been in this closet since she left earlier in the day. Her small carry-on bag was on the opposite side of the closet from where she had left it and it wasn't zipped. She glanced at the cheap laminated dresser provided for guests. The third drawer down was open a crack. Neither she nor Stan had used that dresser. The bedspread was pulled up over the pillows but not tucked under. It looked as if someone had pulled the spread off and then hastily remade the bed. Someone had been in this room, she concluded, searching for something. Vic's papers?

A knock at the door made her jump. She whirled around. "Stan?"

"I'm sorry to bother you. Mrs. Remington?" The tall man standing in the doorway wore a black suit with a white clerical collar. His broad, ready smile seemed insincere.

At her nod, he continued. "I'm Father Paul Rydelle. I spoke to your husband on the phone this morning. We'd talked about meeting."

"I'm sorry, but he's not here."

"Are you sure?" the priest persisted.

Emily worked to keep her annoyance in check.

"Do you expect him back soon?" He made a point of looking at his watch. "There are some personal papers of Father Virchow that I am supposed to pick up. Would he have left them with you?"

Emily felt her stomach lurch.

"Father Virchow?"

"This is standard procedure when a diocesan priest passes away. It's my job to collect his personal effects."

"What makes you think Stan has them?"

Father Rydelle frowned. "I understood from Father Virchow's sister that she had given your husband papers that really should have come to the bishop."

"Well, as you can see, Stan's not here. And I don't recall seeing any papers." Emily wondered if the priest could see through her lie. Was it a mortal sin to lie to a priest? On the other hand, he was likely lying—or at the very least putting a spin on the truth—to her.

"Do you know where I can find your husband?"

"I honestly couldn't say. Why are these papers so important?"

"They are only of value to the bishop."

"So you're looking for official diocesan documents?"

"That and papers pertaining to some other work Father Virchow was doing."

"I understand he was writing his memoirs."

"Anything he was writing is property of the church."

Now who's lying, she wondered.

137

"I'll certainly have Stan contact you when he gets back. Now, if you'll excuse me, I have work to do."

She shut the door firmly in the man's face. Peering through the peephole she watched as he stood on the step for a moment, frowned, and then walked briskly to his car. Gravel sprayed from his tires as he left the motel lot and turned right toward the village.

CHAPTER 21

Now think, she berated herself. Where could Stan have gone? He must have the suitcase with him. He had an insatiable appetite for primary research. And Vic's papers would certainly qualify as material worthy of intense study. However, the motel room was in no way conducive to the kind of sprawl Stan required when delving into a new subject.

At home Stan lived for days at a time in the college library. He'd usually commandeer a small conference room and hang a sign warning intruders that he had squatters' rights. He managed to talk the head librarian into letting him have a key so that that he could come up for air occasionally without having to pack up the mountain of books and papers spread out over the large rectangular table, the chairs, and the floor.

A library. Hadn't she noticed one in the village the other day? Where was it? She closed her eyes, envisioning the sign out in front of a building on the west side of the street. Of course! It was attached to the village hall. And it was only a ten minute walk from the motel.

Emily grabbed the room key and raced for the door. Five minutes later, she was relieved to spot Stan's familiar figure, a couple of blocks up, hauling a suitcase behind him and heading her way. She waved. A sudden fatigue overtook her and anger replaced the anxiety.

"Where the hell have you been? And why don't you have your cell phone with you?" she snapped. "I was worried."

"Sorry. I was at the library. Don't I have the cell phone?" He patted his pockets.

They walked together back toward the motel. Silence loomed between them, a sure sign of her irritation and Stan's remorse. However, she also knew that the tension would dissipate if they just gave each other space for a few moments.

As they walked they passed homeowners raking leaves into tall piles. Emily nodded to a middle-aged woman in blue jean overalls and a red sweatshirt who was bagging her leaves on the sidewalk. Stan steered the suitcase onto the grass to avoid a collision.

"A priest was just asking for you at the motel. A Father Paul something. Wasn't too happy when he drove away. He seemed pretty anxious to get hold of Vic's papers."

"Paul Rydelle? He called this morning, while you were with the motel people. That's why I went to the library. That and some nosy TV reporter." Stan paused a moment to regain his breath. Emily opened the door to the room and held it for him as he pulled the suitcase in.

As she shut the door behind them she said, "That's not all. I was just at the RV."

In response to his questioning look, she said, "Audrey couldn't find those silly reading glasses of hers. Thought maybe she'd dropped them that night. So we went over there. The place was trashed. Somebody is obviously looking for something. On top of that, it turns out, Vic's rectory was broken into."

"When?"

"Sometime Saturday. Stan, these break-ins are not a coincidence." She looked down at the suitcase.

"You don't think they're looking for this, do you? My god, Emily."

"Stan, someone's been in this room."

"What do you mean?" His eyes glanced around the room. "Nothing's out of place."

"Trust me. It's the little stuff."

Stan shrugged. "I think you're overreacting."

"Nevertheless, we need to make sure we don't let this bag out of our sight."

Stan turned to her then, his face bewildered and tight looking. "I need to talk to you about..." he hesitated. Then, "About Malcolm."

"Malcolm?"

"Something's not adding up."

Emily sat on the edge of the bed. "Tell me."

He resisted. "I need time to think about things a bit. I'm feeling hot and grubby. Maybe a shower will help clear my head." He rubbed her hair and gave her a quick peck on the cheek. "Sorry about the cell phone thing."

She smiled. "We can talk about this over dinner. I know it's early, but I'm getting hungry. I seemed to have skipped lunch. Go take your shower. Wish I could change into something less grubby myself."

An hour later, Stan maneuvered a red Honda out of a rental lot and up the highway toward Sister Bay. Vic's suitcase was safely stored in the trunk.

"Any particular place in mind?" he asked.

"People keep talking about this Swedish restaurant. Let's see if we can find that."

It didn't take long to locate the log cabin style building. They laughed at the sight before them. Roaming free on the restaurant's grass-thatched roof were two goats, munching the crop of lawn that grew there.

"Do they really do this in Sweden?" Emily wondered out loud.

"It's not uncommon in Sweden for barns and vacation homes to have grass roofs," Stan said, falling into his professorial cadence, much to Emily's amusement. She'd decided long ago not to interrupt. Once in awhile she even learned something interesting. "The sod provides a not too shabby insulation against the cold. Of course, they don't all have goats. But I did see one like this in Norway when I did some traveling in college. Goats and all. And, it's not unheard of in Africa for huts to be grass-covered. Of course, whether they can even afford a goat is an entirely different matter. And it seems to me I read a travel blog on the Net one time that described this archaic architectural phenomenon up in the mountains of Argentina. Of course, the huts were made of mud to begin with. Didn't mention if they used goats for landscaping purposes there, either."

Emily was relieved when the hostess offered to seat them. And she was especially glad to get a table near the window and away from the few other patrons who had also come this early. They poured hungrily over the ample menu decorated with faux Swedish rosemaling. Homemade Swedish meatballs, Norwegian salmon smothered in cilantro Hollandaise sauce, fresh Lake Michigan perch served with Swedish limpa bread and lingonberries, the menu went on and on; but suddenly neither of them had an appetite.

"Give me the chicken Caesar salad and coffee." Emily closed the menu with a sigh.

"Oh, geez, I don't know. Uh, make it a ham and cheese on rye, extra mayo, with a side order of fries," Stan said. "And a glass of ginger ale, no ice."

After the waitress had delivered their drinks, Emily said, "Okay. Give. What's got you so distracted?"

Stan sipped at his ginger ale a moment before answering. "I found something disturbing in Vic's notes about the university bombing."

Emily frowned.

"What?"

Stan took a deep breath. "Vic's draft of his memoirs. He goes into some pretty significant details about that time. And part of what he remembers was a conversation at one of the protest meetings when Malcolm bragged about how easy it would be to build a bomb. Remember, he was a chemistry major. And, Emily, now that I think about it, I remember that conversation, too."

Emily nodded encouragement, but said nothing.

"And there's something else I remember. That morning. Right after the bombing. He didn't seem surprised."

Stan looked at his wife with stricken eyes. "Malcolm couldn't have been involved without my knowing it, could he? They caught the guy who did it. He never implicated Malcolm. But what if Vic knew something more? No, I'm sure he didn't."

The waitress interrupted them to deliver their food, then slipped quietly away. Emily poked at hers with her fork.

"Eat," she said to her husband.

"Not hungry."

"Doesn't matter. That brain of yours needs fuel."

Stan nibbled distractedly at his sandwich.

"I know we have to give these papers to the sheriff," he said. "But I need more time with them."

"There's another angle we need to be looking at," Emily suggested. "Why is the bishop so adamant about getting Vic's papers?"

"Oh, well! There's a whole file on secret negotiations the bishop was engaged in to cover up some of those sexual abuse cases. It looks like there's a big settlement in the offing."

"You think he was trying to keep this out of the public eye?"

"I don't know the details. I only glanced through the files. But Vic seemed to have thought there was more to the story than the diocesan office was giving out."

"Enough to murder over?" Emily asked.

"Millions of dollars are exchanging hands over this. And in some cases, bishops are being asked to resign. I think this is something worth looking into."

"Why don't you keep that suitcase a little longer?" Emily suggested. "I think I'd like to have a chat with the bishop, and maybe look at the trial transcripts and some of the police records from that bombing incident."

"Well, how are you going to do that?"

"I still have some contacts from when I worked with the campus police in Madison. I could drive down there first thing in the morning and be back by dark. Pelletier wouldn't even have to know I'm gone."

CHAPTER 22

Emily was glad to be on the road again. She hadn't slept well the night before—too many "what ifs" and "whys" running through her brain. Rolling out of the lumpy motel bed while it was still dark, she showered and kissed the still sleeping Stan good-bye. As she pulled onto the highway, she watched for a place to stop for coffee on her way out of town.

There was a certain freedom driving early in the morning, when the only traffic was the occasional milk truck trundling along. She almost felt guilty because Stan had to stay behind. It was tough being under suspicion, and she knew how it rankled him. But she was on a mission, and that always felt good, even if it was a bit clandestine.

She was quite sure she could predict the sheriff's reaction if she had told him she was going to Madison to...to do what? Research a decades old bombing in an effort to clear Stan's best friend? Interview a bishop to get information that might implicate him or, at the very least, one of his assistants in murder? Emily was on a fishing expedition and she knew it.

The sheriff would be pissed. And she knew that, too. Even if she was still on active duty, Emily would have no jurisdiction in this case. And Fred Pelletier did not strike her as the kind of lawman who appreciated having his investigation called into question by a snooping retired cop. But she was willing to risk his wrath to get to the bottom of Vic's murder and to vindicate Malcolm.

Today she was following a policy she'd often adopted when conducting investigations in her home territory—so long as it wasn't illegal, act first and deal with the questions and the consequences later.

Emily guided the car along the state highway out of Fish Creek and headed south toward the sleepy little hamlet of Egg Harbor. She searched for glimpses of the bay, but it was still too dark in the west. However, the eastern sky was just beginning to lighten up. Patches of frost lay on rooftops. Smoke curled from chimneys. The morning had been bitingly cold, but the car had warmed quickly and she suspected the day would, too.

She resisted the temptation to hunt for an NPR station on her radio. She needed time to think. She could understand why Pelletier had included Stan and Malcolm on his list of suspects. If the situation were reversed, she would have followed the same trail, kept her eye on the same group of people.

The sky grew lighter as the secondary highway she'd been traveling merged with the main state road heading into the already bustling community of Sturgeon Bay. Pickup trucks surrounded roadside produce stands, as local farmers unloaded their crops. Emily ached to stop and browse the baskets of apples, winter squash, carrots and onions. Then she spotted a house where a man and woman were setting up what looked to be a garage sale. She slowed down and craned her neck to get a better look. But mid-week? Must be one of those perennial yard sales that drove the neighbors crazy because it was a semi-permanent business, rather than a weekend highlight. This kind of sale didn't interest her as much, maybe because they seemed to lack spontaneity.

Emily focused on the Bay View Bridge ahead, the structure that connected the tip of the Door Peninsula with the mainland. Below the bridge ran the Ship Canal, a waterway built well over a century ago, a conduit for vessels traveling from Lake Michigan to Green Bay whose skippers preferred to avoid traversing the infamous "Death's Door" at the northern tip of the peninsula.

A traffic light in the middle of the bridge caught her up short, and she braked to a stop. Settling back in her seat, Emily knew it would take several minutes for the hidden counterweights to pull the double-leafed drawbridge open, like two hands in prayer. Emily watched in awe as a 700 foot Great Lakes freighter glided through the narrow opening, the rays of the early morning sun glinting off its white-washed bridge. As it pushed on toward Lake Michigan and likely Chicago, she thought wistfully of the trip she and Stan had suddenly had to postpone.

They'd been on their own "maiden voyage" with the ten year old RV. For the first leg of their journey, they had mapped a route to Boston to visit Megan and the kids. Then they planned to hit the open road. No specific destination. Just a road trip, much like the kind they used to take when they were young and first married. But Vic's violent and untimely death had put a definite kink in their travel plans. She was quite sure that when this little episode was over, Stan would want to go home. He was so caught up in the questions posed by Vic's papers that he hadn't had time to grieve for his friend. And of course, they would want to be available for the funeral and to give Beverly the emotional support she would need right after.

Emily let a soft sigh escape her lips. She watched as the stern of the ship slid through the bridge abutments. Silently, the bridge arms lowered into place, and she pushed on toward Madison.

Madison. That's where she and Stan had first met all those years ago. He was a senior, she a rookie campus cop. It was her job to process his arrest after a peaceful Vietnam protest turned into a nasty riot.

Emily had been chafing to do patrol work. But her department wasn't yet ready to let its women face the escalating violence that was becoming a daily occurrence on campus as a result of the protests. Her captain kept finding excuses to assign her and the only other policewoman on the force to desk duties. So that's where she was when yet another ragtag group of Vietnam protesters were hauled in. She was immediately taken by the intriguing young man with the torn Grateful Dead t-shirt and the sweaty dark locks.

"Name?" she asked, her fingers poised over the IBM Selectric.

"I am guaranteed by the First Amendment to the Constitution to the right to free speech as well as the right to peaceably assemble," he declared.

"Then please exercise your right now and speak your name."

"Stanford Remington." His voice was loud and proud.

She tapped the keys.

"Address?"

He had been maced and handcuffed. His eyes were burning, sore and swollen, and he was arguing and expounding on his civil rights far too much to have taken any notice of Emily, she was sure. But for her it was love at first sight. Emily grinned at the memory.

"You'll get plenty of opportunity to peaceably assemble in lockup," she had informed him as she bagged his wallet, belt and shoelaces.

"I don't suppose you'd consider having dinner with me and debating the pros and cons of urban policing in an egalitarian society?" he'd asked.

"No."

"How about just talking about our favorite movies? Or favorite songs? Mine's 'Let It Be.' The Beatles."

His eyes, she noticed, although still puffy from the mace, were the most incredible blue. He held her gaze, unfazed by her burgeoning authority or the possibility of rejection because, as he told her much later, he knew they were meant to be together forever.

"I have your phone number." She pointed to where he needed to sign on the release form. "I'll call you."

The city limit sign for Green Bay—population 102,000—reminded Emily that she wanted to make a phone call. She could also use to find a bathroom, so she pulled into a convenience store parking lot and reached for her cell phone. She was glad Stan hadn't waited for her to call all those years ago. He'd shown up at the police station of his own volition before the week was out. And this time he was successful in his pursuit of her. Emily smiled as she waited for her cell phone to connect.

"Emily Remington! I can't believe it's you! How many years has it been?" The delight in Chief Mary Nebel's voice was evident.

"Too many, and I apologize for that," Emily said to the woman on the other end of the line. "I'm afraid this isn't really a social call."

"I'll accept any excuse. How could I not? I've been no better than you at keeping in touch. What's up, honey?"

Emily relaxed as the familiar voice took her back to her campus days. She and Mary had started their law enforcement careers on the campus force some nearly forty years earlier and Mary had stuck with the department, doggedly working her way up to Chief. Emily knew that Mary was closing in on retirement, but she suspected that her friend would resist sitting back and letting the younger generation have its turn at the helm.

"I'm hoping you'll have time to see me today." Emily got right to the point.

"I'll make the time. Did I hear you're involved in that nasty business with Victor Virchow up in the Door?"

Damn, news travels fast within the law enforcement community. "Stan and I found his body. We were with friends. Do you remember Malcolm Hoover and his wife Audrey? Malcolm was Stan's roomie in college."

"Sure, I remember them. Don't think I've seen them since your wedding, but they were an awfully nice couple. This must be pretty hard on Stan. He was pretty tight with Father Virchow, wasn't he?"

"They were still good friends."

"How can I help?" Chief Nebel wanted to know.

"Stan dug up some stuff in Vic's—Father Virchow's—personal papers that raised some questions about the 1970 bombing."

"The bombing? That was an eon ago."

"It might be a stretch, but I want to look into it anyway. I'm on my way to Madison, and I was wondering if I could come and poke around in the files for a bit."

"Of course. I'll get someone to bring up the evidence boxes and set up a conference room for you to work in. Anything in particular you're looking for?"

"I'm mostly fishing. But I'm looking for anything that's tied to Father Vic."

"I'm on it. You can fill me in when you get here."

Emily agreed to meet Mary at the campus headquarters building on Monroe Street.

Emily used the convenience store's bathroom, then purchased a tall cup of steeply brewed coffee to go. She was tempted to put in a quick call to Stan, but decided against it. He'd been up late the night before poring through Vic's notes. Likely he was still sleeping. She could always call him later from the road.

Emily started the car and quickly turned the heater from the red zone down to the blue, letting the sun do its work through the car windows. Minutes later she merged onto U.S.

41. She turned on the radio. A few seconds of classical piano told her that NPR just wasn't going to do it for her today. Instead, she found a classic rock station and cranked it up as she hit the gas pedal.

CHAPTER 23

Closing the bathroom door behind him, Stan set the plastic razor and miniature can of shaving cream—compliments of the hotel desk—on the only flat surface available, the edge of the sink. He shaved as best he could, grimacing into the aging mirror. His elbow brushed a damp towel hanging from a small rod. Emily's. He fingered the towel, brought it to his nose. It was still sometimes hard to believe that he'd found the perfect woman so many years ago. He turned the shower on hot and steamy and stepped inside.

Stan was grateful that Emily was willing to drive all the way to Madison to investigate and, hopefully, exonerate his buddy Malcolm. But he wished he could go with her. He suspected that the sheriff would be all over him, however, if he skipped town. As it was, he'd likely be all over Emily. But that sort of confrontation never seemed to bother her. And anyway, there were tons more papers in Vic's suitcase that he wanted to sift through.

Stan worked a dab of shampoo into his hair, but the water was beginning to go cold already. He cranked it up as hot as it would go. Tepid. He sighed. He quickly finished soaping and rinsed. As he turned off the water, he reached out for the dry towel—too small and too rough—and briskly rubbed himself dry. Good reason to travel in a motor home, he thought. You can bring your own soft, fluffy, over-sized towels along.

He wrapped the motel towel around his waist, tucking one side in under the other, a tenuous job at best and then grabbed for another to towel his head. A rapping on the motel door caused him to groan. Damn! He wished those news people would leave him alone. He decided to ignore it, but a deep voice called out.

"Mr. Remington? Sheriff Pelletier here. I need to speak with you."

Double damn! Stan had no illusion that he could avoid the man all day, but he'd hoped he'd have some time to himself and Vic's papers before facing the lawman with the new information he'd dug up.

"Just a minute." Stan quickly wiped the bottom of his feet with his hand towel. Tightening the one around his waist, he padded his way to the door.

"Kinda early. You go home last night?" he asked the sheriff.

"Not spending much time at home lately," Pelletier said, holding out a cardboard tray with three cups of take-out coffee. "The missus up yet?"

"She was up and out before I ever got out of bed. Damn, that smells good."

He reached for one of the cups, but just then the towel around his waist gave way. "Crap!" He let go of the smaller towel in his left hand, grabbed for the bigger one just as it was sliding toward his knees, toppling the tray with the three coffees onto the floor, the hot, steaming liquid just missing his bare feet.

Pelletier politely hid his smirk as Stan hustled into the bathroom, showing more of his derriere than he cared for anyone but Emily to see. When he came back, wearing pants wrinkled from days of overuse, the lawman had attempted to mop up some of the java mess with the hand towel.

"Sorry to show up without calling first. I was in the neighborhood."

"No, that's okay." Stan glanced nervously over at Vic's suitcase, before throwing the bigger towel onto the coffee. "What's on your mind?"

Pelletier let his own eyes drift in the direction that Stan had glanced, but didn't appear to think there was anything unusual about a suitcase in a motel room.

"Tell ya what, let's go over to the café. We can get coffee there and they serve an omelet that will knock your socks off."

"Omelet? I'm your man!" Stan grabbed his shirt and pulled it over his head. "Hey, do you mind if I store my suitcase in your car? I know I'm sounding a bit paranoid, but things are really crazy around here with all the break-ins. I'd feel better not leaving it in the room."

"No problem." Pelletier let his eyes linger on the bag a bit longer this time. "Did you bring that from the RV?"

"No! No. I...uh...Malcolm loaned it to me. With a few things. Fresh clothes and what-not."

"Uh-huh." Thankfully, Pelletier didn't say anything about Stan's obviously days-old wrinkled pants and shirt. "What about Mrs. Remington's?"

"Mrs. Remington's what?"

"Did your friend loan a suitcase to Mrs. Remington as well?"

"Oh. No. No need. Her stuff's in here. Toiletries. Extra shoes. Undies." Stan realized he was blathering again. And he was sweating now. Would the sheriff notice? But all he did was shrug his shoulders.

"Better take it along, then."

Out in the parking lot, the sheriff unlocked the back of his squad car long enough to let Stan stow Vic's suitcase. Then the men walked over to the busy little café.

"Sheriff Pelletier! Thought I might see you today," the hostess exclaimed as she grabbed two menus. "Come right on back." She led the two men past a small waiting crowd and through the busy café.

"Joe! How's the fishing?" Pelletier stopped by a table, gave a middle-aged man a good-natured slap on the back.

"Well, Fred! Haven't seen you all summer." Joe put down his fork, quickly wiped his mouth with his napkin, and reached a ready hand to grab the sheriff's in a hardy handshake. "Gettin' my share o' walleye up near Gill's Rock. You been out?"

"Nope. Not the last coupla weeks anyway. But I hear they're bringin' in northern pike by the bucketsful up in the harbor on the island. Thought maybe I'd take a run up there if I can get a weekend off. This your son?" Pelletier asked.

"This is Danny. Took a couple days off, so we're trying to get out on the boat as much as we can while the weather's good."

Pelletier leaned over the table and shook hands with a handsome eighteen-year-old. "Thought you were going to the UW?"

The boy shook his head. "Marquette University. Milwaukee. But I won't be starting until January."

"He got a scholarship," said the proud father. "Hate to see him go, but someone's got to make use of his brains in this family."

Pelletier chuckled. "Well, listen, you tell the missus hello for me." He waved at several more people as they wound their way toward a booth tucked away in the back of the small eatery. Stan wondered if the sheriff knew everyone in this small community. And whether he, perhaps, had a reserved booth in each of the small towns on his beat.

"How are you today, Tammy?" The sheriff winked at the waitress as he and Stan took their seats.

"Short on wait staff. But other than that, can't complain." Tammy directed her next comment at Stan. "We love it when he comes in 'cause he's such a good tipper. But we generally would rather see him under better circumstances. I still can't get over what happened to poor Olga the other day. You're not a suspect, I hope?"

Stan blushed at that and Tammy touched his arm playfully. "Oh, I'm just kidding. Can't imagine the sheriff takes suspects out to breakfast. You men want to start with some coffee?"

Before they could respond, Tammy had hustled over to the coffee bar, picked up two pots—one with an orange tag—and was back to pour.

"I know the sheriff likes his full strength. What'll you have, hon?" As Stan indicated the decaf, Tammy poured them each a hot steaming cup in large ceramic mugs. "I'll give you a minute to look over the menu."

"A couple of omelets will do," Pelletier ordered for them both. "And bring that pastry tray by."

"Sure thing. You like cheese on your omelet?" she asked Stan. He nodded his assent, and she bustled away to put their order in.

The sheriff took a first cautious sip of the hot brew. "You doing okay?" he asked.

"Yeah. Oh, yeah. I'm okay." Stan blew on his cup then took a tentative drink. The coffee was hot but excellent.

"It's hard when it's a good friend. I've been through it," the sheriff offered.

Stan looked into Pelletier's eyes. The man was being sincere. Stan had to fight to keep his own eyes from welling up. He appreciated Pelletier's concern. He knew from experience that a police officer feels it just as deeply as a civilian when a friend is killed, maybe even harder. Emily often talked about how helpless she felt when someone close to her was a victim of a crime, like she should have been able to do something to prevent it.

Stan shook his head slowly. "I don't think the reality has hit me yet. This whole investigative process—it's pretty surreal."

The lawman nodded as Stan went on.

"I mean, this is what Emily does. She's the cop—was, before her retirement. I was just the one she came home to at the end of the day."

"She's quite the lady." Pelletier leaned back as Tammy placed large plates of eggs and hash browns in front of the two men, then refreshed their coffee cups.

"You men enjoy," she said with a wink. Then she was gone.

"Where is she anyway?"

Stan blanched. He had been reaching for the pepper and his hand stopped in mid-air. "She, uh, mentioned a lead she wanted to follow up on." He peppered his omelet vigorously.

Pelletier lifted an eyebrow. He didn't say anything, but stared at Stan for so long that Stan blurted out, "She went to Madison."

"Madison! Why?"

"You tell your wife every lead you're chasing down?" Stan said, bringing a forkful to his mouth.

Pelletier looked at Stan skeptically. He clearly didn't believe that Emily hadn't told her husband why she'd driven the three and a half hours it would take to get to the state's capital. But he didn't pursue it.

Stan could tell by the look on Pelletier's face that the lawman would have a few choice words to say to Emily when she got back.

Tammy was back, this time with the pastry tray. Stan chose a cheese Danish and set it down on his plate. Pelletier picked out no less than three items. Stan marveled that the man didn't weigh twenty pounds more if he ate like this regularly. Or maybe, he only got to eat this way when there was a murderer in town. Stan silently chided himself for his morbid thought, and took a bite of his Danish.

"I had a nice long chat with Beverly Thayer, Father Virchow's sister, yesterday," Pelletier said. "She mentioned that the priest was writing a book."

Stan nodded. "His memoirs. We'd talked about it a couple of times, Vic and I. I was helping him with some of the research."

"He must have had a draft going. Maybe some files he'd been collecting?"

Stan nodded again. "Sure. Of course."

"Any idea where he would have kept those files?"

"Gee, you'd have to ask Beverly about that." Stan was starting to feel uncomfortable about the direction this conversation was going. He masked it by smothering his hash browns in ketchup and then peppering the mess.

"I did. She said to ask you."

"Oh. Well. I, uh, I mean, Vic never gave me any of his files." Geez, what am I doing? Lying to a police officer? Well, okay, not exactly a lie. But honesty was about more than semantics, Stan knew.

"We found his laptop at the rectory."

"You did?" Stan's forkful of ketchuppy hash browns stopped in mid-motion then fell onto the table.

"We processed it, but didn't find any reference to a memoir." The sheriff watched as Stan scooped the potato mess back onto his plate. "I find that odd, don't you?"

"Maybe I could take a look at it for you." Stan would love to get his hands on Vic's laptop. And yes, it was odd that there were no files on it pertaining to the memoir.

The sheriff thought about his offer for a moment. "Maybe you could. I'll let you know." He took a bite of his eggs. "From the research you did for Father Virchow, from what you know of this book he was working on, is there anybody in particular who may have felt threatened?"

"Someone who'd want to kill him? No. I mean, it's just a memoir."

"Beverly said the bishop was putting a lot of pressure on him not to write the book."

Stan thought about the list of priests on transfer. A chill went through him. "Well, I can't imagine a bishop—any man of the cloth, for that matter—would kill someone over a book. For any reason."

"There are more things in heaven and earth, Horatio, than are dreamt of in your philosophy," the sheriff said quietly, waving to Tammy for the check.

"A fan of Hamlet?" Stan looked at the beefy lawman in surprise.

"The library here stocks more than just Agatha Christie novels." As a confused Stan reached for his wallet, Fred interjected, "Nah, I got this. I'll put it on my expenses."

Walking toward the squad car, Pelletier asked, "What do you know about Beverly's husband? Ex, I guess."

"I don't really know the man," Stan replied. "I only met him a couple of times. A real jerk, from what Vic used to say."

"In what way?"

"Well, he was pretty abusive, I understand. That's why she divorced him finally. Vic had tried to counsel them, but Harvey, that was his name, he would get pretty belligerent about it. I think he drank, too. He seemed to think the divorce was Vic's fault." Suddenly Stan looked over at the law man. "You don't suppose...?"

"I'm not supposing anything. But I am checking every angle."

Stan nodded. He wondered if Emily had given any thought to the possibility that Harvey Thayer might have had a motive to hurt Vic. From what Vic said, Harvey had never forgiven him for encouraging Beverly to get out of that marriage.

Sheriff Pelletier pulled the remote from his pocket and clicked it to unlock the doors of his vehicle. He was just heading toward the rear to get Stan's suitcase when his radio squawked to life.

"Pelletier here," he said into the communications device.

Stan could hear the buzz of the caller's voice, but couldn't make the words out.

"Okay, I'm on my way. Better call the state boys." The sheriff holstered his radio, then said to Stan, "Looks like we need to take a ride. Seems your friend Mr. Hoover has been fishing."

In response to Stan's quizzical look he added, "He apparently reeled a body in from the bay."

CHAPTER 24

Emily turned the car radio down as she turned off the freeway. It wasn't long before she caught the first glimpse of the Wisconsin state capitol building. The large edifice with its gleaming white dome sat on an isthmus between two beautiful, if increasingly urban, lakes located just blocks apart from each other. As she drove up East Washington Avenue, she noted how the statue of Miss Forward atop the dome beckoned, straight and center down the boulevard. Turning off, she zigzagged through the older neighborhoods of student housing, past James Madison Park along the shore of Lake Mendota.

Moments later she wound her way through campus, up Observatory Drive past the carillon tower, the lakeside dormitories, and the old Washburn Observatory. The first notes of a familiar melody on the radio caught her attention.

She pulled over and rolled down the car window, breathing in the essence of the moment. Had all those years really gone by since she had sat at this very spot looking out over Picnic Point, a spit of wooded land jutting out into the lake? She'd always loved this campus with its mix of old and new buildings and an energy that exhilarated her. The mellow tones of Simon and Garfunkel filled the car taking her back in time.

The air on the lake-side foot path leading to Picnic Point had hung heavy and damp, the stench of algae overwhelming. Strains of Simon and Garfunkel wafted from an open dorm window. Emily, a rookie officer, ran the beam of her flashlight along the edge of the water.

"There!" The young man, sporting a Delta Upsilon t-shirt, pointed toward a tangle of logs bobbing up against a clump of six-foot tall cattails. He wrapped his arms tighter around a young woman whimpering against his shoulder.

"I see it." Emily's new partner, Clay Braxton, swung his flashlight, the beam intersecting with hers. Now Emily saw it, too. One of the floating logs had the shape of a body, half submerged, face down.

"I'll call it in," Braxton said, reaching for the radio on his belt. "I'm guessing it's that kid that went missing last week. The one they found his canoe out at the end of Picnic Point."

Emily nodded, flicked off her flashlight, and went over to comfort the young couple that had flagged them down just moments before. They had obviously been doing some heavy necking; the young woman tugged at a summer blouse only half buttoned across her chest.

"We'll need to take a statement from you. Get your contact information. Then you can go home," she told them.

The student nodded as he glanced warily in the direction of the floating body. "We weren't doing anything. Just, you know, having a good time. Then we saw it."

Emily could smell alcohol on his breath. A bottle hidden in the brush behind him caught her eye. These kids had done a good deed, reporting their sordid find. But they were going to be in a world of trouble with the university and their parents. The girl started crying again. Emily gave what she hoped was a comforting smile, but it didn't seem to help.

The wail of distant sirens announced the coming of the investigative team. The coroner arrived to take charge. Emily, just a rookie, shuddered watching the men pull the bloated form out of the lake. She had only been on the job for six months and this, her first night on patrol, was her first dead body.

Although they had hours of paperwork ahead, it was not yet midnight and early in their shift. With the campus police force short on staff, she and Braxton were ordered back out on foot patrol after the coroner's van pulled away. In the silence left behind, the buzz of cicadas and the chirping of tree frogs swelled, filling the air with the indifference of nature to the grotesque images she couldn't seem to shake.

The moon over the lake had been fighting with a series of pop-up storm clouds for domination of the late night sky. The moon won and the clouds dispersed, much like the crowds of drunken students after bar-closing on football weekends.

As Emily and Braxton walked across campus, music and laughter spilled from nearby dorm windows, the students blissfully, perhaps drunkenly, unaware that one of their own had been found dead and floating in the lake.

It was odd how normal everything felt, yet nothing was normal about this night.

"You ask that guy for a date yet?" Braxton asked as he tugged on the door of the carillon tower to make sure it was still locked.

"What guy?" Emily's psyche was jarred. It amazed her that her partner seemed unfazed by their encounter with death.

"That guy you processed after the sit-in. The one you couldn't keep your eyes off." He jabbed her in the arm good-naturedly.

She felt the heat of a blush rising into her face. She was glad he couldn't see her in the dark. She didn't think anyone had noticed the sexual energy that had passed between her and the long-haired student she'd finger-printed the day before.

Braxton must have sensed her embarrassment because, when she didn't respond, he quickly changed the subject.

"I gotta tell ya, I'll take this graveyard shift anytime over the mess those hippies have been makin' with all their protests and sit-ins, floatin' dead bodies and all. They're here for an education. What business they got skipping classes and makin' life miserable for everyone? They don't like Vietnam, they should sign up and go over there. And don't tell me they're just tryin' to make a difference. Something's gonna happen. I'm tellin' ya."

Emily grunted neutrally. She'd learned quickly during her short time on the force that this was an argument not worth pursuing.

The two officers turned up the path between a row of dorms. A sleepy quiet had finally settled over the campus buildings; it was nearly three in the morning, and those students who were on campus for the summer term had finals to face when the sun came up. She felt her body relax and took a deep breath. He was right about the job, though, she conceded; the late-night beat was somehow oddly and satisfyingly tranquil. The image of the body in the lake dissolved from her thoughts, and she smiled at the memory of the blue-eyed young man she'd processed after the sit-in arrests the day before. Stanford, he had told her his name was. Stanford Remington.

Suddenly, a blue-white flash ripped through the night sky, shattering the calm. A thunderous roar shook the air and slammed against the buildings around them. Fighting panic, Emily clamped her hands over her ears and dropped to her knees next to her partner. A bright orange fireball rose above the trees and burst into a cascade of debris and flotsam. Windows cracked and ruptured. Lights all over campus blinked out.

The ringing in her ears deafened her to the cacophony of shouts and screams as students, dazed and frightened, tumbled from the shaken buildings. When Braxton turned and shouted at her, his voice sounded tinny and far away, as if he were yelling underwater. She followed his lead as he sprinted toward the source of the blast. Shards of glass, books, furniture and lab equipment, as well as bits and pieces of building material, rained down on them.

"In here!" he shouted, pulling her by the arm into the safety of a nearby portico.

Moments later, daring to leave their shelter again, they scrambled through a thick cloud of dust and debris. The older officer's lips moved, mouthing their coordinates into his radio. Suddenly he stopped, Emily almost slamming into his back. She looked up. Was that the bio-chemistry building in front of them? The smell of burnt plastic, metal, and wood assailed her nose. She strained to make sense of the gaping hole where the front door was supposed to be, smoke and flame spewing from the bowels of the building. She shook her head; distant sirens competed with the ringing in her ears.

She coughed and gasped for air, blindly following Braxton into the building. He turned and yelled something at her, pointing. Then he ran toward the specter of a man stumbling toward them.

She lurched in their direction, tripping over debris. She looked down, horrified. The bloody form of a man lay face down at her feet. This would be her second dead body that evening.

Emily blinked as a group of laughing students tramped in front of her car. As the final notes of the song faded away, she sighed at the memories and reached for her cell phone, punching in the number for the Madison Chancery.

CHAPTER 25

"Diocese of Madison, Bishop Metzler's office. This is Father John Hauser. How can I help you?" said the voice on the other end of the line.

"Father Hauser, my name is Emily Remington. I'm assisting Sheriff Fred Pelletier in the investigation of the death of Father Victor Virchow." She winced at the little white lie. "I'm in Madison today, and I was hoping to get a few minutes with the bishop."

"I'm sorry. Bishop Metzler's calendar is full today. We usually schedule him two to three weeks in advance."

"Father Hauser, Victor Virchow was not dead two to three weeks ago."

"Yes, of course."

Emily could hear the hesitation in his voice, hear him flipping through pages. The bishop's calendar? Then he came back on the line. "I could squeeze you in for a few minutes this afternoon. Three o'clock?"

"I'll be there."

"I'm sure the bishop wants to help in any way he can. We are all deeply disturbed over this event."

Emily noticed the priest didn't say they were disturbed over Vic's death, just over the event of his death. A knot turned in her stomach.

"Thank you."

Emily closed her cell phone. She wanted to make one more quick diversion before keeping her first appointment.

She pulled the car out into traffic and drove toward a multi-storied, red-tiled building with a faded scar on its brick façade. The biochemistry building.

Students hurried in and out of the front door, newly rebuilt in the early '70s. They hadn't even been born when the psyche, as well as some of the physical structure, of the campus had been so violently ripped apart that night all those years ago. Some of the profs might still be around, the ones who'd been just neophytes back then. But most had retired, moved on, died. Life moves on. Not the lives of the student and the night watchman that had been so callously disposed of in the incident. But everyone else's life, including Emily's.

She tapped the accelerator and drove on through the bustling campus, already busy with pedestrian traffic, until she found the university's police headquarters across from the football stadium. She had to circle the block twice before capturing one of the precious few parking spots near the building.

Chief Mary Nebel greeted Emily in the small foyer with a big hug and took her back through the door marked "Employees Only."

She introduced her to the on-duty staff before leading her into a small, cramped conference room. A squad of molded-plastic chairs left-over from when Emily still worked on the force surrounded a large laminated table. A dozen or so dusty evidence boxes stood sentry along one wall.

"You had anything to eat yet?" Chief Nebel asked as she reached for a bag on the table.

"Coffee. On the road."

Emily watched appreciatively as her old friend pulled a large Styrofoam cup of coffee, a half dozen bagels, and a plastic container filled with cream cheese out of the bag.

"Figured you'd need something to sustain you. You're going to be here awhile."

Emily bit into a bagel, not realizing until that moment just how hungry she was. She followed that first bite with a swallow of the most delicious coffee she'd had in a long time.

"How long have you been retired?" the chief inquired.

"Three months," Emily replied, spreading more cream cheese onto the bagel.

"Took you three whole months to get yourself involved in a murder investigation?" the chief chided her friend.

"Well, you know. I had to redecorate the bathroom. Renew my library card. Learn to play bridge."

"You play bridge?"

Emily laughed. "Oh, sure! And pigs in the Upper Peninsula have learned to fly."

"I won't say I'm not a little bit jealous," Mary said thoughtfully. "It's not that my bathroom needs redecorating or I want to watch pigs fly. But the library card part, I wouldn't mind having more time to myself to read. Maybe even do a bit of writing."

"You like to write?" Emily was surprised. This was a side of her friend that she hadn't known.

"Oh, well, you know. I've been collecting ideas for a murder mystery series. I doubt I'll ever do it. But you never know."

"I used to think I'd like to work my way up to a police chief's position," Emily said. "But when it comes right down to it, there's way too much politics attached for my tastes."

"You would have been a natural as a police chief. But, yes, the politics can get quite annoying at times."

Mary sipped her coffee. "So what's going on? Two murders in two days is a bit much even for a city the size of Madison, let alone a little tourist hamlet like Fish Creek."

"We haven't figured out yet if the two are related," Emily said. "But it seems more than a coincidence. Do you know Fred Pelletier, the sheriff up there?"

"We've met at a conference or two. One of our students drowned up at the tip of Washington Island a couple of years back, trying to swim to Rock Island. So we've had occasion to pick up the phone. The word is, he's a straight shooter. Comes across as a bit of a curmudgeon. But he knows what he's doing and he can be counted on to dig through the crap and get to the bottom of things."

"Well, I hope he gets to the bottom of this thing. And soon," Emily said.

"And you're going to make sure he does."

"Damn straight, I am."

Emily gave Chief Nebel a rundown of everything she already knew including the information Stan had dug up in Vic's papers about the 1970 bombing. She admitted that she and Stan were worried that Pelletier thought there might be a connection with Malcolm.

"I remember he was one of the initial suspects. But he was cleared, wasn't he?"

"Yeah, but I want to take another look at the evidence from that part of the investigation anyway."

"Well, we were pretty thorough back then. And the guy that was convicted, that Winchowski, admitted to making the bomb. But have at it. I'm afraid I can't stay to help. I've got three meetings scheduled for this morning. Oh, and before I forget, I made an appointment for you to go over the trial records at the courthouse."

Emily smiled her gratitude. "I owe you a big one."

"You can buy me breakfast next time." Chief Nebel grinned as she got up to leave. "Holler if you need anything else."

As the door closed behind the chief, Emily surveyed the stack of boxes, wondering where to start. Finally, picking one off the top, she set it on the table, signed the chain of possession form, and broke the seal.

A tinny *Für Elise* vibrated in her pocket, but it was a moment before she recognized the sound. She pulled out her cell, glancing at the LCD display. Megan. She flirted with the idea of letting it go to her voice mail, but she knew that ignoring the call would only worry her daughter to the point of distraction.

"Hi, Megan. What's up?" She opened the phone with trepidation.

"I am going nuts here, Mom. Wynter won't speak to me. And Philip refuses to discuss the matter with her."

"What matter?" Emily looked up as a young campus police officer entered the conference room carrying yet another box.

"We found another one, Mrs. Remington. Where would you like me to put it?"

"Over there." Emily indicated a spot on top of the existing pile.

"You know, that business over her expecting to get her ears pierced," Megan reminded her. "Who was that?"

"Oh, just one of the campus cops."

"Campus? Mom, where are you?"

"Madison."

"Madison! What are you doing there? Is Dad with you?"

"No, honey. He stayed up in the Door."

"But why?"

"It's complicated. But your dad, well, he's not supposed to leave the county right now." Emily pulled file folders and manila envelopes from the box in front of her.

"He's not a suspect, is he?" Megan sounded on the verge of hysteria now. "They haven't arrested him, have they?"

"No, honey. He's fine. As I said, it's complicated." She thumbed through a stack of forms. "I'm here following a couple of leads. So what is Philip saying about Wynter's earrings?"

170

"I swear he's gone off the deep end, Mom. I honestly don't see what the big deal is."

"Uh, huh." Emily opened a manila envelope, dumping a pile of forensic photos onto the table.

"And Wynter's not helping things any. She stomps around the house glaring at him. It's like one non-stop pre-pubescent hissy fit."

"I see." She picked up a picture of a building, a jagged gap where the doors belonged, broken windows up to the second and third floors.

"This whole situation is nuts!"

"Remind me again? Who started it?" Emily flipped the eight-by-ten print over.

"Oh, Mom. Now you're not being fair."

A handwritten label on the back revealed a photographer's name, the date, and the location. She recognized the handwriting. It was her own.

"Mom? Mom, are you still there?"

"Listen, honey. I sympathize, I really do. But I have to go now. I'll call you in a couple of days."

"Mom—"

But Emily had already hung up. She studied the photo of the bio-chemistry building in her hand. The violence of the blast was evident in the ragged edges of the concrete blocks that rimmed the hole and in the amount of debris scattered around the damaged building.

"I need you on perimeter duty." Emily could hear the words of Chief Haynes that day. She had had to watch the Chief's lips closely to make sure she understood what he was saying, because her ears were still ringing from the blast.

"This crowd could get nasty. I don't want them any closer to that building. Parts of it could collapse any time. You are not to let anyone but authorized personnel past the police line. Understood?"

Emily shuddered as she remembered watching the coroners remove the body she had tripped over that night.

She twitched her nose; even today the smell of burnt plastic and metal could awaken in her the horrors of her first encounter with such massive destruction. And she would forever remember the sight of the two bodies, one a researcher, the other a night watchman, mangled by the force of the blast.

CHAPTER 26

Feeling dizzy, Stan breathed deeply to keep from hyperventilating. This whole crazy weekend was taking on more and more the proportions of a horrific nightmare.

"Mind if I roll the window down a minute?" he asked the sheriff as they sped along in the police cruiser.

"Be my guest."

Stan appreciated that the sheriff made no other comment, even though the air conditioning was running. He was also grateful that, while Pelletier had his emergency lights spinning, he hadn't felt the need to run the siren as he sped toward the small inlet where Malcolm had been fishing. Pelletier pulled the car into a small gravel parking area near a boat launch. Out on the bay, Stan could see several boats moored under the watchful gaze of the Moose's Leap lighthouse, perched on a cliff jutting out into the bay. One of them he recognized as *Audrey's Dream* bobbing on the gentle swells.

The tranquility of the water, however, was marred by the scene in the parking lot. A fire truck, ambulance, two squad cars and a coroner's van vied for space in the too small clearing. *A bit of overkill*, Stan thought, *for one body. Oh, god,* was his next thought. *Did I really use that word—overkill?* Two firemen guided a gurney toward the coroner's van. On it was a black body bag.

Malcolm sat, head in hands, half in half out of the back seat of one of the squad cars. He glanced up as the men slid the gurney into the van.

"Wait a minute," Pelletier ordered.

The men stopped in mid-lift. Pelletier strode over, unzipped just enough to get a look at the face. Stan caught sight of something white and swollen and turned quickly away. He worried he might vomit at any moment.

The sheriff zipped the bag back up and signaled the men to complete their task. He walked over to where Malcolm was sitting.

"Some catch."

"My line snagged him," Malcolm said. "I guess he was down toward the bottom."

The sheriff nodded. "He didn't drown."

Malcolm looked up sharply. "What do you mean?"

"That man was dead before he hit the water."

"Why? How do you know?"

"His face was pretty battered. Crushed in like he'd fallen off something." The lawman observed Malcolm's reaction for a moment. "You have anything you want to tell me?"

Malcolm seemed flummoxed. "What are you suggesting? Do you think I had something to do with this man's death?" Now he was getting angry.

"Sheriff, I don't think—" Stan interrupted the two men.

The sheriff signaled Stan to back off. "Mr. Hoover, I'm not suggesting anything. Just looking for the facts. Tell me what happened."

"I cast my line into the water. I thought I'd snagged a log. When I reeled the line in, there it was. The body. Honestly, I don't know how it got there."

The sheriff turned to one of the waiting deputies. "We'll need to impound the boat." Then he turned back to Malcolm. "Mr. Hoover, we'll find you and your wife accommodations in town for tonight. Perhaps for a couple of days."

Malcolm nodded. He looked up at Stan with anxious, but resigned eyes. The sheriff moved off to consult with his deputies.

"Geez, Malcolm. I...I don't know what to say." Stan stammered.

Malcolm lifted himself out of the police car. "Audrey's going to be pissed."

"Audrey! Where is she?"

"In town. Shopping." Malcolm walked over to a stone bench and sat down heavily.

Stan followed him, but was too edgy to sit. The sun was rising in the sky and despite the season, the heat was becoming intense. Rivulets of sweat trickled down his back and he wished for shade.

"She wanted to go back to Milwaukee yesterday," Malcolm continued. "But the sheriff wouldn't let us. Can you believe that guy?" He looked over at the lawman, huddled with a small group of deputies. "Thinking I had something to do with—jeez! That makes two dead bodies in three days."

"Three," Stan responded morosely. "Three dead bodies."

"Three?" Malcolm stared at his friend, shocked. He shaded his eyes against the sun. "Damn, yes. That poor woman in your motel. You don't think all these incidents have anything to do with each other, do you?"

"I don't know. It's hard to tell." Stan looked up as the fire truck's motor growled to life. He watched it back up, almost taking out a small tree before pulling forward. The driver gave a perfunctory wave to the sheriff as the truck rumbled out onto the road. The ambulance followed, empty, having had nothing to offer the victim. "I can't imagine how they could be related. But it's a hell of a coincidence to have three murders in such a short time. And in a little burg like this."

175

One of the deputies approached them, his dark sunglasses screening his eyes, beads of sweat on his forehead under his hat. "The sheriff asked me to drive you both back into town." He nodded toward Malcolm. "He said he'll have more questions for you later. And your wife, too."

"Audrey is going to be so pissed," Malcolm moaned.

CHAPTER 27

Emily completed her examination of the boxes and carefully replaced all the files, photos, and evidence bags. Her search recalled a lot of the details that she'd forgotten.

It had been unclear at first how many people were in the building that day in 1970. Two students monitoring research projects on the north end of the building had been injured but were able to get out. They told Emily and Braxton that they thought there were people still in there, another student maybe, and a security guard.

Erratic flames from downed electric lines and broken laboratory gas pipes licked at the night air and cast eerie shadows. Emily and her partner, flashlights in hand, stepped over rubble and dodged falling debris.

They found the night watchman first when Emily stumbled over him. The blast had blown him through a window, shattering his bones and crushing his chest. Blood seeped from his nose, ears, mouth and eyes. Although she did not expect to find any, Emily felt for a pulse.

Several hours later the fire fighters found the body of the student. His internal organs had been pulverized by the force of the shock wave. Emily had to fight the nausea and anger rising in her gut as she ordered people back and away from the small group of fire fighters carrying the young man's body out of the rubble on a stretcher. Strobe-like flashing of the emergency vehicles painted the grim faces of the emergency personnel with a surrealistic, nightmarish patina.

Emily forced herself to move on from the forensic photos to the interrogation transcripts and the investigators' notes. She found the description of the bomb material—a combination of ammonium nitrate and diesel fuel—and a photo of the receipt from the farm supply store where the fertilizer had been purchased. It had been paid for in cash, but the store had required a signature on the receipt. And the bomber had stupidly signed it with his own name. There was no indication that Malcolm had been involved in any way.

The detective's notes mentioned that several students claimed they had heard Malcolm bragging he could make a bomb from materials found in any chemistry lab, any pharmacy, any farm store. Hell, he could make a bomb from ingredients found lying around any Midwest farm, he'd boasted. This had been cause enough to haul Malcolm in.

However, the investigators had quickly dispensed of Malcolm as a suspect. An alibi, provided by a particularly pretty cheerleader, had corroborated Malcolm's statement that he was otherwise "engaged" at the point in time the bomb had been detonated. And the farm store owner had described the man who purchased the fertilizer as being white and five foot-ten or eleven inches. The six-two African-American had been eliminated from the suspect list. All his talk had been nothing more than braggadocio. That had been Malcolm's word. "Braggadocio." He'd admitted he'd been showing off for friends. But, he said, he'd been trying to make a point. In those heady, volatile times Malcolm understood how easy it would be for someone to cross the line.

However, rumors had persisted that perhaps he'd had a role in advising the bomber, Dan Winchowski, on the particulars of bomb making. And that bothered Emily more than she cared to admit.

Emily stretched, drank the last of a cup of tepid coffee one of the duty officers had been kind enough to bring to her sometime in the past hour or so. She had just closed the last box when Chief Nebel walked in.

"Anything?" the chief asked.

Emily shook her head.

"Like I said, the investigation had been pretty thorough."

Emily agreed.

"Want to grab some lunch before heading over to the courthouse?" Mary asked.

"I'll have to take a rain check. I'm pretty tight on time today. Mary, thank you so much for the help and the hospitality."

"No problem. I just hope you find what you're looking for."

The two women hugged again, and after thanking the duty officers, Emily headed out to her car. It took her less than ten minutes to drive to the courthouse and find parking.

The campus police chief had paved the way for her, setting up the appointment and requesting the appropriate court records. Again, Emily was ushered into a small conference room. Again, she was given a box, but this time just one, filled with expandable file folders holding the transcripts from the three-week-long trial. She knew she wouldn't have time to read the entire record, so she skipped the pre-trial material: the jury selection, the opening statements.

She skimmed through the expert testimony, looking for references to the chemistry of bomb making. An expert in explosives had explained how the materials were likely used. Again, there was nothing pointing toward Malcolm. Emily rubbed her weary eyes, wishing she had another cup of coffee. She was about to put the transcripts away when Jeremiah Douglas's name caught her eye. She had forgotten that he had been a witness in this trial. It was his car that had been stolen by the bomber and used to get away.

Emily read through Jeremiah's testimony, but nothing new leaped out at her. She glanced at her watch. It was almost time for her meeting with the bishop.

CHAPTER 28

Emily eased the car out onto University Avenue and toward the far west side of the city. As she neared the tract of land that housed the diocesan chancery, in what used to be a seminary for high school boys, she was amazed how much Madison had grown in the years since she'd lived there. When Emily was a rookie cop, the seminary had been just beyond the edge of town, surrounded by farm lands. In the ensuing years strip malls and condo complexes had invaded the corn fields. Now a massive fitness center sat at the chancery's doorstep.

She had never visited this institution, had only seen it from a distance. And so she was pleasantly surprised by the perfectly coiffed, tree-lined drive designed to draw the eye to the tall spire stretching toward the heavens. The wings of the three-story, red brick building spread out from the central portico like the arms of Christ.

As she parked the car, Emily glanced at her watch. Two minutes to the hour. Perfect timing.

Inside the bishop's outer office, Emily approached a middle-aged priest busy behind a heavy oak desk. He seemed to be doing three things at once: finishing up a phone call and writing in a large calendar, while stapling papers and dropping them into an out-basket.

"Ms. Remington?" he asked, setting the phone down and looking up and over the rim of his slim reading glasses.

"Yes. You must be Father Hauser. Thank you for penciling me in at such short notice."

"I'm afraid he can only give you twenty minutes. He has a reception to attend."

The priest scuttled over to an interior door. Opening it, he announced her arrival.

"Your Excellency, Ms. Emily Remington is here."

Oh, god, Emily thought, *how do you greet a bishop? He's not going to expect me to kiss his ring, is he?* But when she entered the inner sanctum, it was very un-sanctum like. The man behind the simple office desk, rising to greet her with his hand outstretched, was wearing black slacks, a short-sleeved black shirt with the trademark white collar, and a simple cross hanging from a chain around his neck. A matching suit coat hung on a nearby rack. She had somehow drawn a picture in her mind of a cleric in red robes and miter sitting on a throne. His outstretched hand was most definitely positioned to be shaken, not kissed. It was with some relief that Emily complied.

"Thank you for taking the time to come out here today," the bishop said as he came from behind his desk and motioned for her to sit down on a small leather sofa. He commandeered an arm chair opposite. Two other chairs and a coffee table completed the grouping. Obviously the bishop was used to hosting informal meetings in his office. He and the Virgin Mary, who held court from the center of the table.

"Thank *you* for making the time to meet with me," Emily responded.

"Losing Father Virchow is a real tragedy. We didn't always agree on, shall we say, the disposition of his duties, but he was a dedicated priest. Would you care for something to drink? Some tea or coffee?"

Emily shook her head. "Thank you, no."

"I understand you were in the party that found his body?"

Emily was taken aback for a moment at the use of the word "party." It too closely described the context of that horrible evening. "Yes. He and my husband were good friends."

"Give my condolences to your husband then. We will, of course, be bringing his body back to Madison for the funeral Mass."

"Of course." Emily fervently hoped he meant Vic's body and not Stan's.

"Once the autopsy is complete and the authorities have released it," the bishop added. "Father Rydelle is making the arrangements."

"I met Father Rydelle yesterday."

"Did you? Poor man. He was especially devastated by Father Virchow's death."

"How so?"

"He and Father Virchow were quite close."

"Were they?"

"Oh, yes." The bishop smiled sadly. "Father Rydelle was closely involved in mentoring Victor's—Father Virchow's—creative efforts."

"Creative efforts?"

"Well, I understand that Victor was writing a book. A memoir of some sort," the bishop said.

"Oh, yes. Father Rydelle did mention something about some notes he was looking for. Was that in connection with the book?"

"Paul is hoping to follow up on the book, perhaps find someone to help finish it. See it through to publication."

"Is that right?" Emily couldn't decide whether this cleric was being genuine or trying to pull something over on her.

"Paul was closely monitoring Victor's progress. This was a personal interest of his."

"Do you know what the focus of the memoir was to be?" Emily asked.

"Well, Victor had quite a lively career as a priest. He was involved in a variety of social movements over the years. Paul was mentoring Victor through the writing process."

Mentoring? Is that what you call it? Emily thought.

"Vic had a sister. Wouldn't the responsibility for the disposition of his papers lie with her?" she asked.

"You have to understand that a priest's relationship with the Office of the Bishop is different from that of a secular employee's relationship with his employer. The priesthood is a family. As with any family, in the absence of a will..."

"Father Virchow didn't leave a will?"

"Well, of course there is a will."

"So his will would determine the disposition of his personal papers, his notes and journals?"

"Yes, of course. Our legal staff is reviewing the matter as we speak."

"Bishop Metzler, was there anybody you can think of, lay people or perhaps even among the priests in the diocese, who might have taken issue with what Vic, Father Virchow, was writing?"

"Oh, heavens no, I doubt it. There are a lot of people, even some priests as you say, who didn't agree with Victor's perspective and choice of causes. He was a bit confrontational—but to the extent that they would engage in murder? No. Absolutely not."

"Perhaps there were some jealousies?"

"Again, there are always people who are jealous of those in the limelight for whatever reason. But in this case, I just don't see the relevance."

Emily wanted to dig deeper. "Your Excellency, why was Father Virchow put on administrative leave?"

The bishop seemed startled for a moment. Then his eyes lifted upward into the smile of a kindly, worried father. He put his hands together, fingertips pointed upward as if in prayer, but letting them touch his chin. He leaned back casually in the armchair. "Oh, it was for his own good."

"Really?"

"He was under a lot of stress. Quite exhausted by his work; pulled in too many directions. And I think he wanted time to sort things out for himself. He seemed to appreciate the opportunity to focus on writing his book."

"I was under the impression that you'd put him on leave in order to leash him," Emily said.

"Well, that's always the assumption in these cases, isn't it?" The bishop opened his hands as if in acquiescence.

Emily was tired of the tiptoeing. She decided to go for the kill. "Bishop Metzler, there's been some suggestion that you are unhappy with Victor's questions about your handling of the sexual abuse cases in the diocese."

The bishop sucked in his breath, seemed for a moment to glare at her, but recovered his composure quickly. He fingered the crucifix hanging over his chest.

"Father Virchow was clearly overstepping his authority in this matter," he said.

"Is it true that you are negotiating settlements that have not yet been made public?"

"Now *you* are overstepping *your* authority, Mrs. Remington."

He stood up. As if on cue, Father Hauser appeared at the door. "Your Excellency, it's time to prepare for your next engagement."

"Thank you, John."

Father Hauser backed out with a brief nod.

"Thank you again for meeting with me." Emily said as the bishop ushered her toward the door. "I suspect the sheriff will have more questions as he continues his investigation."

"I'm sure he will." The bishop smiled tightly and lifted his right hand as Emily turned to leave. In blessing? Or dismissal? Emily wasn't sure.

As she walked down the corridor toward the exit, she puzzled over the bishop's responses to her questions. She knew for a fact that Vic had not been happy with the directive to take a year's leave. He had phoned Stan shortly after a rancorous confrontation with the bishop. He had needed to vent and he knew better than to confide in anyone within the religious community. Word tended to get back to the bishop all too quickly.

"Mrs. Remington!"

Emily swung around. A man was striding quickly toward her.

"Father Rydelle."

"I heard you were paying a visit today."

Word does get around fast, Emily thought. "Yes. I had an appointment with the bishop."

"May I walk you to your car?" Rydelle asked.

"Of course."

Father Rydelle was quick to get to his point.

"Can I assume that you are here in an investigative capacity rather than for spiritual counsel?" He held the door for her as they left the building.

"You can assume whatever you like." Emily was a little surprised by her curt answer. But her conversation with the bishop still rankled.

"And you are within your jurisdiction? As an officer of the law?" Father Rydelle was obviously conducting his own investigation.

The warm flush of another menopausal "power surge" discombobulated her for a moment. She tugged at the neckline of her shirt, fanning her chest. The priest's eyebrows rose. Was he blushing? But, thank heaven, this was a short one. The air quickly cooled her skin.

"About as much as you are, claiming ownership of Vic's papers on behalf of the bishop." She wasn't going to give this priest the satisfaction of a straight answer.

Father Rydelle blinked, but accepted her words with equanimity. "The bishop has many individuals under his jurisdiction whose best interests he must always be considering."

"Are we talking about spiritual interests or political?" They reached her car and she stopped and looked up at him, squinting against the sun.

"Sometimes, I'm afraid, the two are one and the same in these unsettled times." He flashed an enigmatic smile at her. "Victor seemed to tread a fine line between the two most of his career."

"Yes, I expect he did."

"So you can understand that he may have, among his papers, certain information that could hurt some of those under the bishop's trust."

Are you one of those individuals? Emily wondered. But this time she held her tongue.

"If you come across those papers," Father Rydelle said, "I expect you will contact me. It is important that I edit them before they enter any kind of public forum."

An interesting word choice, Emily thought. She would have used "censor."

"I will keep that in mind," Emily pulled the keys out of her pocket. "If I come across the papers. Can I ask you a question?"

"Of course."

She pushed the button on the keyless remote, disengaging the locks on the rental car. "Would the nature of the information in any of Father Vic's papers be a cause for murder?"

The priest's brow furrowed. "Murder? Are you thinking...? No! No. Some of the issues he was most passionate about were very personal and certainly could cause the ruin of some careers. But, murder? I think not."

Emily studied the man's weathered and handsome face. She suspected he had years of practice presenting an inscrutable visage while appearing friendly and supportive. It was impossible to discern whether he was being genuine or not.

"As I told the bishop," she said, "the investigation is only just beginning. There will be a lot of questions. No one is out to ruin careers. But a man is dead. And in order to know who killed him, it is important to know why."

"Of course. And I will do everything in my power to help." He pulled back his sleeve to check his watch. "Thank you for your time, Mrs. Remington. The bishop and I have an engagement that I must get ready for."

He gave the slightest of bows, and turned on his heel. Emily watched him walk back toward the chancery building. His step was purposeful, the stride of a man who was always walking toward something, and never away.

CHAPTER 29

Stan clutched Vic's suitcase to his chest and took a deep breath before reaching for the door of the RV. Emily would be furious, not to mention Pelletier, who would throw him in jail if he knew what Stan was doing.

After the deputy had dropped Malcolm and Audrey off at their accommodations, Stan asked the officer to take him to the small community library. He wanted to get back to Vic's papers, but his motel room was getting to be too much like Grand Central Station for him to get any work done. He was nervous about that priest looking for him, and he was sure the reporters would be back, especially now that a new body had been found. So he had decided that his cozy little corner in the library was the best place to hide out.

However, after the squad car pulled away, Stan had stood in front of the locked glass doors, fruitlessly pulling on the handle.

"Not gonna get in there this afternoon. Don't matter how much you tug on them doors."

Stan swung around to face an eighty-year-old man, a bright red VFW cap perched cock-eyed on his thatch of white hair.

"Millie takes Tuesday afternoons off. She's taking classes down at Green Bay. You got something you wanna drop off, there's a book slot over to your left." The old man pulled his jacket together and engaged the zipper, tugging it up to his half-shaved chin. "You must not be from around these parts. Everybody knows Millie's hours around here. Anything I can do for you?"

Stan stared at the man, the old guy's words not registering. He tightened his grip on the suitcase handle.

"Were you thinkin' of movin' in?" the man asked with a chuckle, nodding at the travel bag.

"Oh. No. I...I'm doing research. I was...I thought...Hell, I don't know what I'm thinking."

"Well, you'll just have to put your bag back in your car and go on back to your motel. You are staying at a motel, right?"

"Yeah. Well, no. I mean. I can't go there. And I don't have a car. My wife's got the car."

"Anywhere else you wanna go? I can take ya."

That's when it hit him. The RV. Nobody would disturb him there.

"Actually, we're staying at Moose's Leap. Wouldn't mind a lift there if it's not out of the way."

"Young man, nothin' round here is out of the way. C'mon. I was just headin' out myself. Happy to drop you off."

Less than twenty minutes later, Stan found himself being dropped off in front of an Airstream fifth wheeler waving at the old guy driving off. Stan waited until the late model Buick had gone around the bend, then he walked the quarter mile back to his own campsite.

What was that the old man had been chattering on about? Something about Indian braves leaping over moose to impress the young maidens? Stan shook his head. That was one he hadn't heard before, he mused as he strode toward the lot where the Remington's Winnebago was parked.

The sight of the yellow police tape caught him up short. His stomach lurched. This was where they'd found Vic, dead. Was he nuts? He couldn't go in. This was a crime scene. He looked back down the road. No way he was going to walk all the way back to the motel. He was here. He might as well take advantage of the privacy. He would deal with the consequences later.

Stan pulled the key from his pocket and let himself in. If the shock of the yellow tape had set him back, he wasn't at all prepared for what he saw inside the RV. The interior of the motor home was a shambles. Thick layers of fingerprint dust covered everything. He knew, from talking with Emily, that the vehicle had been ransacked, but he had been unprepared for the emotional shock of seeing their possessions strewn about with such disrespect and disregard. Now he understood what people meant when they talked about feeling violated after a home break-in. The giant travel van had quickly become their home-away-from-home, and to see its contents trashed with such abandon was unnerving.

Righting a chair at the small dining table, he gingerly set Vic's suitcase down. Already he was getting smudges of fingerprint dust on his pants. Damn! Avoiding dust-covered, broken dishes and mugs scattered around the counter, he reached for a broom to sweep up the broken glass from framed photos knocked off the walls. A set of plastic tumblers, which appeared to have been pushed out of the cupboard with the sweep of an arm, managed to survive whole.

It took him about an hour of picking up, sorting, and sweeping before he felt like he could sit back and think about the contents of Vic's suitcase again. A quick check of the liquor cabinet showed that while the contents were in disarray, nothing was broken or spilt. But he'd have to drink his brandy out of one of the tumblers. He and Emily had a bit of shopping to do to replace some of the essentials of their small traveling kitchen.

Stan put on a pot of coffee, then lifted Vic's suitcase onto the small dining table. Dealing with the aftermath of a break-in was nothing compared to dealing with Audrey Hoover when the squad car had pulled up in front of a local art gallery. She had been at first embarrassed, then pissed off, to learn that the officer was there to pick her up. She was not happy to be told she and her husband not only were going to have to stay even longer, but were being displaced because the boat had been declared a crime scene, a floating replica of the RV.

On the sheriff's orders, the young deputy had placed a call to dispatch asking for help arranging a motel stay for the Hoovers. Dispatch was quick in getting back to him with the name of an upscale condominium hotel on the water that had units available, this being the off-season. Stan cringed thinking about how Audrey would have reacted had they been housed in the little motel he and Emily were staying in.

Stan located an unbroken mug and poured himself a cup of coffee and topped it off with a generous helping of brandy.

Three dead bodies. His head was spinning. He was sure they were all somehow connected. But it unnerved him too much to think about it, especially considering one of those bodies was that of his good friend, and the third had been fished out of the bay by another good friend. And the one in the middle? That poor woman? Was she somehow connected with all this? Or was she simply an unfortunate soul caught in the wrong place at the wrong time? Stan took a long sip of the alcohol-laced coffee and decided it was better to let Emily do the thinking; he would focus on the research.

He rummaged through the contents of the suitcase. He had read most of Vic's journals and looked through many of the files. He wondered if Vic had started a draft of the memoir. But he didn't see any sort of manuscript among the various papers. Ah, but what was that? Tucked into a side pocket of the bag was a single file folder. Stan opened the file and a photocopy of a newspaper article slid out.

He studied it for a few moments, grabbed one of Vic's journals and flipped through its pages. As soon as he found what he was looking for, he fumbled in his pocket for his cell phone. The battery bars were diminishing, but he hoped he had enough time to tell Emily of his find.

"Hi there," Emily's voice sounded hollow in the earpiece. "I hope you're having a more productive day than I am."

"Hard to say. Where are you?"

"I'm on the road. I just left the Chancery. Where are you?"

Stan hesitated. "I'm...holed up with Vic's papers." *Please, don't ask where.* "I found something puzzling and I wanted to see what you thought."

"What is it?"

"I'm not sure what to make of it, but I found an article about the trial," Stan said.

"I read through the transcripts this afternoon," Emily said wearily. "There was nothing in them we didn't already know."

"Well, this article mentioned Jeremiah's testimony."

"About how it was his car that was stolen? Yeah, I read about that, too."

"The thing is, Vic had written something in the margin. It said, 'Not the way I remember it.'"

"What does that mean?" Emily asked. "He wasn't even around at the time of the trial, was he?"

"No. And that's the point. He was off at seminary, hadn't followed what was going on. The whole bombing episode rattled him so much, he just wanted to remove himself from everything."

"So, why the article? Why the note?"

"That's what I was wondering," Stan said. "So I dug through Vic's personal journals again and I think I found it. But it's really weird."

"What do you mean?"

"Vic wrote that he remembered having asked Jeremiah if he could borrow his car that night for a date. Jeremiah was driving that little red Mustang convertible back then, and Vic wanted to impress this girl he'd been hitting on at a bar we used to hang out at. She was a waitress, and he'd been trying for weeks to get her to go out with him. She finally said yes. Vic wrote that he'd been miffed because Jeremiah had agreed to let him have the car for the night; then later when Vic went to get the keys Jeremiah sort of blew him off. Told him one of the frat guys had beat him to the punch."

"I bet I can guess which frat guy that was."

"Dan Winchowski," Stan confirmed.

"Maybe it's time we go directly to the source."

"Jeremiah? Yeah, I suppose I can try to talk to him. But he's pretty hard to get a hold of these days. "

"No. I'm talking about the frat guy. Winchowski. He's up at Waupun. I can stop on my way back to the Door."

"You can't just pop in at a prison and ask to speak to a convicted felon!" Stan exclaimed. "Can you?" A beep from his cell phone puzzled him.

"I'll have to make a few phone calls. But I think I can make it happen."

"Well, be careful, Emily. I don't like the direction any of this is going."

"I think right now it's more important that *you* lay low. I just ran into your Father Rydelle. I don't trust him any farther than I can throw him. Where exactly are you, anyway?"

"Me? I'm okay. Had breakfast with your buddy Fred. He hasn't let me out of his sight since Malcolm found—Oh shit, I forgot to tell you."

Beep!

"Malcolm found a body, reeled it in with his fishing pole." He paused, waiting for Emily's reaction.

"Emily. Emily! Are you there? Can you hear me?"

Nothing but dead air. He looked at the phone's display; it was blank. Where the heck was his charger anyway? The motel. Crap. She would just have to hear this news later, when she arrived back in Fish Creek.

CHAPTER 30

"Malcolm found what? And where did you say you are?"

When there was no response, Emily said, "Stan? Stan? Are you there? Can you hear me?"

Frustrated, she dialed his number but was thwarted when the call reverted to the voice mail. "Stan, I'm off to the prison. You stay put. I don't like the way this is looking."

Emily sighed. She was worried, but she told herself he was not a stupid man. He knew how to keep himself out of danger. However, he was a dreamer, a philosopher, and he was always so absorbed in the details of the past that he tended to ignore the details of the present—the very details that Emily depended on to do her job and do it well. Stan could usually be depended on to lose track of time, even his whereabouts, when he was deeply engaged in a research project.

As Emily maneuvered her car onto the highway, she glanced at the clock on her dashboard. She had very little time to make the multiple phone calls it would require to bypass the prison regulations regarding visitors. And she didn't have time to pull over to make those calls.

Emily sat in the small, featureless room facing a glass divider. The air was stale; the room reeked of fresh paint. She couldn't tell if the new color was green or gray or yellow. A muffled key rattled in a lock and a middle-aged man in a dark green prison jumpsuit shuffled in followed by a prison guard, who locked the door behind him, leaned on it and crossed his arms.

Dan Winchowski regarded Emily for a moment before he sat and reached for the phone hanging on his side of the divider. Emily, fresh from the files of the investigation and the trial, recognized him only by the gentle brown eyes that stared at her. The pictures from years ago had depicted a youthful man, full of vigor and strength. The man in front of her was sallow and paunchy. His formerly lush brown hair had thinned across the top and gone gray along the edges. He looked sad and beaten, Emily thought. Although he observed her warily, there was no curiosity about why she was there.

She picked up the phone on her side of the glass. "Dan Winchowski? I'm Emily Remington of the Escanaba, Michigan, Police Department, lately retired. I'd like to ask you a few questions if I may."

"Yeah?" The voice was hollow over the wires, but challenging. The defeated look had disappeared, and along with more life, there was a hint of resistance. "Whatever you want doesn't have anything to do with me. I've never been to Escawhatsit." He shrugged his shoulders. "And I've been here for over thirty years."

"This is about what happened in Madison thirty-some years ago. I want to verify some of the facts of the bombing you were involved in."

"Involved in? Look, lady, I did it. You're one of those do-gooders who go around looking to get guys outta here, aren't you? Well, forget it. I made my confession. I'm good with the law and I'm good with God. That priest from Green Bay came by and I told him everything. Made me wanna retch just lookin' at him, him and his kind. They're all perverts. But I cleared my soul."

"Are you talking about Father Virchow?"

"Yeah, that's the guy. First priest I've talked to since that old one diddled with me when I was a kid, serving as his altar boy."

"You were molested?" Emily sat up taller, her conversation with the bishop suddenly taking on a new light. "By a priest? Did the bishop know?"

"Nobody knew, until my confession. Hadn't planned on telling Virchow either. Funny thing is, he was actually shocked. Like he really cared. Told me to write a formal complaint to the bishop."

"Did you?"

"I thought about it. But hell, that was forty some years ago. What's he going to do now?"

Emily thought a moment before replying. "There are a lot of priests being investigated right now. The bishop is on the hot seat. He's going to have to do something about what went on—even forty years ago—whether he wants to or not."

Winchowski pushed the chair back with a scraping sound.

"What the hell difference does it make now?" He started to hang up the phone. "I got my get-outta-jail card secured now, thanks to Virchow. I'm moving on."

Before he could hang up, Emily shouted, "Wait! What get-out-of-jail card?"‟

He hesitated then leaned forward again. "Jeremiah Douglas."

"What about Jeremiah Douglas?"

He grinned. "I know something his electorate would be very unhappy to discover about him."

"What is that?"

"Why should I tell you? This is my ace-in-the-hole." He started to put the phone down again.

Emily was desperate to keep the man talking.

"At the trial, Jeremiah Douglas testified that you had stolen his car."

"Yeah? So?"

"Is that the way it happened?"

"Why don't you check out the trial transcript?"

"I have."

"So why are you asking?"

"I'm asking because I don't think you stole that car."

"Then how'd I get it?"

She had him hooked. His body, slithered back down into his chair.

"You tell me," she said leaning in toward the glass.

He regarded her silently for several moments, the fingers of his left hand drumming the small counter in front of him. He closed his eyes. Emily waited.

Finally, he spoke. "I guess it doesn't matter now. I thought for a while that maybe..."

He was struggling with himself over something and Emily was afraid if she spoke, she'd tip the balance somehow. Years of experience had taught her to just let people speak. The finger-drumming stopped.

"I thought I could use it, maybe. Maybe get out of here on some technicality. Maybe put some pressure on Douglas. If he didn't want it out, maybe he'd see to it that I'd get pardoned or something. I don't know. I don't much care anymore." He paused. "Douglas's old man was a real piece of work. Bought off my lawyer so I would keep my mouth shut. Said it wouldn't make a difference in my sentencing either way."

Emily sat up straighter. She bit her lip to keep from prodding the story from him.

"Ya know? Everybody in those days talked about making a bomb. Every party I went to, someone was bragging that they were gonna bring down the ROTC or the admin building. Or hit a car with some general or senator in it. There was this black guy—a chemistry major. Damn, what was his name? Like a vacuum cleaner."

"Hoover. Malcolm Hoover." Emily broke her silence.

"Yeah him. He said he knew several ways to make a bomb. But I didn't need help from his kind. I did it myself. I took a chemistry class or two myself. It's not really that difficult, you know. Just get yourself some bags of liquid fertilizer. And boom! Bricks flying in the air, dust and papers, earthquake, window glass, then silence a moment. Then screaming. Two guys dead. I guess I made my point. Funny. I don't even remember my point anymore. It seemed important at the time."

Emily waited a moment before responding. She could see the defeated look in the man's eyes, scared almost. But scared of what? He'd been convicted, sent to prison for life. "Tell me about Jeremiah Douglas's father. What exactly did you do for him?"

"My mother needed money for treatment for her breast cancer. I was happy to take his money. Do you know it saved her life? The money I mean. Without it, she'd have died within months. But it doesn't all matter now anyway." Tears sprung to his eyes and he began picking at a hangnail on his index finger.

"Why not?"

"She died anyway. Drunk driver got her. Ain't that a piece of cake? Guy's here now. Got 15 years."

"Jeremiah Douglas's father?" She prompted.

"Yeah. Wanted to keep his kid out of trouble. Paid me to twist the facts. I never stole anything. Jeremiah handed me those keys. He was always lending out that little convertible of his. Made him look like a hotshot."

"So Jeremiah lied on the witness stand."

"No shit. If you've got money you can say whatever you want." He looked at her, straight for the first time during the interview. "You know, that priest was also asking me about this old stuff."

"Father Virchow?"

"Yeah. He's my other ace-in-the-hole. If I ever need him, he'll back me up. He knew Douglas personally. And he knows I'm telling the truth."

"I'm afraid he's not going to do you much good," Emily said.

Winchowski frowned. "What are you talking about?"

"He's dead." She watched his expression carefully. "Murdered."

"Oh." Winchowski's face fell.

His chair squawked as he pushed it back. This interview was over. He turned to go, but he picked up the phone one last time.

"Probably deserved it," he snarled. "They all do."

He shuffled out of the room as the guard held the door for him and slammed it shut.

CHAPTER 31

Stan looked in disgust at the dead cell phone in his hand. Technology was a wonderful thing, except when it didn't work. He tossed the device onto the counter and reached for the brandy bottle. He filled the cup about half way, added some coffee, then topped it off with another slosh of brandy.

He carried the cup back over to the small dining table where the contents of Vic's suitcase were scattered. He looked at the mess. He was puzzled. Here were all the notes and files, but where was the draft of the memoir itself? Stan was sure Vic had told him it was a good three quarters of the way completed.

He opened an unmarked binder. Nothing but newspaper clippings.

Stan looked at the suitcase thoughtfully. He moved off his chair and got down onto the floor where he could open the bag fully. He pulled out all the remaining files and notebooks. He emptied the contents of a small zippered pencil bag onto the floor; a variety of colored pens, paperclips, a highlighter, and a small stapler tumbled out. Then he turned the small nylon case inside out to see if there was anything he had missed. Nothing.

He stared at the empty suitcase. After a moment he unzipped and dug into all the side pockets. Nothing. He sighed, reached up for his coffee cup and took a long draught.

As he lifted his arm to set the mug back up onto the table, he felt a familiar twinge in his back. Damn! One little movement was all it ever took. He tried to straighten his legs out to stretch his back, but there was no room. Time to get up off the floor.

He rolled onto his knees and positioned himself to push off with his hands. Growing old was hell! And this motel room on wheels needed to be bigger. He pushed against the floor with one hand; there was no room to place his other had except into the suitcase to get the leverage he needed. As he started to push off, he felt a lump under his palm. He sat back down, groaning against the twinge, and fumbled at the lining of the suitcase. Something was there.

Running his hand along the edge of the lining, he looked for an opening. A small zipper ran the full circumference of the suitcase, but was hidden in the seam of the lining. He tugged at the zipper and pulled the lining back. A buff colored envelope was taped to the bottom of the suitcase. Stan's face lit up in triumph. Vic, you old scoundrel!

He tugged at the envelope, peeling away the tape, and dumped the contents into the palm of his hand—a key chain.

Stan suddenly found himself fighting tears as he fingered the pewter cross attached to the key ring. The ancient Celtic design brought back vivid memories. He had given this key chain to Vic on the twenty-fifth anniversary of his ordination. Several years before, in the mid-90s, Vic had accompanied Stan on a research a trip to Ireland. For Vic, it was a spiritual journey. At least, that's how Vic had described it to Stan afterward. Vic had been intrigued by the melding of Catholicism with the ancient pagan traditions and symbols in Ireland. He had become obsessed with the Celtic cross—a flared crucifix encircled by a halo-like ring, representing the eternity of God's love, an eternity to which Vic himself had so suddenly and so recently journeyed.

Stan had commissioned this particular keychain to be cast by one of the metalsmithing students at his college, a gifted young artist who'd created a unique design of intricately carved knot work. However, there were no keys on this key chain. Instead, on the other end was a flash drive, a small data storage device for a computer.

Stan pushed himself off the floor with a grunt, ignoring the multiple twinges that were now screaming for attention.

Hobbling down the short hallway to the bedroom, he fumbled for a leather case buried under his golf shoes in the bottom of the closet. He sighed with relief. *Thank god, that burglar wasn't very thorough.*

Back at the dining table he pulled his laptop out of its case and powered it up, thrumming his fingers impatiently, waiting for the start-up programs to load. Finally he inserted the tiny drive into a port on the side of the machine. The computer did its magic, bringing up a single file from the small storage device—the manuscript of Vic's memoir.

Now that Emily was on her way back to the Door, she wished she could enjoy the scenery—the farms bathed in the golden light of an early October evening, crossing the expansive Lake Butte Des Morts on the four lane highway bridge just north of Oshkosh, the geese dotting the sky in their V formations, crowding the fields of already shorn corn. But scenery was the furthest thing from her mind right now. The visit with Dan Winchowski had been revealing, but deeply disturbing. She was worried about Stan.

Was Jeremiah responsible for Vic's death? Had Vic found out about the perjury? That one single choice over thirty years ago, if revealed, would crush Jeremiah's political ambitions today. It was obvious to her now that whoever killed Vic was also trying to get his papers. That would explain the break-ins at the RV and the rectory. And now that she thought about it, likely whoever killed the woman in room eighteen thought it was the Remington's room and that the papers would be there. And that meant that whoever was behind all this— Jeremiah?—knew that Stan had Vic's papers.

Emily pushed the accelerator. She ran through the scenarios over and over, and none of them boded well. The drive from Oshkosh to Sturgeon Bay seemed to take forever.

As she finally crossed the Door County line, Emily tried Stan's cell phone again. Not surprisingly, there was no response. Someday she was going to glue that phone into the "on" position and tape it to his forehead. A sudden sense of panic rose inside her, as she realized he had avoided telling her where he was. Did he have a clue as to the danger he was in? She guessed not.

She flipped the cell phone open again and punched in 911. When the dispatcher picked up, she explained that it was an emergency and she needed to get in touch with the sheriff. A few moments later the annoying *Für Elise* jangled.

"Pelletier here," his voice rumbled.

"Sheriff, this is Emily Remington."

"Where the hell are you?" he growled.

"On 57, just crossing the bridge at Sturgeon Bay. I've been trying to reach Stan and there's no answer on his cell. You wouldn't know where he is, would you?"

"You've been gone all day." His voice was testy. Emily knew she'd crossed a line when she left the county without telling him.

"I had some research to take care of."

"You couldn't let me know you were going?"

"I let my husband know."

Pelletier simply grunted.

"I have some information that I think you will want to hear," Emily told him. "But first I need to find Stan. Do you know where he is?"

"My deputy dropped him off in town."

"Your deputy? Why was he with your deputy?"

"Turns out we have another body."

"What?" Emily was stunned "Where? When? Does this have something to do with Vic's death? And the woman at the motel?"

"That's what I'm trying to find out. Coulda used a little help here today."

Emily knew she was being chastised for ducking out on him. She grimaced at the back end of a milk truck that she'd quickly caught up to. She tapped the brakes once to disengage the cruise control until she could get around the big rolling cylinder.

"Is Stan okay?"

"Your husband's fine. Your friend, Mr. Hoover, found the body this morning."

"Malcolm!?" Emily's internal alarms kicked into high gear. Something was going on that she couldn't figure out, and it was plenty dangerous.

"What did Malcolm have to do with this? Where was the body?" she asked. "And who was it?"

"I suggest you get back here as quickly as possible," the sheriff said.

Emily knew that he wasn't about to give sensitive details out over what could easily be public airwaves.

"If you found out anything of interest in Madison, I could use the information sooner rather than later."

"I should be there in forty minutes," Emily said.

"Make it thirty. Door County doesn't get one murder in three years, much less three murders in three days. A little help from Ms. Marple would go a long way right about now."

Emily winced at the "Ms. Marple" moniker that seemed to be sticking all of a sudden, but any irritation she felt about Fred's nickname for her took an immediate back seat to Stan's safety.

"Where exactly did your deputy drop Stan off?"

"The library, I think. Said he had some research he wanted to do."

Emily relaxed. The library. That was Stan. And what could be a safer place? Unless—

Emily leaned harder on the gas, flying around the milk truck.

"Where do you want me to meet you?"

"I'm on my way to our number three corpse's abode. He's got a cabin in the woods up here. If you take 57 up to Bailey's Harbor, I'll have a deputy meet you at the Town Square Market on County F."

He clicked off, leaving Emily with dead air.

She tossed the phone down onto the seat next to her and kicked the auto into high gear. Wishing she had an emergency flasher to clear the way, she drove as fast as she safely could—maybe even just a little faster.

CHAPTER 32

It was like coming up for air after having been under water for a long time. Stan was so immersed in Vic's memoir that he hadn't noticed the clock ticking away, much less the light beginning to change as the late afternoon wore its way toward dusk. When he finally did look up and at the clock and then out the window, it took a moment or two to register just where he was. He blinked. There was that banging again.

This time his brain deciphered the sound that had brought him up out of the depths—a knocking at the RV door. Stan opened it to find a paunchy man of about sixty in a Chicago Bears sweatshirt and frayed Cubs hat.

"Sorry to bother you," the man said, a belch escaping under his words. "Blew a fuse this afternoon. Ol' Lady dropped her hairdryer in the damn toilet again. Wouldn't have a spare, would ya?" Another belch.

"Fuses? Hell, I don't know. Where would they be kept?"

"You don't know where you keep your spares?"

"This is all new to me. My wife's the mechanic."

"Damn!" He burped again.

This time Stan stepped back away from the wave of beer and salami wafting in the air between them.

"Well, if ya got any, they'd probably be—"

"You know, she did mention fuses. Just this morning. Said she was going pick some up," Stan lied. *If he burps one more time, I'm gonna belt him.* "Wish I could help you. But we're all out."

He offered up a conciliatory smile and pushed the door to close it. But the Bears fan caught it with a fleshy fist. Stan found himself staring at a thatch of black hair on the back of the guy's hand.

"Say, I wanted ta ask ya. What's with all the yellow tape, anyway? You get broken into?" The guy seemed genuinely worried.

"Are you a new arrival?" Stan asked.

"Yeah, got here early this afternoon. So, what's the deal. This not a safe park?"

"Just a prank. Nothing to worry about. I should have pulled it all down, but I got busy." Stan tried again to close the door.

Again, the hairy fist pushing back. A burp slipped from the man's lips. "You wouldn't have a spare beer, would ya?"

"Sorry, all I have is coffee," Stan said, hoping against hope that the brandy bottle was not sitting in full view on the counter behind him.

"Nah, that's okay. Caffeine does a number on my stomach. Makes me burp." The beefy hand waved in farewell, as the man step back down the steps and lumbered across the road.

After finally closing the door and locking it, Stan poured himself another brandy, this time with no coffee. *Hate to start burping,* he thought. He sipped at his drink, staring at the computer screen but no longer seeing the typescript. Having spent the afternoon reliving the priest's life, he felt the loss of his friend even more acutely.

Stan had thought he knew Vic, but was discovering a new dimension to his friend. This was a man who had had a love/hate relationship with his creator his entire life. Vic had devoted his life to doing what he believed was God's work, but often as not blamed God for the injustices, cruelty, and perversity that he believed was inherent in the universal exercise of free will.

The narrative Stan had been reading was definitely a draft, rough and unfinished. However, Vic's story needed to be told. Beverly had urged Stan to consider finishing the book, and now Stan was determined to accept the mission. There was a great deal of research yet to be done, but digging into history never daunted Stan. Rooting out multiple versions of the facts, unlocking the mysteries hidden in individual narratives—the whole process got his adrenaline running, much the same way investigating a crime scene did for Emily.

Stan's stomach growled. He winced at the surge of acid rising up toward his esophagus. An afternoon of brandy-laced coffee was taking its revenge and he realized he was hungry. A quick check of the cupboards reminded him that he had promised to do the grocery shopping before they left on their trip...and hadn't quite gotten around to it. Emily hadn't been happy with him, but he had promised her that they would stop and stock up over the weekend. He would have to remember to ask her whether they needed to buy any spare fuses, he thought. If they got around to it. The grocery shopping that is.

With a resigned sigh, he reached for a box of bran flakes and plunged his hand in for a fistful, popping it into his mouth. Immediately, he regretted it. With a curse, he shoved the open box back into the cupboard. He took a slug of brandy to rinse out his mouth. He pondered where he go to get a bite to eat. More specifically, how could he get there?

Recognizing he had no options for pacifying his hunger, Stan returned to Vic's papers, which were strewn about the RV in stacks and piles that made sense only to him. However, with the light fading fast, he started to get antsy. He thumbed through a couple more folders, but the words were blurring. He rubbed his eyes, wondering if it was fatigue or the brandy. He switched on a light, but obviously the spell had been broken and he could no longer concentrate. Tucking the flash drive into the envelope, he zipped it back into the lining of the travel bag. Then he picked up the folders, notebooks, and binders and repacked them neatly into the suitcase. He carried the suitcase into the bedroom and hoisted the foot of the double-size bed, revealing a storage space filled with suitcases. He wedged Vic's bag in amongst the others.

A second round of banging at the door caught him up short.

Damn! He's back. If he doesn't have food to offer, I'm not letting him in—unless he has a car and knows where there's a good steakhouse.

When he opened the door, it took a moment for it to register that the woman standing there was not his belching buddy.

"Mr. Remington."

"Yes?"

"I'm Shannon Lambert. Remember? We met at dinner the other night. Senator Douglas' campaign manager." She was wearing khaki slacks and a jeans jacket over a pink designer t-shirt. Cross country trainers replaced the business style heels that had defined her stride when they first met.

"Miss Lambert! Yes. I'm sorry. Come in! Come in!" He opened the door wider and stepped back to let her through.

"I hope you don't mind my stopping by. I took a chance that you'd be here. I went to the motel first, but they told me you'd been gone all day."

Stan swung a chair around for her to sit down, but she shook her head no.

"I really don't have time," she said. "The Senator, as you can imagine is quite distraught. As I'm guessing you are."

"It's been a rough couple of days. I can't believe all that's happened."

"I know for a fact that the Senator hasn't slept since... well, since you found your friend's body. I've canceled or rescheduled most of his events and appearances."

"I suppose it's created some havoc for the campaign," Stan commiserated.

"Yes, but that's not why I'm here." She hesitated. "Mr. Remington—"

"Stan."

"Stan. I'm concerned about Senator Douglas. He's obsessed with the notion that he can help discover who killed Father Virchow. He won't let it go. He's been going over and over lists of everyone he knows who had anything to do with the priest."

"I guess we're all doing that," Stan offered. "It's natural in a situation like this."

"He spoke to Father Virchow's sister the other day and she mentioned the priest had been working on his memoirs. He apparently had a suitcase of some sort? Filled with his notes and journals?"

"She mentioned that to me, too.

"Is it true she entrusted those papers to you?"

Stan hesitated. "I have them," he admitted.

"Well, the Senator was hoping...he..."

"Wants to know what's in them?"

"That's why I stopped by. He's is spending a few days up at his house on Washington Island. He was hoping you'd come out and review the papers with him."

"Actually, I was just thinking that perhaps he and I needed a chance to talk."

Shannon glanced quickly at her watch. "There's one more ferry before they shut down for the night. If we hurry we can make it."

Stan nodded. The vision of a t-bone dissolved. Maybe he could talk her into stopping at a drive-thru.

Reaching for his windbreaker, he followed Shannon out the door. She turned and frowned impatiently.

"Father Virchow's suitcase?" she reminded him.

"Of course."

Stan fumbled his way back inside and to the bedroom. As he emerged, nylon suitcase in hand, he glanced out the window at the woman pacing by a late model Lexus. He grabbed a pad of paper and quickly jotted a note to Emily, just in case she came looking for him here when she didn't find him at the motel. He stuck the note to the refrigerator door with a Bugs Bunny magnet.

Then he stepped out into the damp, evening air. Shannon had already slid into the driver's seat, her grim face barely lit by the fading dash lights. The motor growled to life as the headlights beckoned him to take his place next to her.

CHAPTER 33

Wisps of ground fog, ghostly white in the fading light of dusk, hovered over the corn fields and blanketed the cherry orchards. Emily's stomach grumbled and she realized she hadn't eaten since the bagels at noon. Too bad, she thought, but it wouldn't be the first time her body had to run on reserve fuel. Might even be a good thing, she reflected ruefully, especially considering the couple of extra pounds the scale had most recently attributed to her small frame. But when the fuel gauge dipped past its own reserve mark and she stopped to fill the tank and grab a cup of coffee, she gave in and bought herself a Snickers bar.

A short while later, she met the deputy at the market on County F in Bailey's Harbor and followed him along County Highway V for about a mile, maybe a little less. Then they turned right onto A. Kind of like alphabet soup, Emily thought, but it was actually easier than reading place names on the small road signs through the deepening mist as they zipped past. Finally, they turned down a two-lane county road.

It was dark now, and she wished she could switch on her high beams but was following too closely behind the squad car. Thank goodness, she didn't have to find her way by herself. Finally, the deputy's car ahead of her slowed down and he turned onto a narrow dirt road. A quarter of a mile later, she eased her car behind him onto a bumpy two-rut drive and into a stand of cedars and birch.

Fred's police cruiser was parked in front of a small structure, a little cabin hidden from the view of the road. The headlights of the cars lit up the edge of the woods, leaving the unlit parts of the property in milky shadows so deep Emily couldn't tell whether they were surrounded by brush or trees. She guessed it was a combination of both.

Leaving her headlights on, Emily nestled her car under a canopy of cedars. The air was unexpectedly cold, much colder than the past few nights. Glad she'd thought to throw her hooded sweatshirt into the back seat this morning, she pulled it on.

"'Bout time you got here," the sheriff grunted. Wearing a light windbreaker, he stood outside his vehicle, radio mike in hand.

"Rush-hour traffic. Have you heard from Stan?"

"Not since he was dropped off."

Emily grimaced. She hoped he had the sense to stay put at the library. It irked her that he could never seem to remember to charge his phone. But there was nothing she could do about that now.

"What have you got here?" she asked.

"Turns out our third body was one of the groundskeepers at the park."

Emily glanced over at the cabin. "This is where he lived?"

"Thought maybe we'd come up with a clue or two as to who would go to the trouble of throwing him off a bluff."

"A bluff?"

"He was floating in the bay when your friend Hoover reeled him in."

"Yeah, but, how do you know he didn't just fall off a boat?"

"His body had multiple contusions, consistent with having fallen off something pretty high up."

"Sounds like you're pretty sure it was murder and not an accident." Emily said.

"I'm not sure of anything at this point. But it would have been a pretty complicated jump—or fall—if he did it on his own. People don't generally fall off bluffs and directly into the water in that part of the bay."

"What?" Emily chided, "Are you saying people fall off your bluffs on a regular basis?"

"You know what I mean." He offered her a pair of latex gloves. "Think you want to take a look inside?"

Emily accepted the gloves and followed him toward the small building, tugging them on as she went. A cold light escaped from a single dingy window next to the open front door. Fred had been generous calling this a "cabin." It was more of a shack than anything. Made of clapboard siding, it had once been painted green, but years of rain and wind had worn the color away.

Inside, a bare ceiling bulb cast a stark glare over the interior of the room. A twin bed, a porcelain sink, a two-burner stove and a small refrigerator crowded the single room. A chipped toilet peeked out from behind a grimy, ragged curtain. There was no shower. A small table with a single webbed lawn chair shoved under a window served as the dining area. There was not enough stuff in the cabin for it to ever be considered cluttered.

"His name was Casey Lambert."

"Lambert?" Emily thought out loud. Why was that name familiar?

"Turns out our latest body had a sister you might know."

Emily turned a quizzical eye toward the sheriff.

"Shannon Lambert."

"Jeremiah Douglas's campaign manager?" Emily felt a little jolt. This was the second of the three deaths that had a direct link to Jeremiah. She felt like she was staring at a puzzle board, but the picture was murky and pieces were missing. And how did this piece—the death of someone related to Jeremiah's campaign manager—fit in with the others?

"Apparently she's his only next of kin," the sheriff said. Seems their parents have been deceased for a number of years now. Grew up around these parts, but was more of a drifter lately. Was doing odd jobs for the park service out at Moose's Leap. We're trying to locate his sister now."

"Do you have a photo of him?"

"Only his driver's license. He didn't keep much by way of family memorabilia out here." Fred took a plastic card out of his shirt pocket and handed it to Emily. The card was streaked with dried, muddy water.

"Casey Lambert. Twenty-eight. Not much taller than his sister by the description here." She studied the little rectangle outlining the young man's face on the license. "I know this man."

Fred's eyebrows shot up.

"He was at the golf course, watering the plants. He yelled at me to move my RV. There was another time, at the campground. He was picking up trash or something near our site."

Fred frowned.

"I didn't think much about him at the time. Except he seemed a bit whacked out."

"Whacked out?"

"On weed or something. Maybe a crystal meth user. Looked like he hadn't slept in days."

Fred nodded, not ready to make any judgments. He reached into a cupboard with a gloved hand and pulled out a zipped plastic bag filled with a green leafy substance and another plastic pouch, secured at the top with a twist tie, half filled with a white crystalline substance.

217

"Doubt they're oregano and sugar," he said with a wry grimace. He put the bags back.

Emily nodded. She turned slowly, her eyes sweeping the room, gathering impressions of a man she'd only met briefly, one whose young life had come to such a violent end.

The bed with a ratty sleeping bag stretched out on it looked like it hadn't been slept in for some time. A single dish towel hung neatly over the back of the lone chair. The Formica tabletop had been neatly wiped clean, but the chrome legs had years of grime matted into them.

A crack in the window over the table was splayed with cobwebs. She opened the grimy door of the refrigerator that stood no taller than she. A couple of cans of beer, a tub of margarine, and a container of orange juice that had separated were all that sat on the wire shelves. The washed dishes in the dish drainer—two plates, a mug, a knife and a couple of forks—spoke of a man who liked to keep things neat among all the grime and shabbiness, a trait uncommon in drug users, in Emily's experience.

Emily glanced down at a faded Persian rug covering the rough wooden floor. Something nagged at her. Squatting to get a closer look, she ran her fingers over the worn threads of the dark floral fabric.

"The rug," she said.

"What about the rug?" Fred asked.

"The one Father Vic was wrapped in wasn't the one I bought that day."

"What do you mean?"

"This is the rug I bought."

CHAPTER 34

Once the last car had been loaded onto the ferry and the boarding ramp raised and secured into its upright position, the engines came to life with a quiet rumble, pushing the large boxy craft away from the dock at the tip of the peninsula.

"It's a thirty minute crossing, so we might as well make ourselves comfortable," Shannon suggested as she pulled on a dark blue hooded sweatshirt.

Stan shifted the suitcase from one hand to another as he followed the nimble woman up a short flight of steps to the mid-deck with its open-air seating. He stopped at the head of the stairs to read an informational placard. This was one of the newer vessels in the fleet, christened the *Arni J. Richter* in honor of the ferry line's original owner. At 104 feet in length, it easily held twenty cars. An all-weather vessel, this ferry served double duty as an ice-breaker in the winter to keep traffic moving between the island and the mainland.

"Come on!" Shannon grabbed at his sleeve and pulled him toward the chairs out on the deck.

He set the suitcase at his feet and leaned over the rail, watching as the water churned beneath the hull. Shannon had led him away from the few other passengers to where they could have a little privacy. In the darkness, a fog had settled over the six mile expanse of water, blotting out three small smudges on the horizon—Plum, Pilot and Detroit Islands. A gust of wind cut through the fog, sharp and cold, and the water suddenly got choppier. Stan understood why Shannon had thought to bring a hooded sweatshirt which she wore under her jeans jacket, but he enjoyed the motion of the boat as it ate through the waves, slapping the bow up and down, sending a fine mist of spray into his face. In weather like this, he usually found his lined windbreaker to be all he needed to stay comfortable.

"You and Senator Douglas go back a long way," Shannon spoke, breaking the silence that had settled over them like the fog.

"Since college. He was always organizing to support some cause or another even back then."

"Then you know how important this race is for him. How much it means to him to be governor." Shannon pushed a wet strand of hair from her face.

"I admire his drive, if not always his politics."

"He represents everything I believe in," Shannon said. "I've built my entire career around him."

Stan turned to look at her, her profile muted by the mist as she gazed out over the water.

"This is just the beginning," she said, almost as if talking to herself. "He is destined for great things. He can be president someday. He will be."

"So...this office is just a stepping stone for him? A term as governor and then on to higher office?" Stan was not entirely surprised that his friend's ambitions ran that high.

"This country needs men like Jeremiah Douglas." Shannon looked like she was going to say more, but the ferry's fog horn blasted, cutting off all conversation for the moment. Out of the mist, another ferry approached, passed, and rumbled on its way toward the mainland. The captain of the *Arni J. Richter* blew his horn twice in acknowledgement.

Stan reflected on Shannon's last statement. He liked Jeremiah, but he wasn't sure his friend was exactly what this country needed. He watched as seagulls swarmed the ferry, dodging and swooping, then soaring on the feeble air currents, their cries piercing the air.

"Porte des Morts," he said, by way of changing subject.

"What?"

"Death's Door. The early French explorers named it that." Was he imagining it, or did Shannon shudder at his words?

"The name appears to be apropos," he continued. "Maritime folklore credits this site with having more shipwrecks than in any other body of fresh water."

"There are commercial excursions that take people out scuba diving for sunken ships here," Shannon commented. "I grew up on the Door, but I'm only here during campaign season anymore. And then I'm thinking about the future, not the past."

"Ah, but the past is where we learn how to interpret the future," Stan said.

She shrugged her shoulders as if dismissing the notion.

Clearly rebuffed, Stan lapsed into silence. He leaned over the rail and tracked the wake of a passing Coast Guard patrol boat, already disappearing into the mist. The deep, mournful sigh of a foghorn called to them from the abandoned post at Plum Island. He knew from a conversation he'd had with an old mariner he'd met years earlier that the Coast Guard had an outpost on Washington Island, called Station Small. It was manned by a combination of active duty and reserve "summer stock" personnel working out of a remodeled chalet overlooking the cozy island harbor.

The original rescue station with its four-story lighthouse at Plum Island had been abandoned in 1990, the victim of years of stormy weather, man-made contaminants, and a physical facility too costly to repair and maintain. However, the

221

foghorn was still located on the smaller island, and was now activated by radio control from commercial vessels such as the ferry. Stan looked down into the black water.

"Did you know it's six miles across?" he asked. "From the tip of the peninsula to Washington Island."

"Too far to swim," was Shannon's only comment.

Before long the ferry blew its fog horn again, and the vessel entered a small harbor on the south end of Washington Island. Stan and Shannon clambered down the narrow stairs to her car as the ferry pulled up to the dock. Stan barely felt the bump as the large vessel snugged up against the pier.

Shannon guided her car off the ferry ramp and up the road away from the harbor. In the dark and the deepening fog Stan could barely see the small buildings housing a restaurant and gift shop, a bait and tackle shop, and a shack advertising bicycle and moped rentals. He hoped Shannon knew the area well enough not to be confused by the fog as they turned onto the two-lane county highway toward the east side of the island. They'd barely gotten a half-mile down the road when the car suddenly started swerving and bumping wildly.

"Damn it!" Shannon hissed under her breath. "I don't suppose you have experience changing tires?" she asked hopefully.

"Oh, I've changed more than a few in my day. Pop the trunk. We'll look for the jack. Do you have a flashlight handy?"

Shannon turned on the emergency flasher. A few moments later, while Shannon held the narrow-beamed flashlight, Stan jacked up the rear of the car, then used the flat end of the lug wrench to pry off the hubcap. He leaned his weight on the wrench to loosen the lug nuts. Suddenly the beam of light expanded and grew. They were caught in the glare of an oncoming vehicle. Stan straightened up and watched as a pickup truck pulled in behind them.

222

"Hey, there!" said a man in his late forties as he climbed out of the truck. "Need help?"

"No. Thank you. We've got the situation under control," Shannon said.

The man adjusted his baseball cap and came around to where Stan had knelt to pull the old tire off the car. He ignored Shannon and took the tire from Stan, handing him the spare.

"You here on vacation?" he asked, glancing up at Shannon who pulled the hood of her sweatshirt up over her head and stepped out of the direct beam of the light.

"Business," she said.

"Don't suppose you do any fishing?" he asked Stan.

"'Fraid my rod and reel's been collecting a few too many cobwebs these days," Stan responded amiably.

"You get a chance, the one to go for here is smallmouth bass." The man reached for the lug wrench and handed it off like a nurse attending a surgeon.

"That so?"

"There's quite a population all around the island. But the place you want to drop your line is right up there at Detroit Harbor where the ferry comes in. You musta come in on the ferry."

"Can we get this job finished?" Shannon jiggled the keys in her hand.

Stan frowned at her.

"Well, you don't want to be right at the ferry dock," the man continued as if Shannon hadn't spoken, "but farther along where it's shallower. The smallies love the shallow-water rocks, specially in the early morning and just before the sun sets."

Stan finished tightening the lug nuts. His new friend reached out and tested them, nodding his approval.

"You wanna stay in water less'n twelve feet deep. The more rocks the better. Gravel will do. Any kind of sunken rock piles."

"I'll keep that in mind. Thanks."

Stan stood and stretched his back. The bass fisherman grabbed the dead tire and tossed it into the trunk and started pumping the lever to lower the jack.

"You come here to fish, you're gonna wanna make sure you have the right bait. Tube jigs are the way to go for smallies. Use the lightest jig head you can find. But you still want to maintain contact with the bottom. The trick is not letting the tube jig drop too fast. Most people just let it drop like a stone. What you wanna do is let it glide, sort of swim along the bottom." He demonstrated with his hand. "Or you can use a topwater lure. Maybe throw a buzzbait or a plug. The smallies can't resist 'em. They'll attack either one. But if you're gonna be topwater fishing, you're best to do it early in the morning."

"You ever use live bait?" Stan asked as he put the tools away and closed the trunk lid.

"Hell, yes."

Shannon was already back in the car, starting the engine.

"If you're not an experienced jig fisher, you wanna stick with live bait. Not as much fun, but when I'm out with a novice, I always give 'em live bait. Smallies aren't terribly particular."

Stan held out his hand, and the fisherman gave it a hearty shake. "Yer little woman's not much for fishin', I take it."

Stan glanced toward Shannon, impatiently tapping the steering wheel. Her hand balled into a quick fist and she punched it, producing two high pitched toots of the horn. "No, seems like she's got another agenda altogether."

"Well, you have a good evening. Don't get lost in the fog."

The man tipped his baseball cap and ambled off to his pickup. Stan climbed in next to Shannon. He barely had the door closed, when she stomped on the gas, fishtailing and spraying gravel as the car shot into a vortex of swirling gloom.

CHAPTER 35

Emily looked up at the sheriff. The expression on his face was a clear indication he wasn't tracking her as she studied the floral rug in Casey Lambert's cabin.

"See this stain?" she asked, pointing at a dark splotch.

Fred look confused.

"I had talked the people at the garage sale down because of the stain."

"Okay...?" He prodded her.

"The patterns in the two rugs are similar, but not the same. It didn't occur to me the night we found Vic, but I knew something wasn't right. But this is my rug."

"So, if your Padre, our first victim, was wrapped in a different rug, how did yours get here?"

"That's the question, isn't it?" She stood up and brushed off her pant legs.

"I'd say it's pretty clear two of our victims have a connection," Pelletier said. "I doubt our groundskeeper just somehow happened upon your rug and decided it would look good in his cabin."

"I've got another new wrinkle for you as well." She shook her leg to relieve the cramp in her calf that had developed while she was on the floor.

"I was hoping you hadn't spent all day having tea and crumpets with old college friends."

"Bagels. We had bagels," she said. "I did some checking around. I wanted to find out more about Vic's relationship with the bishop."

"I had a long chat with that lackey of his. Father Rydelle. Some piece of work he is," the sheriff commented.

"I had a little chat myself with both of them. They certainly were not happy with the idea that Vic might use his memoirs to do some whistle blowing. But I don't see them resorting to this level of violence to muzzle him."

The sheriff nodded. "I did a little digging too and I'm not inclined to suspect them of foul play. Foul attitudes, maybe. But not murder. So, that shifts the spotlight back to your Mr. Hoover."

"Yeah, I wanted to talk to you about him. Stan was worried that Malcolm was one of your suspects."

"Shouldn't he be?"

"No. He was just in the wrong place at the wrong time."

"Twice?" Fred asked.

"Quite a coincidence, I know. However, I drove to Madison today to check into a possible connection Stan had found between Vic and the bombing that took place in Madison back when I worked for the university."

"Whoa, Ms. Marple! Bombing?"

"It was our questions about Malcolm that led us there."

"Back up, back up. Are you talking about the protest bombing of the bio-chemistry building at the UW?"

"Stan's been digging through some of Vic's papers."

Pelletier's eyebrows shot up. "And where did your husband get the good Padre's papers?"

"It's a long story," Emily said. "I'll fill you in. But right now you need to know that Father Vic was privy to some information about that bombing that has the potential to hurt Jeremiah Douglas' campaign."

"Are you saying the Padre dug up dirt that could cast aspersions on our good candidate's character?"

"Perjury."

"That would do it."

"Jeremiah's Mustang was used as the getaway car by the bomber back in 1970."

Fred Pelletier's eyes widened.

"Jeremiah always claimed it had been stolen. And in fact, that's what Dan Winchowski, the guy who was convicted of the bombing, testified during his trial some dozen years later."

"So, where's the connection with our priest?"

"Father Vic was off at seminary when the trial took place. He wasn't aware of what had been said. But as he was researching for his book, he came across the bit about the car being stolen. Problem is, he remembered that night differently."

"How so?"

"Vic had arranged to borrow the car himself, for a particularly hot date. But when he went to pick it up, Jeremiah had already lent it to one of his fraternity friends."

"And that fraternity friend..."

"Was our convicted bomber."

"So Mr. Douglas perjured himself on the stand."

"And his father bribed the defendant."

"You can corroborate this?"

"I stopped by Waupun and had a chat with Mr. Winchowski on my way back up here."

"You've been a busy lady, Ms. Marple."

Emily grinned despite herself.

"The problem is," he said. "I don't see Mr. Douglas going to this extreme because of a rumor of perjury. He has more to lose by the connection to these murders than any accusation of perjury."

Emily nodded. Her eyes continued their survey of the room. Something leaned against the wall near the small kitchen table.

"That's odd," she murmured.

"What?"

"Why would an outdoorsy young man need a cane?"

Pelletier picked up the wooden cane with the carved knob.

"Good question," he said.

"Father Vic used a cane. He had broken his ankle in a parish softball game a number of years back, and it never healed properly. He had to have a permanent pin put in it. I remember, he limped when he walked and used a cane with a carved bone handle. I can't say if this is his or not, but Stan would know."

Emily flipped out her cell phone, hit the number for Stan, then cursed when the call immediately went to his voice mail again. She closed the phone and shoved it back into her pocket.

Pelletier signaled to one of his officers. "Can you get some prints off of this?" he asked.

Emily pointed to some dark spots along the wood. "You might want to check for blood as well."

"Looks like we need to start treating this as a crime scene," Pelletier said dryly. "Jacobs, call the state crime lab. Have them send somebody over here." He turned to Emily. "I think it's time I had another talk with Jeremiah Douglas."

"Do you even know where he is?" Emily asked.

"Hell, yeah. Politicians are easier to keep track of than a possum in a pine tree. He's got his boat moored over at Bailey's Harbor. Trying to get the commercial fisherman to cough up a few campaign bucks with the promise of unlimited catches, no doubt."

"Do you need me at that interview?" Emily asked.

Fred shook his head. "I can handle Mr. Governor-Wanna-Be. I get the feeling you want to be looking for your husband."

CHAPTER 36

Emily resisted the urge to nudge the gas pedal even closer to the floor. The light of her low beams bounced back at her from the thickening fog and barely illuminated the unfamiliar road ahead. Trees crowded the edges of the pavement, closing in on her. She knew that beyond the fog lay farm fields and cherry orchards that she couldn't see.

Watching the sheriff maneuver his squad car out of the small clearing in the woods and turn east toward Bailey's Harbor, Emily had been torn by the desire to follow him instead of turning west toward Fish Creek and the library. She desperately wanted to confront Jeremiah Douglas herself, to hear his side of the story. It was hard to believe that this man, whom Stan had cared for and trusted for so long, could have had a hand in Vic's death. However, she fully knew that ambition could drive even the best of people to desperate actions. A perjury conviction would surely end Jeremiah's career. The politician's connection to the body that had been found floating in the bay was too much of a coincidence to ignore. It wasn't unreasonable to assume that the two men knew each other or at least had met. Jeremiah could easily have hired Shannon Lambert's brother to do his dirty work without her knowledge.

But why? There were easier ways to stop the inevitable political train wreck that would come as a result of the candidate's past action.

In Fish Creek, she parked her car in front of the small town hall and ran up to the doors. They were locked and the building was dark. A sign on the door alerted her to the fact that the library had been closed the entire afternoon. Odd, she thought. He must have gone back to the motel.

But a quick check of the motel room proved her wrong. Now her instincts were sounding warning bells. But her investigative experience overrode her rising anxiety. She searched for Malcolm's number in her cell phone and hit the call button.

'I haven't seen him since about noon," Malcolm said in answer to her query. "Maybe he went to the campground."

"Well, that's off limits," Emily countered.

"Your point being...?"

Emily knew that Malcolm was right. If Stan had decided to go to the RV, chances are a little yellow police tape wouldn't keep him out. It hadn't kept her out earlier.

As she pulled into the Moose's Leap campground, a dull pain throbbed in the back of her head, rising up from her neck. She worked her jaw to loosen the tension and forced herself to wiggle her fingers and release the grip on the wheel. Her concern over Stan's sudden disappearance was tempered by annoyance. He knew better than to take off without telling anyone. It would serve him right to learn about his friend's culpability in this whole nasty affair from a breaking news report. However, she knew she needed to be the one to confirm Stan's suspicions before it became public.

Gravel crunched under her tires as she pulled up next to the RV. A subdued light shone through the window. He must be there. As she hurried in, she noted that Stan had made good use of his time, picking up and straightening the contents of the tiny living area. The chairs had been uprighted, the mess from the broken jar of jam swept and mopped.

"Stan?"

No answer.

"Stan!" She checked the bedroom. Now she was really unnerved. Where could he have gone now? He had no transportation.

The grumbling of hunger pangs reminded her she was subsisting on a Snickers bar downed hours earlier. Maybe she could find something quick, a piece of fruit or a slice of bread. As she reached for the refrigerator, she spotted Stan's note tacked to the door with the Bugs Bunny magnet. Bless his heart. The man had some consideration after all, if no common sense.

"Gone to meet JD on Wash Is w/SL"

"Oh, crap!" Emily's jaw tightened. *He doesn't have a clue what he's walking into.* "Tell me you didn't take Vic's suitcase," she said to the room. She glanced around, but didn't see it. "Damn." That suitcase was exactly what Jeremiah wanted to get his hands on.

Emily whipped out her cell phone and punched in 911. "This is Emily Remington, again..."

As much as she had wanted to follow the sheriff to Bailey's Harbor, if Jeremiah was on Washington Island, Emily knew now it would have been a wasted trip.

"Ms. Marple." The sheriff's voice sounded grim when he returned her call for the second time.

"Fred, Stan's in danger."

"What do you mean?"

"He's on his way to meet with Jeremiah."

"So what's the problem?"

"The problem is, they're meeting on Washington Island. I think Stan wants to confront him about Vic's perjury allegations."

"Doesn't make sense," the sheriff said.

"What do you mean it doesn't make sense?" Emily asked.

"Mr. Douglas isn't out on the island," Fred answered. "He's here with me. On the dock at Bailey's Harbor."

Emily was confused. She pulled the note off the fridge door ignoring the magnet as it clattered to the floor.

"His note says, 'Gone to meet JD on Washington Island with SL.'"

"JD. Jeremiah Douglas. Who the hell's SL?"

Emily was at a loss. Stan had gone with someone, thinking he was going to meet with Jeremiah. But who? Oh, shit, she thought.

"Fred, ask Jeremiah if he knows where Shannon Lambert is."

Emily was putting the dots together, and she didn't like the picture it was making.

"Ms. Lambert's been unavailable since we found her brother's body. Nobody seems to know where she is."

The dots were getting more numerous. Vic murdered, likely at Casey's shack of a cabin. Casey himself found dead and floating in the bay a couple of days later. And an innocent tourist brutally murdered in the room Stan and Emily had recently vacated. And while Jeremiah was the common thread to the mystery, he wasn't the one who posed an immediate threat to Stan.

"Fred, we have to find her. I think Stan's with her."

"I'm on it, Ms. Marple," Fred's deep voice became suddenly businesslike. He had been connecting the same dots.

Emily breathed deeply to dispel the panic rising inside her.

"I'll contact the Coast Guard," Pelletier said. "You drive to Gills Rock. I'll have them pick you up there. Mr. Douglas has offered the use of his cruiser. We'll meet you on Washington Island."

Emily slipped the cell phone back into her pocket. No use trying to dial Stan again. She closed her eyes and stood still for a moment, taking several deep breaths. Then she moved purposefully toward the driver's seat. Slipping her hand under the seat, she felt for the barely perceptible latch release in the hard plastic lining and pressed firmly. A moment later a small compartment opened. Lifting a petite, black gun out of its hiding place, she fingered the familiar grip of the Keltec P-32. She was thankful that the sheriff's crew hadn't been thorough enough to discover her custom-made hiding place. She inserted a loaded magazine into the grip, locking it into place, then shoved the weapon into her other pocket.

Grabbing a hooded jacket from the hook by the door, she slammed out of the RV and jumped into the car. Gravel flew as she gunned it. She forced herself to slow down; the fog still obscured her view of the road and despite the nearly empty campground, midweek in October, she would hate to be swerving around pedestrians in the dark. The deer would have to manage to keep out of her way on their own.

Wheeling the car onto the main highway heading north, Emily let the speedometer hover at a rate that no law-abiding police officer, active duty or retired, ought to be traveling, especially on a foggy night.

CHAPTER 37

Stan clutched the leather door grip of the Lexus, as Shannon negotiated a series of tight curves, one tire slipping off the edge of the narrow highway. Peering into the gloom, Stan gasped as a deer leaped out of the fog-shrouded trees and bolted across the road in front of them. Shannon slammed on the brakes, throwing the car into a skid, but the deer was long gone. Without a word, she hit the gas and the car sped up again.

"What's the rush?" Stan asked, willing his thudding heart to slow down.

Shannon eased off the gas. "Sorry. We're almost there." After a few moments, she slowed down even more and pulled into a darkened drive.

"This is it," she announced. "The Senator couldn't have picked a nicer spot. This is the sandy side of the island, though you can't tell in the dark."

She cut the engine, but left the headlights on in a futile effort to illuminate a misty, shrubbery-lined path.

"Which way is the house?" Stan asked, squinting through the windshield, trying to orient himself in the dark. He realized there were no lights on anywhere. Something wasn't right. "Where is Jeremiah?"

"He's out on the lake. He wanted to get in some night fishing. We'll take the runabout. He's likely not more than a hundred yards out."

Stan didn't like the feel of this but climbed out of the car, grabbing the suitcase from the back seat.

"Watch your step," Shannon said as he followed her up the path, the long beam of the headlights swallowed up in the fog.

A large structure, which Stan assumed to be the house, loomed off to the left. In the distance he could sense, rather than see, the lake. The curtain of fog momentarily parted, and Stan could make out the edge of a small creek, its mouth opening out to the larger body of water. A runabout, tethered to a wooden dock jutting out into the mouth of the creek, floated silently. As they trod along the rough-hewn planks, their footsteps clumped in eerie contrast to the silence of the night.

Shannon switched on a small camping lantern that hung from a post on the dock.

Stan turned to face her. "What's going on, Shannon?"

"We have to meet the Senator." Her voice sounded tight, controlled.

"I don't think so. I'm going back to the car." He turned away from the dock.

"No!" The severity of her voice caused him to swivel back. She was pointing something at him that glinted coldly in the faint light of the lantern. Stan's eyes widened. She was pointing a gun at him.

"Get into the boat," she hissed.

Stan took only a moment to evaluate the situation. He could turn and walk away and risk a bullet in the back. Or he could go along with her and hope that he might be able to gain some advantage when they were out over open water. It wasn't a hard decision. He climbed into the boat, tugging the suitcase in after him. Shannon motioned him to the bow of the small craft.

As she climbed in after him, careful to keep her distance and to keep the gun leveled at his gut, Stan wondered what Emily would do in this situation. Would she try to overpower the petite woman? Should he try? Not with that gun staring him down. Certainly biology dictated that he was the stronger of the two, but he couldn't very well outmaneuver a flying bullet.

"What's going on?" he asked again. "Where is Jeremiah?"

"Senator Douglas is on his way to becoming governor of this state," Shannon replied evenly. She tilted the motor into the water without ever taking her eyes off him. She opened the tank vent, moved the gearshift to neutral and set the choke. Twisting the throttle, she pressed the small electric starter button. The motor coughed once, then purred to life.

"Untie the bow line," she ordered. Stan reached over and unknotted the rope that held the front end of the boat to the pier. "Now sit down and don't move."

Stan settled himself uneasily into the front of the boat. Casting off the stern line, Shannon revved the motor and maneuvered the small craft away from the dock, out through the mouth of the creek and into the glassy water of the open lake. Shivering—was it against the dampness or from fear?—Stan wished he had on something warmer than just a windbreaker.

"Why are you doing this?" Stan kept his voice purposely level, even though his heart was beginning to race. "Whatever it is that Jeremiah did, we can work through this."

"He didn't do anything. This mess is all the fault of that priest friend of yours."

"Vic?" Stan felt the bile rising in his throat. "Vic's dead. How can this be his fault?"

"This country needs Jeremiah Douglas. He is a great leader. He has vision. Clarity. He knows how to make the country great again."

"You killed Vic, didn't you?" Stan gripped the side of the boat so hard his knuckles hurt.

"It was an accident. The priest should have known better. He was Senator Douglas' friend, for God's sake. Loyalty alone should have kept his mouth shut."

"Jeremiah doesn't know we're out here, does he?" Stan asked. "He never asked to see me. It's Vic's papers you want. Does Jeremiah even know about them?"

Shannon's expression was impossible to discern in the darkness and the fog. The glow of the stern running light lit one side of her face in a ghostly halo; the other was in blackness.

"We're going to put the whole sorry mess to rest at the bottom of the lake. What happened all those years ago has nothing to do with the good things Jeremiah Douglas has achieved in his years in the State Senate, with all that he can achieve as governor and someday as president."

Stan would have laughed at the absurdity of the drama in her voice, if he wasn't so sure that she planned to put him to rest at the bottom of lake as well.

"How did you manage it? Getting Vic's body into that rug? And why?" Stan was stalling for time now. He needed time to think. He needed to figure out what this woman's story was. He needed to keep her talking. It seemed like a cliché; in every book he'd ever read, every movie he'd ever seen, the hero kept the villain talking. Hero, Stan grimaced. He was probably the least likely person he knew to be a hero. He just knew that every minute he kept this woman talking was one minute she wasn't lifting her gun and shooting him.

"Casey helped me. Oh, god! Casey! My poor Casey. It's all your fault. You and that stupid wife of yours."

"What? What's our fault? Who's Casey?"

"I tried to warn him off."

"You tried to warn Casey off?"

"No, you idiot! That damned priest. Oh, he claimed he wasn't interested in exposing the Senator. But I couldn't run the risk he'd sabotage the campaign."

Stan sucked in his breath. Despite Shannon's increasing agitation, he was determined to get the full story. "He made a connection between Jeremiah's car and that bombing back in 1970, didn't he?"

"Senator Douglas has always been generous to a fault. How was he to know how that horrid man planned to use his car?"

"Jeremiah testified that the car had been stolen." The bomber had also testified in court that he'd stolen the car, but Stan remembered Vic's scribbled note in the margin of the article about the trial. "Jeremiah lied, didn't he? And he bribed Winchowski to lie."

"The Senator would never stoop to tactics like bribery. He's always been an honorable man."

"But he perjured himself," Stan countered.

Shannon shifted uncomfortably on the wooden plank. "It was his father. His father made the payout. He wanted his son to have a future; he knew he was destined for great things."

"But Jeremiah's future is over if people find out he perjured himself and was party to a bribe."

"Nobody *will* find out."

Stan could see the gun rising, pointing again at his chest.

"Who's Casey?" He was desperate to distract her.

A moan escaped Shannon's lips. "I've been taking care of him ever since we were kids."

"Your brother?"

Shannon moaned again.

"What happened to Casey?" Stan knew he was pushing hard now. His efforts at stalling could easily backfire.

"You killed him!" She stood up in the stern of the boat and aimed the pistol at Stan's heart.

"Whoa! Whoa! Shannon! I didn't even know him."

"I tried so hard to get him on the right track. It wasn't my fault. After he started smoking dope, and then using crystal meth, he became a lost soul. A lost soul!"

"You loved your brother."

Shannon sat down again.

"When I went to him up there at the lighthouse, all I wanted was for him to take care of me for a change. I needed help, and he messed it up. He wouldn't have died if it wasn't for you."

"He died at the lighthouse?" An image of Malcolm's boat bobbing in the waters under the Moose's Leap lighthouse was replaced by the image of a black body bag being pushed into the coroner's van.

"It wasn't his fault. He doesn't know what he's doing half the time. The drugs have messed him up so much. He was so high, he never even defended himself. He couldn't. He would never do anything that would hurt me. But I didn't think he would just stand there and take it. When I shoved him, I thought he would shove back. He never resisted. He went over the ledge to keep from hurting me." She gasped and put her free hand over her mouth. Without a hand guiding the outboard, the boat swung out into a precarious arc. Stan felt the suitcase bump against his leg.

He shivered. He and Emily had climbed the steps of that lighthouse just days before; he remembered leaning out over the ledge, looking down on the rocky outcrop below and seeing the crash of waves as they battered against the cliff wall. He could imagine the argument this crazed woman must have had with her brother: the anger building, the adrenaline rushing through her chest, shoulders, and arms as she pushed and pushed against a man so stoned he didn't have the wherewithal to fight back. Stan closed his eyes against the vision of a falling body that threatened to materialize out of the fog.

"It's your fault," she hissed in a voice so low it was almost a whisper.

CHAPTER 38

Emily jerked on the wheel, sending the rental car into a near spin as she flew into the small gravel parking lot near the Gills Rock boat launch. She jumped out and ran toward the pier where the Coast Guard harbor patrol boat waited for her, its motor already humming.

The familiar tones of her cell phone caught her up short. Stan. She flipped the phone open without looking at the LCD screen. "Where are you?"

"I'm at home, Mom. Where are you?"

"Shit, Megan."

"Mom?"

"I'm sorry. This isn't a good time. I'm expecting a call from your father." Emily stepped onto the pier.

"Where is he?"

"I can't go into it now, Dear."

"Mom, I need your advice. This piercing crisis is driving me nuts."

"What are you talking about?"

"About Wynter wanting to get her ears pierced. Remember? Mom, are you okay?"

240

"Megan..."

"Philip is just really pissed at me right now. And I don't know what to do."

"Well, then tell Philip to get his own damn ears pierced. I really don't have time for this."

"Mom! You're brilliant. We'll all get our ears pierced. I've been wanting to forever. I can't believe I'm thirty-six years old and never had my ears pierced. And Philip won't admit it but he—Oh, geez, Mom, the doorbell. I gotta go. Tell Dad I love him."

Emily stared at the phone. Did this conversation really just take place? And, oh god, am I ever going to be able to tell Stan that Megan loves him?

"Detective Remington?" The voice of the Coast Guard auxiliary officer brought her back to the task at hand. "I'm Petty Officer Lew Mattson. I'm your skipper for the mission."

She took the officer's outstretched hand and climbed down into the thirty foot utility boat that looked more like a large orange rubber raft sporting a portable cabin than a lake-worthy vessel.

Her jaw was set in a grim clench as the boat backed into the small harbor, then headed out onto the calm waters of Green Bay. They rounded the tip of the peninsula and turned east, passing the gently rocking buoys marking the entrance to the straits, their bells clanging to indicate their position. She soon found herself disoriented, however, as the fog thickened and the sound of the buoys bounced back from nowhere.

Suddenly, out of the darkness, a towering black shadow loomed over them. Emily shrank back, gasping. It took a moment for her to recognize that the immense specter materializing out of the fog was an ore carrier. A thousand feet long, it blasted its horn to warn small boats out of its path. The Coast Guard skipper had apparently sensed its presence long before Emily did, because he'd angled his vessel to head into its wake rather than be caught broadside by it. The ore ship quickly slipped past the smaller boat, its engines thrumming, the only other warning that it was so near.

If Stan were here now, Emily thought ruefully, he would have entertained the captain of this small vessel—and annoyed her to no end—with the history of the Great Lakes Coast Guard and the now abandoned Plum Island Coast Guard Station located in the middle of the Porte des Morts straits.

Stan was enamored with the account of the infamous 1913 November gale with its near hurricane force winds and blinding snow that forced ships crossing the Death's Door straits to seek shelter in the harbor on Washington Island. The *Louisiana*, one of the last of the wooden steamers to traverse the Great Lakes, was ablaze and dragging anchor when the crew from Plum Island found it beached in the shallows just off the island. The *Louisiana's* crew had abandoned ship and escaped in a small life boat.

The aged steamer was only one of several ships in imminent peril that day. A barge had been thrown up onto the beach by a monster wave, much to the fortune of its crew who were able to climb overboard and wade to shore. The gale lasted for over seventy-two hours, the Plum Island Coast Guard fighting the entire time to save ships in sub-freezing temperatures.

This was the stuff of history that Stan thrived on. Now Emily's biggest fear was that she would never again have the opportunity to be annoyed by his redundant stories.

When the ore ship had moved out of range, Emily felt the silence as palpably as the fog. Even with Mattson on board, she had never felt so alone. And she had never feared so much for Stan's life. A shroud of dread pulled its heavy weight over her and she had to force herself to focus on the situation at hand.

The crackle of the onboard radio broke into Emily's morbid reverie. The Petty Officer picked up the receiver.

"Detective Remington. Sheriff Pelletier wants to talk to you," Mattson said.

The veil of solitude lifted. Grateful for action of any sort, Emily reached for the radio.

"Emily here."

"Ms. Marple. I'm with Jeremiah Douglas on his boat, heading up toward the east end of the island. His onboard radar indicates a small craft ahead, something too small to be out on the lake this time of night and in this weather."

"Do you think they've taken a boat out?"

"Jeremiah says there's a small runabout moored at his dock. I'm guessing one way or the other, Miss Lambert has Stan with her in that boat."

Emily felt her stomach lurch. One way or the other. One way, he's alive. The other...

"Douglas has tried a couple of times to reach her on her cell, but the signal's not going through."

"Tell him to keep trying," Emily pleaded. "Maybe once you're in range..."

"I will. Hand me back to the skipper, so I can give him the coordinates," Pelletier directed.

The radio crackled again and Mattson spoke a few cryptic words into it. Emily felt in her pocket for her pistol. Its compact grip was reassuring. Unless she let herself think about "the other." The bow of the utility boat dipped as the skipper put it into a tight turn, and she grabbed for a rail to help steady herself as the boat plowed through its own wake.

"Looks like they're heading toward Plum Island," Mattson shouted to Emily over the din of the motor.

"The abandoned outpost?"

"That's my best guess." He opened the throttle; the motor roared, the nose of the Coast Guard boat leveling out as it picked up speed.

CHAPTER 39

Stan stretched his left arm over his head. If he could just ease that nagging pressure building in his chest. He flexed his fingers.

"What are you doing?" Shannon's voice cut through the fog.

"I need my nitro." He watched the gun waver a moment. "It's in my pocket."

"Go ahead."

Reaching for the small vial, Stan noted the incongruity of being allowed to live a bit longer without pain, just to be shot in heart later on. As he slipped the tiny white tablet under his tongue, Shannon cut the motor.

"What are *you* doing?" Stan asked.

"The suitcase," Shannon ordered.

Stan looked down at the small bag, then back at his captor, puzzled. The boat drifted silently, bobbing and swaying as waves lapped at its side. In the distance, a whining hum broke through the blanket of fog. Another boat? Stan's hopes rose. Did she hear it, too?

"Shit." The urgency in her voice rose as the distance hum became louder. "Dump it. Now."

"What?"

"The suitcase. Overboard."

He reached for the handle, but hesitated.

"Now," she barked.

Stan grabbed for the bag, but couldn't get the leverage he needed to heft it over the gunwale of the small vessel. He froze as he heard the sharp click of the gun's safety lock disengage.

"Give me a minute!" he begged. He stood up. The boat rocked wildly under his feet and he had to fight to keep his balance as he bent to lift the suitcase. He gasped for air, panic strangling the muscles in his chest.

"Hurry!" she snapped.

Forcing his lungs to work, Stan heaved the bag onto the side of the boat, gave it a shove, and watched in horror as it plopped into the water and disappeared beneath the surface.

Shannon quickly re-opened the throttle and angled the runabout away from the sound of the approaching vessel.

Stan toppled over onto the slat of a seat and clutched for the gunwale as the boat lurched away. The thudding in his chest seemed louder than the motor of the oncoming vessel. He peered over Shannon's shoulder hoping to see running lights in the fog. How far away is the other craft, he wondered. And do they even know we're out here?

"There's nowhere for you to go, you know." He forced his words out between gasps of air. "And you have nothing to worry about now that Vic's notes are gone." He closed his eyes and took a long slow breath. "I can be your ticket out of here."

"You're just more baggage." The woman's voice was clipped and edgy.

"Vic's death. Like you said, that was an accident. And Casey's. That wasn't your fault."

"Damn right it wasn't my fault."

"You've got a vision. For Jeremiah. For this country. Why risk it?" He knew he was rambling, likely not even making sense. But again, he wanted to keep her talking.

The beep of a cell phone startled them. It sounded oddly out of place in the fog, out on the open water. Shannon edged her knee against the throttle to keep the runabout headed on a steady course; tightening her grip on the gun with one hand and pulling the phone from her pocket with the other, she deftly flipped it open. As he watched her glance at the tiny luminescent screen then hold it up to her ear, Stan noted with a wry amusement the irony of his situation. He was about to be murdered, but his imminent demise was forestalled by the lure of today's most disruptive cultural artifact.

"Senator Douglas!" She listened a moment. "I'm okay. Everything's okay. Don't worry about me." She listened a moment longer. "No. Senator. I've got everything under control."

Stan was amazed at the sudden note of false efficiency in her voice.

"You can't get involved. Promise me you won't get involved."

He could tell she was fighting rising desperation. He wondered if Jeremiah had any clue what was really going on.

"Senator, please trust me. I would never do anything that would compromise your career. You have to trust me."

She shut the phone off and shoved it back into her pocket. The small boat had begun to veer again into a wide arc, but Shannon grabbed the throttle and resumed their course. How she knew where she was going, particularly in this fog, Stan couldn't imagine.

Suddenly out of that fog land emerged. Shannon cut the motor again, letting the boat glide and eventually bump alongside a dilapidated dock. Stan peered into the shroud of mist, trying to distinguish a landscape. What was that boxy structure? A boat house?

The mist parted momentarily and he discerned three oversized bay doors. Definitely a boat house. Beyond, the outline of another building with a forlorn tower caught his eye, before melting back into the fog. Stan had gotten just enough of a glimpse to recognize the lighthouse. But this night there was no light, instead, only an intermittent, mournful "Beee-oh," of a fog horn, like the wailing call of a lonely sea bird. Plum Island, he thought. The abandoned Coast Guard station. Well, at least Shannon hadn't shot him yet and dumped his body into Lake Michigan.

CHAPTER 40

Petty Officer Mattson throttled the small Coast Guard vessel as fast as it could safely go in the fog, keeping one eye on the small, blinking radar screen. In the distance Emily heard the deep groan of a fog horn. As they sped through the mist, she remembered once being so close to the source of a fog horn that it shook the ground beneath her feet. But now she was confused. She knew that there were no automatic fog signals left anywhere in the Death's Door straits.

"Where's that signal coming from?" she asked.

"Plum Island. I can trigger it from my vessel. The ferries and other commercial boats can, too." The skipper pointed off through the darkened haze to a single white light flickering through the fog. "That's the northern range light on the island. You can only see the other light if you're coming in off Lake Michigan. Mariners have used those lights for a hundred years to navigate these straits. I prefer the radar. More efficient."

Mattson throttled down just about the time that Emily discerned a faint shadow of land emerge from the fog. He turned the boat northward and they coasted up the western side of the small land mass. Then he angled their boat eastward toward the spit of land that housed the abandoned Coast Guard station.

A muffled crack—Emily recognized it immediately as the sound of gunfire—broke through the stillness of the night. Stan! Her grip tightened on the railing as she peered out the window of the pilot house and into the curtain of fog. She fought the urge to shout at the skipper to push the boat harder; in fact, she could feel the craft slowing down as they approached an outcropping of rocks.

As they drew closer to the island, Mattson flicked on a powerful searchlight and swept its beam across the shoreline, casting a ghostly ripple over the water. The ribbon of light dissolved momentarily as it caught the edge of a large wooden structure.

"That's the boathouse," the skipper informed Emily. "Hasn't been used since 1990."

Emily strained to see through the dappled mist. Where was Stan? The beam highlighted the length of a wooden dock and broke across the bow of a large cabin cruiser snugged up against the weathered pilings.

"Senator Douglas's boat?" Emily asked.

Mattson nodded. He swung the light again, and this time, in its shimmering beam, Emily spotted a small runabout bobbing against the dilapidated pier. She could see that it was empty. She frowned.

"Can you contact Pelletier?"

"Yes, Ma'am."

Mattson reached for his radio and hailed the other vessel.

"*The Jerry Rig.* Douglas, here." Jeremiah's voice crackled through the airwaves.

"Jeremiah," Emily said. "I need to talk to Pelletier."

"The sheriff went up after Shannon and Stan. He told me to stay put. Frankly, I'm worried. I think she's gone off the deep end."

"Did you see them?"

"No. Just their boat. Emily," his voice hesitated. "I think I heard a gunshot. I don't know what to do."

"You stay with your boat. Keep the line open."

"What are you going to do?"

"The sheriff's going to need backup. I'm on it."

She handed the radio back to the skipper.

"How well do you know this island?" she asked him as she pulled her weapon out of her pocket and checked the magazine.

"If you're looking for another way in, I can take you up the beach."

"Let's do it."

CHAPTER 41

Stan's legs shook as he clambered up onto the dock. Breathing heavily, he looked back down at Shannon as she revved the runabout's motor. Now he understood. She hadn't planned on killing him and dumping him in the lake after all.

"Are you just going to leave me here?" he asked, not sure if death by bullet, by drowning, or by starvation and exposure to the elements on an uninhabited island was a worse fate. He suddenly felt the cold in a way he hadn't all evening.

"You'll be okay. People go by here all the time. Someone will find you." She gunned the motor, but it coughed, sputtered, and died. She tried it again.

"Damn!"

"Sounds to me like you're out of gas," Stan observed.

"Move back!" she barked, pointing the gun at him again. "Far back."

She tossed a line up and around a splintered piling, looping it through itself and pulling it tight, without ever taking the barrel of the gun off its target. Stan was amazed at how nimble she was as she pulled herself up and onto the dock.

For a split second Shannon took her eyes off him. That was all Stan needed. He turned and raced up the pier toward the boathouse. But he had miscalculated the younger woman's speed and agility. He heard a loud crack and felt the zing of a bullet as it whizzed past him and thudded into the side of the building.

"Stop!" she shouted.

But fear hiked his adrenalin into overdrive and he kept running, rounding the corner of the boat house. He grabbed for the handle of a door, yanked, and shoved his shoulder against it. Nothing happened. A rusty, government issue padlock kept a latch firmly in place, and the door wouldn't budge. Gasping, he swiveled around. A ripple of light swept across the old station house. Did she have a flashlight? Stan couldn't remember. A thrumming filtered through the mist. He shook his head in confusion. It didn't make sense.

But the station house couldn't be more than a dozen yards away. He might find some cover there. He reached down and picked up a handful of dirt and stones, just as Shannon rounded the corner, and flung the rubble at her face.

She shrieked and pulled her hands up to her face, brushing the stinging debris away, just long enough for Stan to break for it and run toward the abandoned Coast Guard quarters.

"Bastard!"

The front of the building offered little sanctuary. The row of double-paneled windows was too high off the ground to be accessible. The wood-railed porch sheltering the front door was too exposed. In the dark, Stan stumbled toward the back of the building. A set of steps led up to an enclosed porch.

Shannon's footsteps crackled on the gravel not far behind. His heart thudding in his chest, Stan took the steps two at a time. He slammed against the door. His shoulder screamed in pain, but this door wasn't padlocked, and the latch gave way. He lurched into the dark building, tripping over his own legs, and crashed to the floor, knocking the wind out of his lungs.

Shannon was only steps behind. As Stan rose painfully to his feet, her gun was already in his back.

"Don't be stupid," she said.

He sank back down to his knees, crouching in fear. As he sucked in air, he was aware only of the pounding in his chest and the rasping of his lungs.

"So what's your plan now?" he wheezed.

"Shut up. I have to think."

A beam of light played across the door frame, catching them both off guard.

"Shit." Shannon's voice was barely a whisper.

New hope rising, Stan straightened his shoulders and pushed himself off the floor.

"Shannon Lambert! This is Sheriff Pelletier."

At the sound of the sheriff's voice, Stan felt a relief that died just as quickly as the gun pushed harder into his back.

"Lie down. Don't say a word."

He felt the warmth of her breath against his ear. As he stretched out onto the floor, he realized the sheriff was walking into a trap. In the dark, all he could make out was the open door and faint rectangles where the windows broke the inky blackness. He sensed that Shannon had moved away from him. He saw movement at the door and the beam of the flashlight again.

"Pelletier, don't!" he shouted.

But it was too late. As the sheriff stepped cautiously through the door, his own gun in the ready position, the scoop end of a shovel came smashing down on him. Pelletier's gun and flashlight both skidded across the floor, the narrow beam playing uselessly against a wall.

Stan rolled once, hoping to confuse Shannon by changing his location. But as he struggled cautiously to his knees, he was blinded by a bright light. He covered his face with an arm to shield his eyes from the glare.

"Get up," Shannon ordered, the sheriff's flashlight wavering in her hand. "Take these." She shoved a pair of handcuffs into his hands. She must have pulled them off the fallen officer. "Cuff him behind his back."

Stan felt the nausea rise in this throat as he pulled Pelletier's arms behind him and ratcheted the manacles shut. The lawman moaned.

"Now, you. Sit." Shannon pointed the flashlight back at Stan.

He sat with his back against the wall. Every bone and muscle in his body ached. But he knew that Pelletier hurt worse.

A tiny LCD screen glowed eerily in the dark, and Stan could just barely make out Shannon's grim face for a moment as she raised her phone and nestled it against her ear.

"Senator? Where are you? I need your boat."

CHAPTER 42

Emily slipped the small gun back into her pocket. She watched anxiously as Mattson beached the utility boat in the dark shallows of a small cove about a hundred yards down the shoreline from the abandoned Coast Guard Station. They had agreed that he wouldn't use the spotlight.

"You're sure you don't want me to go with you?" he asked.

"We need a command post with an open communication line," Emily replied.

The skipper nodded.

She accepted the flashlight Mattson handed her, but slipped it into a pocket. She climbed onto the broad rubber gunwale of the rescue craft. Her fingers clutching the life line, she swung her feet over the edge and slid down into a foot of black icy water. She gasped as the shock of the cold hit her legs and soaked through her jeans.

She stood a moment, getting her bearings, then took a tentative step, testing the ground under her feet. The bottom was rocky, but firm. She took another step, then sloshed forward through the frigid water to the gravelly beach. Her feet, now numb with cold, felt like they had weights attached, as she stepped onto dry land.

Her body trembled with cold and the familiar surge of adrenalin as she pulled out her gun again and racked a round into the chamber. Then she switched on Mattson's flashlight and pointed it close to her feet.

The rocky bank was steep. Her feet ached, but she forced herself to move on. Allowing the flashlight beam more play, she swung it across the tree line ahead and found a narrow, sandy path through the scrub grass and errant dense brush. As she crept along, hugging the flashlight close to her again, branches snagged her sweatshirt and she impatiently brushed them aside. One branch snapped back and scraped her cheek; she squeezed her eyes against the sharp burning sting. She swiped at her face with the back of her hand, but kept moving forward.

Finally, the bushes thinned, revealing a small clearing. The curtain of mist opened up, allowing her to discern several buildings. Off to her left stood a small outbuilding. She smelled the faintest odor of diesel fuel. The water pump house, she guessed, the source of the contaminated water Mattson had spoken of as he hastily drew a sketch of the Coast Guard property before she climbed off the boat. If this was the pump house, then she knew she was at the back of the property. She could just barely see a larger building across the yard from her. A squat tower hovered over the structure and wavered in the thinning mist.

Spotting the flicker of a light dart across the lower window of the old Coast Guard house, she snapped off her own flashlight. She flattened herself against the wall of the pump house as the sound of a woman's voice floated through the air. Three shadowy figures appeared in the doorway. The woman's voice grew urgent and insistent.

Emily tightened her fingers around the grip of her gun. Footsteps crunched on the gravel and a ray of light from the flashlight danced across the path leading to the front of the property. One of the figures stumbled and fell to the ground with a deep groan.

The woman's voice rose in anger. "Get up!" Shannon Lambert's voice, Emily thought. Was that Stan on the ground? She resisted the urge to break cover and run toward them. Then she heard his voice.

"Give him a minute, will you? You knocked him out cold. What do you expect? And get that damn gun out of my back!"

Emily could see Stan's figure leaning over the fallen man.

"Pelletier!" Stan's voice was urgent. "Can you get up?" Then he was talking to Shannon. "Are these handcuffs really necessary?"

"Just get him up and get moving," Shannon barked.

Emily watched as the two figures engaged in an awkward, macabre dance in the fog and the dark; finally one struggled to its feet.

She took advantage of the confusion to slip away from the cover of the pump house and bolt across the clearing, staying out of Shannon's line of sight and behind the lighthouse.

As the trio began to shuffle again toward the dock, Shannon's tone changed.

"I just need the boat, Senator. If I can get to Canada, I'll be okay. And so will you." She paused for a moment. "I'll manage. I've done enough boating in my life to know what I'm doing. You'll be safe here with these two. The Coast Guard will find you."

Edging around the corner of the building, Emily found herself no more than a dozen yards away as she watched Shannon nudge the two men toward the boathouse. The woman's head was cocked at an odd angle; she had her phone tucked between her ear and her shoulder.

Beyond them, Jeremiah's yacht rocked alongside the dock; the figure of the candidate paced in the brightly lit window of the pilothouse. Emily noted the absurdity of Shannon and Jeremiah conversing by cell phone when they were no more than fifty yards apart. The distance was quickly closing, and Emily knew she couldn't let the other woman get on that boat. She needed a way to stop her before she got too close to the dock with her hostages.

Emily scanned the ground around her feet. Damn! The property had been left in pristine condition. No junk lying around. She scrabbled in the dirt until her hand bumped against a baseball-sized rock. She pitched the rock, aiming for a small window on the side of the boathouse.

The rock smashed through the window, the crashing of the glass alarming the three ghostly figures. Stan, fearful for his life, rammed into the sheriff; both men tumbled to the ground.

Shannon swiveled, her phone clattering onto the stony path, her flashlight beam swinging frantically. She fired several shots into the dark.

Emily dropped her own flashlight to grip her gun with both hands.

"Shannon! Drop the gun!" Emily shouted.

But Shannon fired wildly again.

Emily aimed and squeezed the trigger. Shannon cried out as the bullet slammed into her shoulder and she crumpled to the ground. Emily ran toward the downed woman and kicked the gun out of her reach.

"Are you okay, Stan?" she shouted.

"Emily?" Stan's voice shook in disbelief. He struggled to get up.

"About time you got here, Ms. Marple." Fred's muffled voice held a note of relief.

Emily and Stan hurried to help the lawman to his feet. He wobbled and Stan grabbed at him to keep him from falling over. Pelletier nodded toward the woman whimpering on the ground.

"She's hurting. But she's alive. Nice shot."

Emily picked up Shannon's phone from the ground.

"Jeremiah? Are you still there?"

"Shannon?" Douglas was clearly panicked.

"No. This is Emily Remington."

Stan fished a small key out of the sheriff's pocket and released the handcuffs.

"Shannon is taking a leave of absence from the campaign," Emily said. "Radio the Coast Guard skipper and ask him to pull his boat alongside yours. We're also going to need an ambulance standing by at the ferry landing."

The sheriff, his hands free again, knelt down to apply pressure to Shannon's wound with his handkerchief. Stan turned toward Emily and embraced her with exhausted relief. Emily held him tightly, then went into her mother-mode, checking that nothing was broken, bleeding, or otherwise missing.

"I'm okay, Emily! I'm okay."

CHAPTER 43

Stan maneuvered the Winnebago off the county highway and onto State Highway 57. A quarter mile further, at the corner where Ridges Road forked off, he found a spot and parked the big bus. He looked across the street at a small, non-descript, one-story white building with a sloped roof. Over the door sagged a sign that read Sandpiper Restaurant.

"Are you sure this is it?"

"There's his car." Emily pointed to Sheriff Fred Pelletier's Chevy Tahoe. They climbed out of the RV and crossed the busy highway.

On the cement patio behind the restaurant, a crowd of people gathered around a fire pit. A waist-high, hand-painted sign announced the All-You-Can-Eat Friday Night Fish Boil—coleslaw, dessert, and a beverage of your choice included. Stan noticed that the beverage of choice for most of the crowd appeared to be a deep amber lager, which flowed freely from the spout of a large aluminum barrel.

Two men, both in summer shorts and t-shirts, and one in a camouflage hunting cap, manned a gigantic black kettle full of water sitting over the open wood fire. At a nearby table, a third man was cutting up fresh fish.

"Bone-in whitefish," the man said as Stan peered over his shoulder. "Still swimmin' this morning."

A rotund woman kicked open the back door of the restaurant and pushed through, followed by a younger waitress. Both carried large rectangular pans of new red potatoes, onions, and carrots, cleaned and sliced.

"Here ya go, Arnie," she said and handed hers off to the man in the camouflage cap. With a grin, he dumped the vegetable medley into the pot, causing the water to rise dangerously close to the brim.

"Ya got that fish ready yet?" he called out to the man at the cutting table.

"Coupla more minutes."

"Over there." Emily pointed to where the sheriff had commandeered a picnic table. Sitting across from him were Malcolm and Audrey. The men were already nursing frosty mugs of beer. Audrey had something that looked like a wine spritzer. When he spotted the two newcomers heading his way, Pelletier lifted his mug in invitation.

"Arnie! Two more!" he called out. "That okay?" he asked Emily.

"Sounds good to me," she replied.

Stan reached out and shook hands with Pelletier and Malcolm. Emily and Audrey hugged.

"I take it you're off duty today?" Stan nodded toward the beer in the sheriff's hand.

"Oh, yeah." Pelletier took another pull at his mug. He signalled the man in the camouflage hat who'd left his post at the kettle fire long enough to draw two more drafts and deliver them to their table. "Thanks, Arnie."

"No problem, Fred. Friends staying for dinner?"

"Couldn't let 'em leave the Door without experiencing a fish boil."

"Welcome to the Quiet Side," the restaurateur said. "Don't know why people spend so much time in that tourist trap over to the other side anyway. Here you get good food, good company, and you won't go away hungry, you betcha." And with that he ambled back to the boisterous crowd that was growing around his kettle.

As the head cook grabbed a large tray full of fish pieces, Pelletier grinned in anticipation. "It's time to go join the fun."

"Did you know that fish boils date back to the Scandinavian settlers and lumberjacks?" Stan's professorial tone elicited a groan from Emily.

"Well, I thank them for their contribution to the culture of the Door." Pelletier raised his mug in salute then swallowed a mouthful of beer. Then he led his guests over to where the jovial crowd had formed a ring around the cooking pot, its water roiling.

Arnie dumped the load of cut fish into the giant kettle. "Okay, folks. Stand back!"

The crowd took a token step backward.

Arnie grabbed an old tin coffee can filled with kerosene.

"Three!" the crowd shouted. "Two! One!" Arnie tossed the kerosene onto the flames. A fireball exploded into the air, an inferno of smoke and flame rising up a good ten feet, engulfing the kettle and filling the air with thick black smoke. The crowd cheered with delight. Feeling the wave of heat blow past her, Emily took a nervous step back.

The flames died down as quickly as they'd flared up. The kettle—superheated now—boiled over. Arnie and his assistant each grabbed an end of a long pole attached to a basket nestled inside the kettle. As they raised the basket, up came the fish, potatoes and other veggies. Dinner was served.

The small group filled their plates, refreshed their drinks, and followed the sheriff back to the picnic table. The savory aroma of the boiled dinner caused Emily's stomach to rumble. Spearing a piece, she brought the flaky fish to her lips, blowing on it to cool the morsel. Then she took a bite, groaning with pleasure.

Later, his hunger satisfied, Malcolm dabbed his lips with his napkin. "So," he said finally. "What do you think? Looks to me like Jeremiah's got a bit of damage control to do now."

Stan nodded, wiping up the last juicy remnants from his plate with a dinner roll. "I'm afraid he's out of the game. Perjury's a bit much even for the local electorate."

"I feel sorry for him," Audrey offered. "I understand his marriage has gone down the tubes, too. Rumor has it that Glenna has packed up and left."

"Jeremiah didn't deserve all this," Malcolm said. "I don't much like the way his politics turned out, but the guy was really trying to make a difference. How could Shannon do something like that?"

"Misguided passion," Stan offered. "Some people just go over the edge."

"Okay, yeah, but how did that little bit of a woman get Father Vic's body into Emily's rug and up onto your RV?"

They all looked at Pelletier. He swung one leg over the edge of the table's bench to give himself room.

"First of all, it wasn't Emily's rug," he said. "When Ms. Lambert shot your Padre in her brother's cabin, she enlisted his help. He's the one who rolled your friend's body into the old rug that he had on the floor of his shack. According to Shannon, she instructed him simply to get rid of the corpse. What she hadn't bargained on was that his brain was so messed up on drugs, he was one egg short of a dozen. In his addled mind it made sense to replace the rug on top of Stan and Emily's RV with the one he'd rolled the body in. He assumed it would drive off into Lala Land."

"But when did he do it?" Audrey persisted, stacking the dirty paper plates into a pile in the center of the table.

"While you were at dinner," Pelletier answered. "If you remember, the RV was pretty well hidden by the trees."

"And it was dark," Stan interjected. "I think he saw his chance when Emily came to pick Malcolm and me up from the golf course. Remember, that guy who yelled at us for parking there? That was him, wasn't it?"

"Yeah, that was him," Emily said.

The party fell silent for a moment, each lost in their own thoughts. A burst of raucous laughter from a nearby table broke the spell. Audrey piped up again.

"What I don't understand is, how did Shannon know about Father Vic's book? Even Malcolm didn't know the details."

"She apparently had been monitoring Mr. Douglas' phone calls," Sheriff Pelletier said.

"It started out simply enough," Stan filled in. "Part of her job was to intercept his phone calls. She had control over who got to talk to him and who didn't. Jeremiah frequently asked her to listen in so he'd have a witness to sensitive conversations. Sometimes the other party knew she was on the line, sometimes not."

"Then she started listening in even when she wasn't invited?" Malcolm guessed.

"Power can be a pretty corrupting force sometimes," Emily commented.

"In the beginning," Stan went on, "when Vic tried to get Jeremiah on the phone, Shannon would often as not play the game of 'He's in a meeting.' But Vic persisted. Finally, by dropping Winchowski's name, he got Jeremiah's attention. Not only did the Senator respond immediately, but he instructed Shannon to put Vic's calls through right away. This piqued Shannon's curiosity, and she began to listen in on their conversations without her boss's knowledge." Stan lifted his glass, catching the eye of the waitress. "Who wants more beer?"

Pelletier waved him off. He had had enough.

"I'll have another," Malcolm spoke up. "I understand the D.A's going for second degree, rather than first degree murder."

"Second degree?" Audrey seemed puzzled. She placed a firm hand over Malcolm's glass and shook her head at the waitress.

"Unpremeditated," Emily explained. She reached out a hand as the waitress set a fresh glass in front of Stan, who automatically plopped his keys into her outstretched palm. "Shannon claims she never intended to hurt Father Vic. She thought she could bribe him into leaving the Senator out of the book and keeping it a secret."

"But it didn't work out the way she planned," Malcolm finished.

"Never does," Pelletier added dryly.

"Sad how someone totally innocent, someone who just happened to be in the wrong room on the wrong night, got killed," Emily said.

"That tourist? The woman in the motel room you'd moved out of?" Malcolm asked.

"Shannon sent her brother to find Vic's papers," Stan said. "He'd apparently checked the register earlier that day and saw that we were in room eighteen. He had no way of knowing that we'd moved."

"But her death was so violent!" Audrey shuddered.

"He was high on crystal meth," said Pelletier. "That drug really does a number."

"So, this perjury business. How exactly was Jeremiah involved in that awful bombing on campus?" Audrey pressed for more details.

"It was his Mustang that the bomber used," Malcolm said.

"I know that," Audrey replied. "It was in all the papers. But they said it had been stolen. When the guy was caught, he even testified about it on the stand."

"That's certainly what everyone believed." Stan nursed his beer. "But when Vic was researching the bombing and came across the newspaper accounts, he remembered that night differently."

"How so?" Audrey wanted to know.

"According to Vic, he'd managed to land a date with a girl he'd been flirting with at one of the State Street bars for a couple of weeks."

"Wait a minute. I thought he was in the seminary," Audrey interrupted.

"This was before the seminary, remember. When we were still in college. Vic wanted to impress this girl, so he asked Jeremiah if he could use the Mustang. Jeremiah agreed, but when Vic went to pick it up, Jeremiah told him he'd forgotten his promise and let one of his frat buddies take it instead. Vic remembered the incident because he'd been so pissed about Jeremiah reneging on the car at the last minute and ruining his date."

"That frat buddy was Dan Winchowski," Emily interjected.

"According to his notes," Stan continued his story, "Vic had been in the seminary at the time of the trial, and so hadn't paid much attention to what was going on. He didn't even realize that Jeremiah had been on the stand as a witness or that he had claimed the car was stolen.

"When Vic started his research and saw the discrepancy between the trial accounts and the way he remembered it, he arranged to visit Winchowski up at Waupun prison. Once he realized Vic was a priest, he seemed pretty eager to talk to him about what went on back in 1970. He somehow got it into his head that their interview was akin to a confession, and that Vic—being a priest—was bound by his vows to keep their conversation confidential."

"Like with your attorney," Malcolm clarified.

Stan nodded. "But, according to Vic's journal, there was never a request for absolution. Rather the prisoner seemed to be looking for an opportunity to rationalize his actions. Apparently even though Vic told the man it was not a valid sacramental confession, Winchowski believed what he wanted to believe.

"Vic contacted Jeremiah, not only because he was concerned about his campaign, but also because Winchowski clearly intended to use the information to get a pardon."

Audrey interrupted Stan in disbelief. "What, get a pardon based on a decades-old alleged perjury charge?"

"Well, understand there was more than just perjury involved," Stan said. "Jeremiah's father had bribed Winchowski to testify that he had stolen the car."

Stan paused for a breath. The fire in the pit had now died to smoldering embers. Emily zipped her sweatshirt against the cold of the night.

"Apparently this was a bomber with a personal conscience," she said. "His mother had been ill, cancer. She couldn't afford the treatments, so Winchowski arranged for Jeremiah's father to pick up the medical costs. It was all done anonymously, through a third party. The woman never even knew who her angel benefactor was."

"When she died," Stan interrupted, "Winchowski had no reason to keep his secret, except to use it as leverage. According to Vic's journal, the guy was biding his time as long as his mother was alive. He planned to accuse the Senator of perjury as his ace card in a new appeal. If that didn't work, then he would try to extort a pardon when Jeremiah became governor." Stan raised his mug, drank, then licked the lingering foam from his lips. Before he had a chance to go on, the sheriff jumped in.

"When Ms. Lambert overheard your padre and the governor-wanna-be talking about Winchowski, she panicked. She also put that messed up brother of hers to searching the rectory up at Ellison Bay and your camper."

"Camper?" Stan looked offended.

"And don't forget that poor tourist's motel room." Emily ignored Stan's bluster. "Shannon's brother was so whacked out on drugs, he just tore things apart looking for Vic's papers. That's why all those places were such a mess."

"But what about the room we moved into, Emily?" Stan asked forgetting about Pelletier's playful insult. "You told me you thought someone had searched it, too. But there was nothing out of order. At least, nothing I could see."

"That one wasn't the brother," the sheriff explained. "Turns out, Ms. Lambert wasn't the only one interested in those papers."

"Father Rydelle," Stan guessed.

"Who's that?" Audrey wanted to know.

"The assistant to Bishop Metzler," Emily explained. "The bishop was determined not to let Father Vic's book see the light of day. He instructed Rydelle to find the papers, and that man did everything short of murder to comply."

"So is it true Shannon threw Vic's paper overboard?" Malcolm asked.

"Turns out she threw Stan's dirty underwear overboard," Pelletier laughed.

"What?" Audrey was perplexed.

"Seems your hubbie's old roomie here pulled a switch-a-roo at the last minute."

"I had stashed Vic's suitcase in the storage space under the bed just before Shannon came by the RV," Stan explained. "When she seemed so eager to get her hands on it, something didn't feel right."

"Stan was making fun of me for not using a laundry basket in the Winnie, but the suitcase seemed just as handy as anything," Emily laughed. "I hadn't gotten around to actually washing that load. Now it looks like they'll be washed for eternity."

"So who has the suitcase now?" Audrey wanted to know.

"I gave it to Fred," Stan said. "It is evidence, after all."

"But I understand Beverly asked you to finish the book," Audrey said. "Are you thinking about it?"

"Vic's story is one worth telling. And worth telling right. I think I owe it to him to take it on."

"It's just too bad he's not here to tell it himself." Malcolm blinked back tears.

Stan suddenly found his own eyes beginning to well. This was their friend's life they were wrapping up so analytically.

Noticing her husband's anguish, Emily reached under the table and took his hand. He squeezed back.

"But I am glad to hear you're planning to take it on," Malcolm said to his friend, blowing his nose into his handkerchief. "If anyone can do justice to Vic's life, you can."

"Oh, god, I hate to keep asking," Audrey said. "But it's the details that bug me. That body that Malcolm fished out of the bay?" She shuddered. "You said it was that Lambert guy? Shannon's brother?"

The sheriff nodded.

"Did she kill him, too?" Audrey asked.

"She's saying it was an accident," the sheriff said. "All indications are that he was still high. She claims they were having an argument when he swung at her, lost his balance, and went over the rail."

"Do you believe her?" Malcolm asked.

"Her story seems to change depending on who she's talking to," Stan observed. "But I don't think she can accept that she was responsible for the death of someone she loved."

"Well, I can't believe it all comes down to Jeremiah lying all those years ago about what happened to his car," Audrey said sadly.

"Seems to me, more often than not, it always comes down to the petty things. Like lying," Pelletier replied.

The somber mood was suddenly broken by the waitress who came out with a dessert tray so big she could barely carry it—homemade cherry pie with ice cream on top. When everyone had had their fill, Pelletier patted his stomach and pushed away from the table, a man satiated.

"Well, folks, it's time for me to call it a night. I'm still a workin' man and the sun comes up early here."

He stood and shook hands with Stan and Malcolm, nodded at Audrey. Emily rose, extended her hand and he shook it with real warmth.

"It's been nice working with you, Ms. Marple." His smile was genuine. "But next time you and your friends plan a vacation—well, I'd appreciate it if you'd plan it for someplace other than the Door."

Emily broke into a laugh.

"Fair enough," she said.

Pelletier gave her a sly smile. "Got something in the car I thought you might want."

Emily couldn't imagine what he was talking about. She followed the beefy man over to the SUV where he lifted up the back end. There inside was Emily's Persian rug—the one she'd bought at the garage sale in Bailey's Harbor, rolled up tight into a tube.

"It's all yours, Ms. Marple. Just might wanna go kinda easy when you unroll it."

ABOUT THE AUTHOR

M. J. Williams is the pen name of sisters-in-law Peggy Williams and Mary Joy Johnson. *On the Road to Death's Door* is the first in what they hope to be a successful series featuring Emily and Stan Remington and their RV adventures. Both writers live in Madison, Wisconsin.

15074398R00148

Made in the USA
Lexington, KY
07 May 2012